An Imperial Marriage

Arthur W. Marchmont

An Imperial Marriage

Copyright © 2021 Bibliotech Press
All rights reserved

ISBN: 978-1-63637-636-3

CONTENTS

CHAPTER I

THE "IMPERIAL MARRIAGE"

When the Kaiser planned the marriage between his kinswoman, the Princess von Altenvelt, and his handsome favourite, the Prince von Graven—the "Imperial Marriage," as the Court gossips styled it—there did not appear to be even the remotest possibility that it could ever be any concern of mine.

The news was almost the last I sent through to my paper, the London Newsletter, for I heard of it just before I resigned my position as Berlin Special Correspondent, on succeeding to my uncle's fortune. I had remained on in the capital, ostensibly to give a lift to my successor, my old Varsity chum, Gerald Bassett, but in reality for a reason which no one knew, except my sister, Bessie. And she only guessed it was on Althea's account.

Sisters have a knack of ferreting out these secrets, and I gathered that she had guessed mine because she had dropped more than one hint that Althea, being a great friend of hers, would be very welcome as a sister-in-law.

That was the position when, at a dance one night, Hugo von Felsen told me with a grin on his thin long malicious face that the Imperial Marriage was in danger because Prince von Graven had fallen in love with Althea and she with him.

I had always detested von Felsen, and had only tolerated him in my newspaper days because, as the son of a powerful Minister, Count von Felsen, he could sometimes be tapped for valuable information. The fact that this news came from him made it seem even worse than it was.

"You can see for yourself," he added. "There they are, together. All Berlin knows about it. Look, everybody is watching them"; and his close-set cunning eyes were fixed on my face as if he knew how his words would affect me, and was pleased.

"They are worth looking at, anyhow," I answered, with a shrug of indifference. They were. In my eyes Althea was the most beautiful girl in the room. The type of a lovely brunette, with perfectly moulded features, large lustrous eyes instinct with tenderness and sympathy, and a figure of consummate grace. But then I looked at her with the eyes of a lover. The Prince was also strikingly handsome. Tall, with a soldierly bearing, and as fair as Althea was dark, his face was marred only by the weakness of the mouth.

"We only want the Kaiser himself and the Princess von

1

Altenvelt to complete the picture, eh?" sneered von Felsen with a chuckle of malice. "How his High-and-Mightiness would enjoy the sight! As much as you do, Bastable."

"Yourself, you should say, rather, judging by your looks," I retorted. "It is nothing to me."

"You wouldn't have a chance, if it were," he snapped.

I was not going to let him see how hard I was hit by the news, and as the band struck up then I turned away in search of my partner. This was Chalice Mennerheim; really Althea's niece, although the relationship appeared a little absurd as there was only a year or so between them. I meant to find out from her whether there was any foundation for von Felsen's insinuation.

Chalice had a remarkable voice, and Althea had brought her to Berlin to be trained by Herr Grumpel, the great professor, whose influence at Court was as powerful as his skill in voice culture was great.

After a couple of turns round the room I led her into one of the conservatories. She was very vain and intensely selfish, and would have been really pretty, had it not been for a certain hard, calculating expression in her light blue eyes. They always suggested to me the eyes of an unskilfully painted picture.

I paid her a number of compliments and then led round to the subject of the Prince, observing casually that I had just heard some news about him.

"Tell me," she said, with a quick side glance and a very musical laugh, as she laid her hand on my arm with a little coaxing gesture. "It's awfully wicked, and Althea is always at me about it; but I love scandal. And I'm scarcely twenty yet. What I shall be at thirty makes me shudder. A regular old scandal-monger, I expect."

"You are not shuddering; only smiling and looking very pretty. The Prince thinks you very pretty too, I presume, by the way he was looking at you when you were dancing with him just now."

She laughed again. "What were you going to tell me?"

"They say the Imperial Marriage is in danger because he——" I left the sentence unfinished intentionally.

"Go on. Go on. Because——? Tell me."

"Haven't you noticed anything which would enable you to finish the sentence?"

"You don't mean—Althea?" Her voice sank to a whisper.

I felt a grip at my heart at this confirmation. "Half the people here were watching them just now as they stood together in the centre of the room."

She burst suddenly into a fit of merry, irresponsible laughter.

2

"Isn't it fun?" she cried. I suppose it was, to her. I did not see the humour of it, however.

"There may not be much laughter in it when the Kaiser hears," I growled.

"Ah, the Kaiser!" and she shrugged her shapely shoulders petulantly. "What business has he to turn matchmaker? Why should not the Prince marry whom he pleases? Think what an ugly thing is that Princess von Altenvelt!" She appeared to be quite indignant on Althea's account.

"It would cost the Prince the Emperor's favour and his position at Court," I replied; "and probably he would be packed off to some fever hole in the Colonies on military service. Nice for Althea, that. The Kaiser can be hard when he likes."

"It is unjust! Infamous!" she exclaimed vehemently. "Poor Althea! But you don't think that really? The Kaiser likes him too well."

"He has done it before, remember." Jealousy plays odd pranks with a man. Here was I finding a sort of morbid delight in drawing this gloomy picture, when in reality I wished Althea all the happiness in the world. But the smart of my disappointment was so fresh that I felt positively spiteful for the moment.

Chalice cast her eyes down, and in the pause a partner came to look for her. She threw me a little nod and a smile, as if we had had the pleasantest chat, and flitted off prattling to her partner and making eyes at him as I had seen her make them to a hundred other men before.

I sat on and brooded. I had been a self-centred ass not to have seen things, and a fool to dream that such a girl as Althea would ever give me a second thought. And then with a sigh I resolved to get out of Berlin without loss of time. I was walking off to the smoking room when I came on Althea sitting alone.

"I believe you have actually forgotten that this was our dance, Mr. Bastable," she said with a reproachful look and a smile. She always spoke English, and spoke it remarkably well.

I had forgotten it, and mumbled a lame apology.

"Let us sit out the remainder of it then. I am rather tired. And you look as if the weight of a throne were on your shoulders. Are you worried?"

I dropped into the seat by her side and began to make small talk, although every pulse in my body was leaping with the desire to speak of the feeling that filled my heart.

At length she spoke of Chalice. "You were talking to her just now," she said, "and appeared to be discussing some very grave subject."

I resolved suddenly to get the truth from her. "It was about you, in fact."

"About me?" she asked in surprise.

"I don't know whether you'll think I'm putting my foot in it, but I should like to tell you something."

"What a grave preface!" she said jestingly, but with an earnest look.

I fidgeted uneasily under her gaze. "The fact is, I heard something from von Felsen, and Chalice confirmed it—about you and Prince von Graven."

She pressed her hands together quickly, and a tinge of colour crept up into her cheeks. "Chalice confirmed it?" she repeated. "What did she say?"

"Well, the fact is—you see, when you and the Prince were standing together in the middle of the room a while back, a whole lot of people were staring at you; and—there was a lot of talk as to what the Kaiser would be likely to do when he—when he heard about you two."

I kept my eyes on the ground and felt many parts of a fool in the pause which followed. Then Althea laughed, and I looked up.

"It is a very awkward position, of course; and equally of course you do not quite understand it. I—I meant to tell you and Bessie all about it. I will do so one day. We must be more careful for the future." And again she laughed.

Her laughter nettled me. It ought not to have done so, of course. She could not possibly know how I felt. "If you wish to avoid the Kaiser's anger, you certainly must be. But I am going off to England by the afternoon mail to-morrow," I declared bluntly.

My reference to the Kaiser stopped her laughter, and she looked very grave for a moment. Then she got up. "I must say good-bye to you then, I suppose."

We shook hands; and then to my surprise she added: "I wish I knew what the Kaiser would do. It would let the thing be cleared up."

"I wish you happiness with all my heart," I replied earnestly.

"Thank you, Mr. Bastable. I am sure you do. I should like—— But of course I can't. Good-bye"; and with this she turned away a little abruptly.

I told my sister as we were driving home that I was going to England on the following day, and she guessed at once that Althea was the cause, and got the truth out of me.

"I don't believe it, Paul," was her verdict; "but perhaps the best thing is for you to go away. A change will do you good; and as Aunt Charlotte is coming here I must stay behind." Aunt Charlotte was

4

Mrs. Ellicott, a wealthy, childless widow, who made a great favourite of Bessie and was to leave her her money.

A sleepless night's reflection confirmed me in my resolve to go away, and the next afternoon found me at the station.

Then the unexpected happened. I was looking after my luggage and Bessie had gone off to buy me some papers, when Althea came hurrying up to me.

"Oh, Mr. Bastable, I remembered you would be here. I am in desperate trouble. Will you help me?"

She was pale and, although she smiled, I could see she was trembling with nervous excitement. "Of course I will. Tell me," I replied quickly. To help her, I was ready to toss every plan I had formed into the melting-pot of change.

"I am to be arrested."

"Arrested! You!" I exclaimed in profound astonishment.

She laid her hand on my arm and made a brave effort to smile again. "I think it is on account of—of Prince von Graven." Her voice died down gradually as she said this hesitatingly, until it was little more than a whisper; and her eyes fell.

"And where is he, then?" I blurted out, like the clumsy lout I was.

I guessed of course that the news had reached the Kaiser's ears and he had taken prompt action. But that the Prince should have left her to bear the brunt of the Imperial anger alone in this way was downright cowardice.

"You don't understand, Mr. Bastable," she said, biting her lip. "But I—— Oh, they are following me now. What am I to do?"

I pulled myself together. "Do you mean the police?"

"I don't know. I was on the point of leaving the house when they came. The maid, Lotta, helped me to slip away; but I think they followed me."

"Do they know you well by sight?"

"I think not. I passed one of them outside. I got a cab, but they followed."

"It will be all right. Bessie is here. Don't worry. We'll see you through."

Bessie came hurrying up with an exclamation of surprise at seeing Althea.

"Don't stop to ask any questions, Bess," I said. "Fräulein Korper is in some bother. Take her into one of the waiting-rooms and change cloaks and hats with her. She can come back to me; but you must drive off somewhere in a cab. Get out when you are a mile or so away, and then go home on foot. There isn't a moment to lose. Quick, both of you."

5

Bessie hurried Althea away almost before I had finished speaking, and I turned to see that my luggage was put back into the cloak-room instead of being registered. I made the excuse that one of the trunks had been forgotten.

Althea returned before I had finished, and I gave her a critical look. My sister had been wearing a long drab driving coat and a very plain, essentially English golf cap; and I could not restrain a smile at the change they effected in Althea. No German would dream of taking their wearer for one of his countrywomen.

She was still nervous, and as she came up she whispered that the men she meant had just entered the station.

A glance in the direction she indicated showed me that I knew one of them—a police agent, named Dormund. Not the one who had seen her, fortunately.

"It will be all right," I said reassuringly. "Now just a touch or two more, and you will pass as English. Put your hair back right out of sight; slip on these sun spectacles, purse up your lip and show as many of your teeth as possible—you know the German cartoon of the average English girl; look as plain and formidable as you can; and only speak to me to snap out a word or so, as if we were quarrelling."

She tried to follow my directions, and I was glad to see her smile in amusement, despite her alarm.

"That's better. I know one of the men, and he will probably come over and speak to me. We are supposed to be brother and sister for a minute or two—he has never seen Bessie—and we are wrangling because you have left one of my trunks behind and caused me to lose the train in consequence. Be looking among those trunks over there, so that you can keep your face averted."

"He is not the man who saw me," she whispered, when I pointed to Dormund, who caught sight of me soon afterwards and came over.

"Why you couldn't see that all the things were brought beats me," I exclaimed in a loud, irritable tone to Althea. "I thought you could be trusted to count as far as four without a mistake. Giving all this infernal trouble. I shall have to go back for it, and so miss the train. Enough to make a man almost swear."

Dormund was now close and had heard much of what I said and was looking intently at Althea.

"Heir Bastable, excuse me," he said.

I turned on him quickly and irritably, and then smiled. "Hullo, Herr Dormund. I wondered who the deuce it was, and was within an ace of venting a bit of temper on you for the interruption. My sister has forgotten a trunk of mine, and now I shall miss the train," I gestured toward Althea. She had her profile toward him, and his face showed me that he had no suspicion.

"Ah, your sister," he said; and raised his hat and looked first at her and then to me as if expecting an introduction. "I heard you were leaving Berlin to-day," he continued, when I did not take the hint. "It is indeed annoying."

A scowl and an angry murmur gave him the measure of my temper. "It's a marvel to me that women can make such blunders," I growled.

"Where are you going?"

"London. And now there's no train till the night mail, and I hate night travelling."

"Have you been long in the station?"

"About half an hour or so. It took my sister that time to find out that she had made any mistake at all"; and I shot another wrathful glance at Althea. There was no doubt about my being in a very bad temper over it.

"Then perhaps you can do me a little service. You know Fräulein Korper, I believe? Have you seen her here within the last few minutes?"

"My dear fellow, I haven't had eyes for anything but my luggage, and not enough eyes to see all that even," I replied with a short angry laugh. "Have you seen anything of Althea Korper here, Bessie?" I called.

"No," she snapped, as irritably as I had spoken before. It was well done.

"Thank you," I replied in the same snappy tone, "I am sorry," I said to Dormund; "don't you know her by sight then?"

"Unfortunately, no."

I lowered my voice. "You're surely not seeking her officially?"

He smiled and threw up his hands, leaving me to infer what I pleased.

"By Jove," I exclaimed. "Can't say I wish you luck, Dormund." Then I turned to the porter. "Here, get these trunks to the cloak-room. I'll drive back for the other and see if I can catch the train after all. Come along, Bessie."

She acted the sulky sister to the life and succeeded in keeping her face almost entirely averted from Dormund.

He remained with me while I got rid of the luggage and then while I chartered the cab; and I began to wonder if after all he had not some suspicion and whether he would let Althea go.

She had kept behind us and when the cab was ready, the door of which Dormund himself held open, she hurried past him and

7

took her seat. He closed the door and stood bareheaded while we drove off.

I drew a breath of relief.

"Will he follow us?" asked Althea nervously.

"Not he. He hasn't a thought of the trick we've played him."

"Oh, Mr. Bastable, how could you do it so naturally? I was positively trembling the whole time."

"You needn't worry about anything now," I said reassuringly. "Try to fix your thoughts on what is to be done next."

"I don't know what to do," she murmured.

Neither did I. Nor did I seem to care. The unexpectedness of it all had taken my breath away. The whole position was so unreal that I was in the clouds.

A few minutes before I had been bent only upon rushing away in search of distraction from the galling rack of my disappointment on her account; and now she had rushed to me in the hour of her trouble, and was by my side, trusting to me to get her out of it all.

I would do it at any cost; but for the moment I was so elated by the proof of her confidence, that I could think of nothing else.

CHAPTER II

COMPLICATIONS

Althea was at first unwilling to go to our house, as such a course might involve us in some way with the authorities; but I would not listen to her objections.

"Let me suggest one precaution," I said as the cab stopped. "That you hold your handkerchief to your face as you enter. We have one German servant, Gretchen, and she had better not recognize you. The other two are English, and will hold their tongues."

She adopted the suggestion, and when we entered the house we found that Bessie had already arrived and had explained that I had missed the train. She kissed Althea and fussed over her in the way girls have, and I could see that she was bursting with curiosity to know everything.

After a few minutes she suggested that I should send a telegram home to say I was not going; and as I saw that she wished to be left alone with Althea, I went off at once. It turned out to be lucky that I did, for Lieutenant von Bernhoff, a man who took a great deal more interest in Bessie than she did in him, was just getting out of a cab as I left the house.

"What has happened, Bastable? I went to the station to see you off, and Dormund told me you weren't going. From what he said I was afraid that something had happened to your sister."

I shut down a smile. "There's nothing the matter. One of my trunks was left behind, and I had to put off my journey. I'm on my way to wire to my people at home. Come with me." He was no favourite of mine, and as a friend of Dormund's, about the last man in Berlin to be trusted with the secret of Althea's presence in the house.

He went with me to send the telegram, and plagued me with a hundred questions about Bessie, the reason for her having to wear spectacles, and so on; and when we reached the house again he wanted to come in and see her.

"You must excuse her to-day, von Bernhoff. The place is all sixes and sevens on account of my intended departure," I said with a shrug.

"You found your lost trunk, I hope? Dormund told me you were in a fine temper about it."

"I am much obliged to him, but he might mind his own business."

"He was minding it in a sense," he replied with a grin. "I had promised to introduce him to your sister. He knows, you know"; and he grinned meaningly.

"A pity you were not there earlier then," I said carelessly, repressing a smile at what would have been the result if he had been.

"I shall bring him some day to introduce him," he declared as we shook hands.

"By all means. He is a good fellow. But not until I get back to Berlin."

"He is awfully keen to know her—now"; and with this somewhat cryptic remark he grinned again and turned away.

I went upstairs wondering curiously whether Dormund had said anything else about the "Bessie" he had seen at the station to start von Bernhoff's suspicions. The complications were beginning already.

But Althea and Bessie appeared to be taking the matter lightly, for a burst of merry laughter from them both rang out as I opened the door.

"Paul of the grave face!" cried Bessie. "Look at him, Althea."

9

Althea's eyes were shining brightly, and the colour had returned to her cheeks, as I saw when she looked up at my entrance.

"It is good to find you like this," I said.

"It is Bessie. She is wonderful," said Althea.

"There is just no trouble at all," declared Bessie, coming toward me with a light of pleasure dancing in her eyes. "It is the most ridiculous mistake, Paul; and all this bother to-day appears to be the result of it. Shall I tell him?" Althea nodded. "About the Prince von Graven. It isn't Althea he cares for at all. It's Chalice. Althea has let every one believe it, lest Chalice's prospects should be injured."

I started and caught my breath in surprise and almost fierce delight at this wonderful news. But Bessie was a thoughtful little body, and she had placed herself purposely so that Althea should not see the effect upon me; and to give me time to recover myself, she added: "You'll have some tea, won't you, Paul? Ring the bell for another cup."

I turned away and rang the bell, and then with a big effort I choked down my delighted surprise and drew a chair close to the others.

"So it's Chalice, eh?" I asked quietly.

"Of course no one must know it except you two," said Althea.

Bessie laughed mischievously. "Even that doesn't much matter, does it, Paul?"

"It makes no end of a difference," I said gravely. "But why on earth have you allowed the mistake to be made? Both you and Chalice herself let me share it last night, too."

"It is for Chalice's sake," said Althea. "You had just come from her, and I saw what she had told you. You know she is in my care, and that I promised my sister on her death-bed that I would look after her."

"You speak as if she were a child and you a grave and sedate matron, Althea," declared Bessie. "And there can't be more than a year or two between you."

"Three years, Bessie. Chalice is only twenty; and I am her aunt, you know."

We all smiled at this. "But that is no reason why you should get into all this bother on account of the Prince," objected Bessie.

"The simplest thing will be to let the truth be known," I put in.

"Oh no, no," protested Althea vehemently. "Anything but that; at any rate for the present. Herr Grumpel declares her voice will take the whole country by storm; and she is to make her début soon. She has a brilliant future before her, and if she were to incur the displeasure of the Court at such a time it would ruin everything."

10

"But Prince von Graven won't wish his wife to be a singer," I objected, "even supposing such a marriage were ever sanctioned."

"Chalice declares she will not do a thing to hurt his interests. That is why she will not have a betrothal."

"But what about you, Althea?" cried Bessie indignantly. "Are you to be packed off to prison or out of the country in order that the secret may be kept?"

"It must be kept, Bessie," said Althea very decidedly.

"I think a little plain talk to the Prince would be a good thing," I suggested.

"He thinks only of Chalice, and will not do anything against her wish."

"Something like a deadlock, then," I murmured. If everything was to hinge only on Chalice's wishes, the case promised to be awkward. We were silent for a while, and then I said: "You will be placed in a very ugly fix. We all know what the Kaiser is when any one opposes him. You surely won't go to the extreme of letting yourself be arrested?"

This appeared to alarm her seriously. "No, no. There are other reasons, too," she exclaimed hastily.

"Then your only course is for you to leave the country."

"I can't even leave Berlin while Chalice is here."

"Then take her with you."

"There is Herr Grumpel. If she left now, it would ruin everything."

I tossed up my hands with a smile. The position was impossible.

"Hadn't you better fetch your trunks from the station, Paul?" asked Bessie.

"I'm afraid there's nothing in them that will solve this puzzle."

"At any rate you will not go home now," she retorted meaningly. "And while you go for them, Althea and I can talk things over. I have made up my mind. She must, of course, stay with us for the time."

"No, no," protested Althea. I rose, delighted at the idea.

"We shall have everything settled by the time you're back, Paul."

"There's Gretchen, remember," I replied as I went out of the room.

I walked to the station and started to think things over, but there was one thought which for the time crowded out all others. Althea was not in love with the Prince! Thank Heaven for that. And compared with that, nothing mattered. I would find some way out of the tangle, and in the meantime—well, I could hope again. And then

11

I began dreaming and planning with the sanguine vanity of a man very much in love and once more able to hope for the best.

Dormund was still at the station, and met me as I entered. "Ah, Herr Bastable, going on your journey after all?"

"Not to-night. I don't travel at night if I can help it."

"Well that is perhaps as well. It will give you more time. All passports have to be viséd afresh. But of course I can see to that for you, if you like."

"Why's that? Anything happened?"

"It would interest you if you were still on your paper. Trouble with those cursed Poles again. A plot to rob one of the Imperial couriers of his papers. We had news from Koln and prevented it; but some of the scoundrels are known to be here in Berlin, and we are watching for them. If we were to behead a few of them it would save a lot of trouble."

"There would be so many less to make the trouble, anyway," I replied carelessly. "Do you know the people in it?"

"I know who is at the bottom of it, and so do you; for you have written about him often enough. That Baron von Ringheim. There's no proof, of course; there never is; but proof or no proof, I'd put him in safe keeping if I had my way. He's the most dangerous man in Europe to our Government."

"I think you have him on the brain, Dormund," I laughed.

"I'd rather have him under lock and key," he retorted almost angrily. "But get the evening paper; you will see something about it there."

I had heard a good deal about this Baron von Ringheim. He had been banished many years before for some offence against the Government, and his estates had been confiscated. He was believed to have allied himself with all parties who had grievances against the Government; had been very active in the work of sedition; and was credited with having originated a policy of combination among them for the common purpose of discrediting the Government. The policy had been very successful, with the result that, whenever a daring coup of any sort was made or attempted, he was credited with the responsibility.

"Then I suppose I owe it to the Baron that if I go to-morrow I must get my passport viséd," I replied after a pause.

"Yes; but of course it will only be a form in your case. By the way, Lieutenant Bernhoff was here after you left this afternoon. He came to bid you good-bye, he said; but I suppose it was more to see your sister. He tells me he has hopes some day of——eh?" and he smiled insinuatingly.

"One never knows what may happen, Dormund."

12

"He is a good fellow, and rich. He would have done me the honour to present me to your sister this afternoon. You may have seen that I was very interested in her."

"We must find another occasion then. I am sure the pleasure will be mutual," I said with a smile, the meaning of which he fortunately did not understand.

"You are very good." He was pleased at the compliment.

I assumed a more confidential air. "By the way, Dormund, I've been thinking a good deal about that arrest you were after—of Fräulein Korper."

"You know her well?"

"She is a very great friend of my sister." I managed to suggest more than the words implied and he smiled. "I can't bring myself to think of her as a criminal of any sort. It took my breath away."

"Of course I can't tell you anything I know officially, but there can be no harm in my saying that the arrest was ordered from Count von Felsen's office."

"I'm not after newspaper copy," I laughed. "But it bewildered me."

At that moment some one came up to him and he excused himself. I bought the evening paper and drove off home with my trunks.

I had not learnt much in regard to Althea, but the fact that the arrest had been ordered from Count von Felsen's office might mean that it was connected with her supposed relations with Prince von Graven. It was certainly unusual, and the Kaiser's hand might well be in the background.

Then I read the account of the affair Dormund had spoken of. It read very much like one of the Baron's coups. The courier had been in possession of some very important State papers, and these had all but fallen into the hands of those who had attempted to steal them. The same thing had been done more than once before, I knew. The object was to get hold of such things, and then make them public at the moment when they would do the greatest damage.

At the present time the Kaiser's naval policy was the target at which they were striking, and the temper of the people was in such a ticklish condition that any well-aimed blow might hamper those in power dangerously. If the old Baron was at the bottom of it, he was certainly a very astute tactician. And if I knew anything of the feelings of the authorities, he and his friends would have a very bad time of it if they were caught.

I was folding up the paper when I had a very ugly shock. I caught the name, "ALTHEA KORPER," in bold type in the centre of a police notice.

It was an advertisement announcing her flight, seeking information about her, and warning all who connived at her escape or gave her shelter that they would render themselves liable to prosecution. To this was added a minute and detailed description.

This was something indeed. It threw a fresh light upon the reason for the arrest. It was impossible to believe that so drastic a step as this would be taken merely because of the affair with the Prince. There must be more behind than I had thought.

Even the Kaiser would not go to the length of setting the police to hound down a girl merely because a man had fallen in love with her, and a Court marriage scheme threatened to go wrong in consequence. The idea was simply preposterous.

But what could the arrest mean then? I must see if Althea could throw any light on it, and warn her. We should have to steer a very careful course, or there would be serious trouble. That was certain.

I tore the notice out of the paper and put it in my pocket, and when I reached home I was careful not to show the real concern I felt.

"I have persuaded Althea to remain with us for a time, Paul," declared Bessie.

"Good. As a matter of fact it would be a little difficult for you to leave Berlin for a day or two," I said to Althea, as lightly as I could. "There has been some bother with the recalcitrant Polish party"; and I went on to give the gist of my talk with Dormund.

"Can I see the paper?" she asked. "I am a Pole, you remember."

I had not remembered it, and the coincidence struck me forcibly. I gave her the paper, and said I would see about my luggage while she read it.

"Don't go, please, Mr. Bastable. I have something to tell you," she said, looking up from the paper. "About this. I must go away at once."

"No, no, Althea," declared Bessie. "We shan't let you go, shall we, Paul?"

"I will tell you, and you will see that I must. You know what is here about the Baron von Ringheim, Mr. Bastable. This is evidently the reason for my arrest. I have misled every one. I did it for Chalice's sake. My name is not Korper at all; it is that"—and she pointed to the paper—"von Ringheim. I am his daughter. Now you will understand why I must hide."

There was a pause. I looked at Bessie, and our eyes met.

I took the police advertisement from my pocket and handed it to her in silence. She read it at a glance, and read also my meaning—that I would not let her decide what to do without knowing all the facts.

14

She gave it back to me with a smile.

"While you were at the station, Paul, I had a quarrel with Gretchen. She was insolent, so I discharged her on the spot."

I breathed a sigh of relief. She was with me in the resolve to stand by Althea, let the consequences be what they might.

CHAPTER III

CHALICE

We had great difficulty in persuading Althea to remain with us, and should not have succeeded if Bessie had not put on her hat and vowed that she would go with her wherever she went. Then we came to a compromise—Althea was to stay that night and decide on her plans the next morning.

By that time I had induced Chalice to try and clear away one at least of the tangles by letting the facts be told about the Prince von Graven, and to get the Prince himself to ascertain the real cause for the steps against Althea.

I sent a note to him, hinting at the reason why I wished to see him immediately, and he answered the letter in person. He professed himself greatly distressed at what had occurred; but it had not suggested itself to him that he should remedy matters by acknowledging the truth.

"I will be frank with you, Mr. Bastable. The greatest pressure has been put upon me to induce me to abandon my—to consent to my betrothal to the Princess von Altenvelt; and this is apparently the result of my refusal."

"But do you seriously think a drastic step like this would be taken on such a slight foundation?" I objected.

"I haven't thought about that. It is drastic, isn't it? But you know the Emperor is liable to fits of temper."

"The order for the arrest issued from the office of Count von Felsen; will you make inquiries as to its real reason?"

"Of course I will. The Minister and I are unfortunately at daggers drawn. He is jealous of the favour with which the Emperor honours me. I will do all I can."

"There is certainly one other thing you can do, Prince!" He

15

began to fidget uneasily at this. "I mean explain the mistake and that it is Fräulein Chalice Mennerheim whom you desire to marry."

"My dear sir, I would marry her to-morrow; but she will not have even an open betrothal. What can I do?" Where Chalice was concerned he was obviously like clay in the hands of the potter.

"I am going to see her at once," I said as I rose.

"If you can prevail with her, you will do me the greatest favour in the world," he exclaimed eagerly, grasping my hand with warmth.

I went off then to see Chalice, leaving the Prince to go to Althea. It required very slight discernment to see that we should do little with him. He had his own battle to fight at Court, and that was more than sufficient to monopolize all the firmness he possessed. And I expected but little more help from Chalice.

An incident, to which I attached no significance at the time, occurred as I entered the house of Frau Steiner, where Althea and Chalice had their lodgings. I gave my card to the servant, and she took it first into a room leading off the hall, and then carried it upstairs. While I was waiting, a dark, striking-looking Jewess came out as if to leave the house. She stopped suddenly, surprised to see me still in the hall, hesitated, and then returned quickly to the room.

I knew her by sight. Her name was Hagar Ziegler. She was the daughter of a money-lender whose shady methods I had had to investigate on more than one occasion while I had been on the Newsletter. I was called upstairs to Chalice a moment later, and thought no more of the incident.

I had not expected to find Chalice very concerned about Althea, and was not therefore surprised when she received me as calmly as though I were making just an ordinary call.

"This is a delightful surprise, Herr Bastable," she exclaimed with a lovely smile, as she gave me her hand. "But you catch me in deshabille. I was practising." As a matter of fact she was rather elaborately gowned, and I knew she was very particular in such matters. There was very little of the girl about Chalice.

"I should ask your pardon for coming at such an hour and without notice; but I have come about Fräulein Korper."

"About Althea? Oh, that is good of you. Of course I've been terribly anxious about her. And worry is so bad for the voice."

"I sympathize with you, I am sure."

Her sense of humour was not keen, and she accepted this as quite genuine. "Everyone is so good to me," she murmured. "And where is Althea?"

"Do you not know what occurred yesterday afternoon?"

"I was at Herr Grumpel's all the afternoon—I had a most trying lesson. He was in a horrible temper, and it quite put me out. Well,

16

when I came home, Althea was gone, instead of having some tea ready for me. And when I asked where she was, that stupid girl, Lotta, said something nonsensical about the police having been here. Such rubbish, of course."

"Unfortunately, it was quite true. An attempt was made to arrest her."

"Herr Bastable! You don't mean it!" Surprise, no other feeling in this. No grief, no concern even. "Whatever for?" As if it had been Althea's fault.

"It was on your account," I said bluntly. "Because of the mistake you have allowed people to make in regard to the Prince von Graven."

She was not in the least embarrassed. "So you know that. I am so glad. It is such a relief not to have to keep these tiresome secrets from one's friends. I couldn't tell you before, could I? You see, it was Althea's secret as much as mine. And the Prince's, too. He is so devoted to me. And such a sweet man."

"You don't appear to grasp the real gravity of the matter, I'm afraid."

"Oh, that is unkind! Of course I do. I wouldn't have dear Althea get into any trouble on my account for the world!"

"Then of course you will let the truth as to the Prince be known at once."

"Herr Bastable!" Eyes, expression, voice, gestures, everything eloquent of indignant surprise at the suggestion. "Why, then they might arrest me!"

"On the contrary, the Prince is eager to marry you at once."

"But my voice. My début! You don't understand. Herr Grumpel declares that I shall make such a reputation as——" She threw up her hands as though it were impossible to estimate the fame awaiting her. "How can you be so cruel? Besides, it would ruin the Prince with the Emperor. You would not have him ruined just for poor little me!"

I was fast losing patience. "It is rather a question whether you are to ruin Fräulein Althea by keeping silence."

Her features drew together as if she were going to cry. "Do you mean that Althea wishes this? That she would selfishly sacrifice my future in this way?"

"She may be in very serious danger if it should be known that she is the daughter of Baron von Ringheim."

"But who is likely to tell that?" she asked with an air of quite artless innocence; and then added quickly: "Besides, in that case it would be of no use to say anything about the Prince."

It was useless to break oneself against the wall of such

selfishness as this, so I tried a different argument. "Let me show you one way in which you can turn this matter to your own great advantage." All sign of tears passed away instantly. "Your future depends upon your securing the favour of the Court. Now, if you were to submit yourself to the Emperor's will in the matter of the Imperial marriage and sacrifice your wishes in regard to the Prince because you have just heard of the Imperial desires, His Majesty would highly appreciate your self-sacrifice; the whole country would ring with your romantic self-denial; and you would gain a bigger advertisement for your début than any singer ever enjoyed in this Empire."

She saw all this in a flash, and her eyes shone with the light of ambitious desire. "Oh, Herr Bastable! But do you think it could be done?"

"Shall I make some inquiries? I have friends on whom I can rely."

"Oh, you would be the best friend a poor lonely girl could have in the world. But we must be quite certain first, mustn't we?"

"You would lose the man you love, remember."

She sighed and cast down her eyes, a picture of beautiful resignation. "It would be terrible," she murmured. "But there is dear Althea to think of, isn't there? It is, perhaps, my duty."

She pressed my hand warmly at parting, and urged me to come again as soon as I had any news to bring; and before I left the house, I heard her rich melodious voice ring out. She had resumed her practice.

As I closed the front door behind me I saw Hagar Ziegler again. She was now in close conversation with Hugo von Felsen; and as I did not wish him to know of my visit to Chalice at such a time, I walked off in the opposite direction.

He had seen me, however, and presently came hurrying after me. "Ah, Herr Bastable! It is you then," he said as he reached me. "How did you find the ladies?"

"I don't know that I am much concerned to tell you," I answered curtly.

"Has Fräulein Althea returned? Isn't that an extraordinary affair?"

"I really have no time to discuss gossip with you."

"I think it will be worth your while," he replied meaningly. "I heard of your change of plans, too, when you were actually at the station. My friend Bernhoff told me. He is a grand fellow, Bernhoff."

"A testimonial from you is certainly a strong recommendation," I replied as nastily as I could speak.

But he only smiled and spread out his hands. "I'm afraid you are still angry with me on account of that chat of ours the other night at the Ohlsen's dance—about Fräulein Althea. But I'm not a fellow to bear malice. And you know, as every one knows, how intensely I admire her."

"I don't care a hang whether you bear malice or not."

"You are very difficult, Bastable; but really I wish to be your friend, and to warn you. People are talking about you."

"Let them talk then."

"This visit to this house here on the morning after Fräulein Althea's disappearance; your sudden change of plans yesterday; the hurried visit of Prince von Graven to your house this morning. These things cause questions"; and he gave me a very sly significant smile.

"As you appear to be asking them, the best thing you can do is to answer them in your own way. Good-morning"; and with that I turned on my heel.

But although I could get rid of him, I could not so easily shake off the unpleasant impression his words had made. He had certainly been spying on me. Why? Could he have any suspicion of the truth?

The more I considered matters, the closer appeared to be von Felsen's connexion with them. It was he who had first told me of the Prince's supposed love for Althea; he had hinted at the probable effect of the Kaiser's anger; it was from his father's office that the order for the arrest had come; and as he was in that office, it was highly probable, almost certain, indeed, that on the night of the dance he had already known it was to be made.

The thing looked like cause and effect; but then there was the fact that he had laid stress on his admiration for Althea. He could not wish to see a girl he cared for in the rough clutches of the police. The thing was absurd.

It was a fair presumption, however, that he was trying to find her. His knowledge of the Prince's visit to me that morning showed that some one was shadowing the Prince, and the spy had carried the news straight to von Felsen. I had certainly blundered badly in letting the Prince come to Althea's hiding-place.

He had known also of my visit to Chalice; and then it occurred to me that Hagar Ziegler had been used for that purpose. The Steiners were Jews, and she might well be a friend. I recalled her manner when she had come hurrying out as I stood in the hall. She had been going to leave the house. Was it to carry word to him, and had she brought him there to wait for me when I left?

The whole business was a very ugly complication, and the best thing would be for us to smuggle Althea out of Berlin while I set to work to straighten it out.

19

I returned home, both puzzled and ill at ease, to report the result of my interview with Chalice; and Bessie met me with news of another twist in the skein.

"Aunt Charlotte has arrived, Paul," she said, with a very long face.

"The deuce! Why she wasn't to come for a week or so."

"Well, she's here anyway. You'd better come up to her room and see her at once"; and she turned and ran upstairs. "She does these odd things, you know."

My aunt was a particularly nervous person, and about the last we wanted to have in the house at such a time. I followed Bessie, wondering what sort of explanation of Althea's presence I could make.

"Have you told her about Althea?" I asked.

"She will only think she is staying with us in the ordinary way," replied Bessie, pausing with her hand on the door-knob. "And you'd better be careful. She has one of her headaches after the travelling. You know what she is at such times."

She was lying on the sofa with her back to the light, her long greyish curls straggling over her shoulder, and a handkerchief pressed to her brows.

"I am sorry to hear you have a bad headache after your journey, Aunt Charlotte," I said as I tiptoed across to her couch.

She gave a faint little moan of pain, and held out three fingers in a way I knew well. I just touched them. "I am very glad to see you," I murmured, as she withdrew them quickly.

"Don't make a noise, Paul," said Bessie, as she knelt down by the sofa. A most unnecessary caution, for I was not moving. "Men are so rough, are they not, aunt? Shall I bathe your head, dear? Get the scent, Paul. On the mantelpiece."

I tiptoed to the other end of the room, and Bessie called "Hush!" in a very aggressive whisper.

As I turned, bottle in hand, I noticed that they were both shaking with what looked uncommonly like suppressed laughter; and as I reached the sofa again, Bessie got up giggling. Then I understood and joined in the laughter, and "Aunt Charlotte" let me see her face.

"You ought to have known her hand, Paul," cried Bessie. "One would suppose you had never seen it before."

"All right. Grin away. You had me. Those curls took me in; they are Aunt Charlotte's to the life."

"They may well be. It's the wig she left here last time."

"Is your head too bad to let you stand up so that I can see your dress, 'aunt'?" I asked.

20

"It is all Bessie's work," said Althea, as she stood up.

"It's great," I agreed. "I believe I should have passed you in the street, and I am sure I should if you had a veil on"; and then Bessie explained how she had been thinking it all out.

"And now, about Chalice? Wasn't she in terrible distress?" asked Althea.

"No. She appeared to think that you would be all right and had not worried in the least."

Bessie coughed significantly and glanced at me. I went on to describe what had passed; and Althea was as firm as ever in her resolve not to do anything which would prejudice Chalice's prospects. I held my tongue about the last argument I had used with Chalice.

"I've seen others beside Chalice," I said presently. "Hugo von Felsen. I have the idea that he is in some way mixed up in this. Can you tell me of any reason why he would be likely to take a hand?"

Althea paused a second and then looked up with a smile. "He wishes me to marry him. He has asked me more than once; and the only benefit I ever had from the supposed attentions of the Prince was a relief from his. Why does that make you look so serious?" she asked with another smile, seeing my grave look.

"I am thinking."

"It's a big effort for Paul," bantered Bessie.

I gestured impatiently. "Tell me, do you think it possible he can have guessed your secret—about your father, I mean?"

"Yes, he knows it. Why do you ask that?"

"Because things are forcing me to the conclusion that in some way or other he is at the bottom of all the trouble. I don't understand it yet; but I will before long, if I have to drag it out of him by force."

But I would not alarm them by saying anything of von Felsen's suspicions that Althea was with us.

I knew it well enough now, however, and recognized to the full the danger which it boded.

CHAPTER IV

EPHRAIM ZIEGLER

Althea's statement—that von Felsen had pressed her to marry him—made it plain to me that he was pulling the strings in everything; although why he should endeavour to secure her arrest in order to further his purpose, baffled me.

If his motive were jealousy, however, it was possible that he would call a halt when he learnt the truth about the Prince. I urged Althea to let me tell him, but she would not. Her quixotic regard for Chalice stood in the way. Nor would she adopt the alternative advice I tendered—that "Aunt Charlotte" should leave Berlin as secretly and mysteriously as she had arrived.

Nothing was left for me, therefore, but to cast about for some other means of dealing with von Felsen. In the meantime I knew he would lose no time in confirming his suspicions as to Althea's whereabouts.

This was soon made plain. I was speaking to Bessie when von Bernhoff's card was brought to us; and when he was shown up, von Felsen was with him. Von Bernhoff introduced him to Bessie, and he made himself insinuatingly polite to her.

A lot of small talk followed: a good deal of it about my interrupted journey; and von Bernhoff asked if I was going on the following day.

"I don't think Aunt Charlotte will let you go, Paul," said Bessie, who was as cool and self-possessed as possible.

"Frau Ellicott has come then?" said von Bernhoff, who had known of the intended visit. "I shall be glad to see her again. She is a charming lady."

"She arrived this morning," said Bessie in the most matter of fact tone.

"You should see Frau Ellicott," said von Bernhoff to von Felsen, who had pricked up his ears at this. "She is a perfect type of an English lady."

"I shall hope for the honour of being presented," he smirked.

"She will be delighted, I am sure. Lieutenant von Bernhoff is a favourite of hers, and any friend of his may count upon her good graces." I thought Bessie was carrying things a bit too far; but von Felsen was keeping an eye on me, and I could not warn her. "To-day she has a bad headache. You may remember how a journey upsets her."

"Ah yes, indeed"; and von Bernhoff shrugged his shoulders with a gesture of commiseration. "I remember too how interested she was in Fräulein Chalice Mennerheim. More than once she has spoken to me in raptures about her voice."

"She is passionately fond of music and used to be a great singer herself," was Bessie's absolutely composed reply.

"This news about Fräulein Korper will interest her greatly, then," interjected von Felsen; and I saw why Chalice's name had been dragged in so clumsily.

Bessie was on the point of replying when we heard footsteps in the room overhead, and the sound of some one singing the jewel song from Faust. Then the door above was opened and the voice sounded nearer. The singer came downstairs.

"One of Fräulein Chalice's songs," said von Felsen, with a grin.

Bessie rose. She was quite cool. "Aunt Charlotte must be better, Paul. I'll go and see if she will not come down to see Lieutenant von Bernhoff."

Von Felsen hastened to open the door for her, and took the opportunity of glancing up the stairs. "She has a young voice, your aunt," he said to me as he closed the door behind Bessie.

"She is no longer a young woman, as you will see."

"If she is well enough to come to us," he retorted meaningly.

"At any rate her headache is better," grinned von Bernhoff; and then we sat in silence until Bessie returned, laughing merrily.

"A most ridiculous mistake, Paul. I don't know how we could be so stupid. It was Ellen singing—our maid, you know," she added to the others. "Aunt Charlotte opened the door to tell her to be quiet. She is very angry at having been woke up."

Then came another mishap. The two men were murmuring their obviously insincere regrets when Ellen entered and said the Prince von Graven wished to see me.

"Show him up," I said, with a sort of feeling that nothing mattered now.

Von Felsen gave such a leer of triumph that I could have kicked him. "He is, indeed, an ultimate friend of yours, Bastable. Two visits in one day"; and with that the two men went, meeting the Prince on the landing.

"I could almost cry with vexation," whispered Bessie.

"It's too serious for tears, Bess. Was Althea coming down here?"

She nodded. "I was just in time to stop her."

"She might almost as well have come," I grunted. "You had better leave me alone with the Prince. Try and persuade Althea to make a bolt of it."

The interview with the Prince was very short. Eagerness to learn the result of my visit to Chalice had brought him together with

23

the desire to tell me he had found out that the arrest was not ordered by the Kaiser, who knew nothing about it. I told him what had passed between Chalice and myself.

"I was afraid of it; but of course she must have her own way," he declared feebly.

"Do you think she has the right to ruin Fräulein Althea, then?"

"It is most perplexing, baffling. I do not see what to do."

"Not to tell the truth is simply cowardly," I said with some warmth.

"Herr Bastable!" and he drew himself up to his full height.

"To place one woman in danger merely for another woman's caprice is cowardly, Prince von Graven. And you are chiefly responsible."

"Do you speak in this way with Fräulein Althea's sanction?"

"On the contrary, she is all too willing to sacrifice herself."

"Then it is scarcely pertinent to the matter."

"Pertinent or impertinent, it is the truth," I declared bluntly, disgusted at his indifference to Althea's welfare.

"Are you seeking to force a quarrel upon me, sir?"

"No. I am merely trying to rouse you to do what you ought to do."

"I am the best judge of that."

"Then we may as well end the interview"; and I threw open the door.

He was bursting with indignation. "I am extremely disappointed in you, Herr Bastable."

"A mutual feeling, I assure you, Prince"; and I bowed him out.

I was glad to be rid of him. His news—that the arrest was not at the Kaiser's bidding—confirmed my belief that I must deal with von Felsen as the chief instigator, and I must lose no time in getting to work to checkmate him.

I knew a good deal about him. He had lived a wastrel, dissipated life, and was deep in the hands of the Jews; and the fact that I had seen him with Hagar Ziegler led me to think I could get from her father what I wanted—something discreditable which would enable me to pull him up short.

Old Ephraim Ziegler was under a considerable obligation to me. During my newspaper work I had refrained from taking a certain line in regard to a very dirty transaction in which he was concerned, and had saved the old Jew from being prosecuted. He knew this, and had more than once expressed himself anxious to show me some practical appreciation of that service.

I was shown at once into his office, and he received me with more than unctuous servility.

"Ah, Herr Bastable, this is indeed an honour," he said, rubbing his fat hands together while his beady eyes searched my face in doubt whether I had again come to undo some of his questionable work.

"So you haven't forgotten me?"

"Forgotten you!" he cried, spreading wide his arms. "You are one of the only friends poor Ephraim Ziegler ever had. You come on business? A little money, eh?"

I shook my head. "Oh no, not that."

This disconcerted him somewhat. He jumped to the conclusion that it must be something unpleasant. I let him think that for a while and, referring to one of the former cases, hinted that I had come to warn him, and that something had been discovered which might mean trouble for him. But I ended with an assurance that personally I would not do anything against him. Then I rose as if to leave.

He trembled and was very frightened; his flabby cheeks paled, and his voice shook as he pressed me to stay. "It is such an honour you do me," he declared. Thus pressed, I resumed my seat, and we chatted about a number of matters until I brought the talk round to von Felsen, mentioning his name casually among several others. "He's one of the flies in your web, you old spider," I laughed.

"He owes me a lot of money, that young man," he said. It was his habit to gloat over his cunning in such matters. "But it will be all right in the end."

"Where's he to get it from to pay you? Not from his father."

"Not from his father; that is true. But he will get it, he will get it"; and he sat pressing his finger-tips together with such an air of satisfaction that it set me thinking. I remembered that he was a Pole, and had been mixed up once before with one of the Polish schemes.

"There are other things beside money to pay debts with, eh?" I put all the significance I could into the question, and winked at him. "You old fox!"

"You almost make me afraid of you, Herr Bastable. You get to know so much," he answered after a pause, and with a leer intended to flatter me.

"Would you like to know what I do know about this?" I laughed. "Your 'almost' would then be 'quite,' I assure you"; and I rose again as if to leave.

"Oh no, no. Don't go yet," he cried eagerly.

Down I sat again with a shrug as if to please him. "You want to find out how much I do know, eh? But I did not come to discuss politics"—I paused intentionally on the word, and the effect satisfied me—"but just to warn you about that old Martin affair. You can't pump me; but you'd better go carefully in both concerns."

His uneasiness showed that my old experience with him stood me in good stead now. He had a wholesome fear of my sources of information. He paused, hunched up in his chair, and asked suddenly: "Why did you mention Hugo von Felsen's name to me?"

I had an inspiration and resolved upon a shot. I took out my cigarette case, selected one with great care, and as I lit it, looked across at him. "Your daughter is a very handsome girl, Ziegler."

The shot told instantly. "You mean something. Herr Bastable," he cried, leaning forward in his eagerness. "You are my friend. You must tell me. I love my Hagar. She is the light of my life. Tell me," he repeated.

I wished with all my heart that I could; but I could only look as if my secret knowledge would fill an encyclopaedia.

This spurred his eagerness. "Ah, my friend, my dear Herr Bastable, you must tell me," he urged.

I shook my head. "You are a very clever old spider but—some one is blabbing. Look out." It was a safe general sort of shot and added to his mystification. He bit his nails and his eyes rolled from side to side rapidly. It was his way when deeply moved. "Do you mean about Hagar?" he asked at length.

I knew by this that there was something more important than Hagar behind. He would always put the less important consideration in front. "No. It's the other affair; about the——" I broke off, and his eyes fastened on mine as if to read in them the rest of the sentence. "But it's no affair of mine," I added with a shrug. "Why should I bother myself? But don't forget my warning."

"Do you mean we have been betrayed? That there is a spy among us?"

I turned grave for an instant. "I name no names, Ziegler; but some one gave you away the other day when you failed."

The effect of this second shot was startling. "God of my fathers, if I thought it was von Felsen I would——." He clenched his hands in rage.

I was almost as excited as he was, but I took care he should not see it. Von Felsen was mixed up in these Polish schemes; and if I could get at the truth, I should have him in the hollow of my hand. "It wasn't von Felsen," I said to reassure him. "He's too deep in, and too much in your power to chatter. You know that. And I shan't give you away. I have too much sympathy with your cause. But it wasn't von Felsen. I assure you that, although I bear him no good-will."

I had succeeded in convincing him that I knew a lot; and he had not a suspicion that I had been merely guessing on the strength of the hints he himself had dropped. He sat a long time thinking, and was greatly disturbed.

"You have startled me, Herr Bastable; but I know you sympathize with the cause. I know that from what you have written in your paper. But why do you bear ill-will to Hugo?"

"Hugo," eh? He spoke or thought of him by his Christian name. The inference was easy. Von Felsen was playing a double matrimonial game. "When may one offer congratulations, Ziegler?" I asked with a smile. I could afford to smile, for I was winning, hands down.

"It is Hagar's wish. She loves him; and she will be a countess, too."

"Two excellent reasons. And meanwhile you find him useful to get——" Again I broke off the sentence and finished with a knowing smile.

"You are the devil, Herr Bastable," he replied with a laugh.

"Well, it is at least useful to be able to get inside information when very important papers are in the hands of an Imperial messenger, eh?"

"I don't know what you mean by that," he answered, wagging his head.

I affected to take offence. "It's enough for my purposes that I do. Is it worth while to try and fool me? I don't take to it easily, you know."

"I am not trying it," he protested.

"Then don't pretend that von Felsen isn't in all this with you. I know too much. And now, look here, I'll tell you the real object of this visit. Von Felsen is trying a fool's game with me, and it has to stop. I know he daren't go against you, Ziegler, and you daren't go against me; even if your friendship for me were less than it is."

My tone alarmed him. "What is he doing? I have influence with him, of course."

"What he is doing may turn out to touch you pretty closely; but never mind what it is for the present. Give me a line to him—that I am your friend and that anything he does against me is the same as if done against you."

"Of course I will," he consented. He wrote a few lines quickly and handed them to me.

MY DEAR HUGO,—

"Herr Bastable is a great friend of mine. Any service to him is a service to me; and the reverse.

"EPHRAIM ZIEGLER."

27

"That will do. And now a last word. Not a syllable to him or any one of what has passed between us to-day."

"I give you my honour, my dear Herr Bastable," he agreed readily.

"I shall hear if you talk, mind; and if I do—well I shall take it as a sign that I am to talk on my side. And I shall." I left him with that and walked out of his office on excellent terms with myself.

I was convinced that von Felsen was so tight in the toils that the letter I had obtained would frighten him consumedly. But I little thought of the grim results which were to flow from that afternoon's conversation.

I hurried home as fast as I could, and it was fortunate that I did so. As my cab drew up at the house, I found von Felsen and Dormund at the open door. I saw the move at once, without von Felsen's smug explanation. "Herr Dormund has a question to put to your sister, Bastable, about Fräulein Althea."

"I trust I am not intruding, Herr Bastable," said Dormund apologetically; "but Herr von Felsen tells me Miss Bastable has expressed the wish to give me important information."

"Von Felsen is wrong. My sister does not know any more than I do; but come into my den here and I'll see if she is at home," I replied indifferently.

"Your servant has already told us she is," put in von Felsen.

"Then I'll go and fetch her"; and I handed out my cigars and left them.

It was a tight corner; but of course Dormund must not see Bessie. It would at once reveal the trick I had played him at the station. Yet to deny her after Ellen's admission that she was at home would be the tamest subterfuge which he would see through in a second.

There was only one course: to call von Felsen out, face him with Ziegler's letter and make him get rid of Dormund. I was about to do this when another blow fell.

Ellen came running up to me, white of face and trembling.

"There are a number of police at the door, sir."

A loud knock at that instant confirmed her words.

It was a pretty fix in all truth, and I stood hesitating in perplexity what to do, when the knocking was repeated more insistently.

Obviously there was nothing for it but to admit the police, so I sent Ellen downstairs, and prepared to meet the crisis with as bold a face as possible.

CHAPTER V

ALTHEA'S STORY

I opened the door and found three men there, two of them in police uniform.

"Herr Dormund is here?" asked one of them.

"Yes," I said, and they entered.

"We must see him at once."

"Certainly." I went to the room where Dormund sat with von Felsen. "Some of your men wish to see you, Herr Dormund."

He jumped up quickly, and the next moment I breathed freely again. Instead of fresh trouble, the visit was a rare stroke of luck. He had left word where he was to be found, and the men had come with an urgent message for him to go to the police headquarters at once.

He excused himself to me hurriedly, and a minute later he and the others had left the house. I had scared myself for nothing.

I returned to von Felsen. "Herr Dormund has been recalled to his office. Why did you bring him here?"

"I thought you would like him to be perfectly satisfied that it was your sister whom he saw at the station?" he replied, forcing a laugh.

"You think it wasn't, then?"

He was still laughing maliciously. "He described her as a dark girl."

"And you thought I had misled him, eh?"

"Fräulein Althea is dark," he replied significantly.

"It didn't occur to you, I suppose, that I might have been doing a good turn for any other dark girl. A Jewess, for instance."

"I don't know what you mean."

"A friend of Ephraim Ziegler's, for instance."

"What are you driving at?"

"It's getting near to my turn to laugh, von Felsen."

"Fräulein Althea is in this house," he rapped out sharply. "You helped her to get out of Dormund's clutches at the station, and you are sheltering her here."

"Assume for a moment that she is here—mind you, I don't admit it. But assume it, what were you going to gain by putting Dormund on the track? I want the truth, you know. Suppose you had succeeded in putting her in the hands of the police, how would that help you?"

He rose. "Mind your own business," he said angrily.

29

"No, it's yours I am minding just now. You are going to stop this hunting down of Fräulein Althea. If you don't I shall turn hunter myself, with you as the quarry. You are not worth quarrelling with, so you needn't trouble yourself to stand sneering there. I shan't take any notice. Just read this."

I handed him the letter which Ziegler had given me. He started nervously as he read it, changed colour, and looked at me with an expression of bitter hate.

"I asked Herr Ziegler when I might congratulate him on Hagar's marriage," I said with a smile. "And that's one reason why I want to know your reason for what you are doing against Fräulein Althea. You profess to wish to marry her, you know; and even the son of a powerful Minister can't marry them both."

His confusion and anger were so intense that he could not find any reply to make to my jibe. He dropped back into his seat and sat biting his nails and scowling. I was delighted with my success.

"Well?" I asked at length. "A bit awkward, isn't it? I told you it was getting to be my turn to laugh. But I'm ready to come to an understanding. Drop this hunting business, and I'll hold my tongue to Ziegler."

"You've cornered me," he admitted with an oath. Then he laughed and swore again. "It wasn't my doing."

"What wasn't?"

"About Althea. I had to seem to wish it. It's my father's plan."

"You did the seeming very realistically," I retorted drily. "What are you going to do?"

"Marry the Ziegler girl when the time comes. I've no choice"; and he shrugged his shoulders and sneered.

"Why did your father wish you to marry a poor girl like Fräulein Althea?"

"If I'm not going to do it, what does that matter?"

"Not much, and I'll see that you don't do it," I replied as I rose. "We'll call a halt on both sides. I shan't talk so long as you run straight. But mind you do"; and with that I let him go.

I was well satisfied with the result of the interview. He was a man on whose fear I could play pretty safely, and his change of manner on reading the letter had convinced me that he went in deadly fear of the ruin which the wily old Jew held over his head.

I did not envy Hagar her prospective husband; but that was her affair. She loved him—Heaven knows there is no accounting for the vagaries of a woman's heart—and if she wished to marry him, she must have her way.

But he should not marry Althea. That I was firmly resolved, whether it was his father's idea or not. Not if the Emperor himself

30

and the whole Court were set upon it. What the real reason might be behind the scheme I had not yet fathomed; but I had done well enough, and would find out the rest.

There was no longer any urgent reason for Althea to leave the house, and elated with my success I ran up to tell the others my news.

I found Althea alone. She did not hear my knock at the door, and was sitting by the window buried in thought, her face resting on her hand, and gazing out across the city.

She started at my entrance and looked round hurriedly. "I am afraid I am disturbing you," I said.

"No, no. Please come in, Mr. Bastable. Bessie insisted on going out to look for some place to which I can go on leaving here. She declares she will go with me; but I——" She broke off with a little shrug of protest.

She was pale, and her eyes had a worried, anxious expression. I had not been alone with her since her arrival at the house. I had purposely avoided that, indeed, for fear lest some sign of my love for her should escape me. While she remained in our care I could not, of course, give even a hint of my feelings. It had not been so difficult to assume indifference in Bessie's presence; but alone with her I was afraid of myself.

"She would go, of course; but fortunately it will not be necessary for either of you to leave," I said in a level tone.

She smiled. "I read in that that you have been able to help me yet further. Tell me—unless you have no time to spare."

"I think I have been able to call a halt in all this"; and I went on to describe von Felsen's trick of bringing Dormund to the house, and how I had succeeded in checking him by means of the information about Hagar.

"You think he will marry that Jewess?"

"I think he goes in terror of her father, and that the Jew holds his fate in the hollow of his hand."

She nodded, and was silent for a space, and then shook her head. "Will you tell me what you know of Ephraim Ziegler?"

"Do you know him?" I asked in surprise.

She paused again, sighed, and glanced at me. "I owe you so much that I am bound to tell you everything. I am sure you will not betray me?" She stretched out her hand and laid it on my arm with a wistful gesture.

My pulses beat fast at the contact. "I hope you feel that."

"Of course I do," she said simply, withdrawing her hand again. For a moment she turned away and gazed out of the window, the red glare of the setting sun lighting her face. "He is a Pole, like my father; and you know the dream of every Pole—national independence. We have been foully wronged, and deep down in every Polish heart burns the desire for retribution. In that I, too, am a true Pole." Her eyes were ablaze with the light of enthusiasm as she turned them suddenly upon me. "I would freely give my life for the cause if it could do good; but, alas! I know it is but an empty dream. I am not blind."

"You have not taken any active part in any movement, surely?" I asked in some dismay.

"It is that which is probably behind the attempt to arrest me. The Government holds us all for enemies of the state. Any step is held to be fair against my countrymen. They are so conscious of the wrong they have done us that that very knowledge urges them farther along the road of oppression. I am my father's daughter and so am suspect. But I have not plotted, as have so many of us, against the Government. I know the uselessness. My father has written me often of the plans, and has urged me to use my opportunities here in Berlin for the cause."

"And yet you venture to remain here?"

"Herr Ziegler is deep in the schemes," she replied, not heeding my question. "You know what the policy is now. To ally ourselves with every disaffected element in the Empire, to stir discontent, to band together every section of malcontents, to lose no chance of throwing discredit on the Government, and when the time comes to raise the cry for Independence."

"And yet you venture to remain here?" I repeated.

"Do you think I am a coward?" and again she laid her hand on my arm. "No, Mr. Bastable, we Poles are dreamers and visionaries, but we are not cowards."

"I should not make that mistake, I assure you."

"I have told you because—well, because I wish you to know. I would trust my life to you. I have never in all my life had such friends as you and your sister."

"I thank you for that," I said in a low voice, averting my eyes that she might not see how deeply her words moved me.

She was silent for fully a minute, and my heart was beating so lustily that I half feared she would hear it.

"And is your father deeply concerned?" I asked, to break the trying silence.

"My dear father," she replied, with a smile and a sigh. "Ah, Mr. Bastable, if you could see him you would smile at your own question. In former years he was a power in the movement; but he is old now, and has brooded so long upon his wrongs that his mind has been affected. He was then indeed an enemy to be counted with, but he is no more his old self. Things are done in his name because of the influence he once wielded, but he himself does them no longer. They have broken him on the wheel of persecution. Pity rather than terror should be the emotion he stirs; but what do the iron rulers of this great Empire know of pity?"

"And the end?"

She tossed up her hands and let them fall on her lap. "Failure, of course, with its accompaniment of more proscriptions, more imprisonments, more tyranny."

"But yourself?"

"I have done no wrong and do not fear. Besides, have I not found a friend in you?" and she gave me a bright smile.

"I wish you would let that friend see you safe out of the country," I said very earnestly.

She shook her head slowly. "I am no coward to fly; but if ever it should come to that and I ask your help, you will not fail me I know."

"On my honour, I will not," I cried, all my heart in my voice. "I shall wait for that day."

"I am sure of you, Herr Bastable," she replied simply.

Again we were silent for a while. I could not trust myself to speak, and this time it was she who broke the silence. "I am very glad I have told you," she said. "Glad because it is good to share confidence with a friend, and glad, too, because you will see why it is not right for me to remain here, to let you and your sister run this risk on my account. She must not go with me when I leave your house. You understand that now?"

"We shall not let you go."

"Spoken like a friend, and as I should expect you to speak. But there is another reason. I scarcely know how to speak of it. And yet why should I hesitate? You will understand now. I would gladly stay, ah, so gladly! But I have had to learn to put aside my own desires. There are two deciding motives in my life—my father's welfare and that of Chalice."

"She does not consider you," I burst out bluntly.

"I won't hear that," she smiled. "I don't wish to hear any discordant note from you. You are not angry that I speak so," she cried quickly, as she put out her hand again.

"I am only sorry that I said it, since it grieves you."

"Well, then, were it not for something you have said now, those motives would drive me to leave you at once. You will think it strange when I say it has to do with Herr von Felsen. Ah, you frown."

"Surprise only. How can he have anything to do with such a decision?"

"I told you, and I think he has told you also, that he wishes to make me his—his wife." Her voice dropped as she hesitated over the word.

"Well?"

My voice must have betrayed something of the feeling with which I heard this, for she looked up and said hastily: "I am speaking to the best friend I ever had, am I not? To one who understands that I have to think of both those who love and trust to me—my father and Chalice? You will have wondered why Hugo von Felsen should entertain such a wish. I will tell you. He knows my secret—I told you that before. You remember?"

"Yes, I remember." Try as I would I could not make my tone other than hard.

"He is one of the few who know also the real facts about my father—that he is no longer a power among the Polish Irreconcilables. And by the influence of his father, the Count von Felsen, a pardon for my father can be obtained, and our family estates can be restored; not indeed to him, but to—to my husband if that husband should be Hugo von Felsen."

There was a long pause. "There is the Jewess," I said then.

"It is what you have told me about that which baffles me," she replied with a gesture of bewilderment.

"How do you know that what he has told you is true?"

"Do you think he is a man to seek as his wife a girl who has no fortune? And I have none at present. Why then does he press this? Just before this attempt to arrest me, he urged me vehemently to marry him at once and secretly. I would not; I could not, I despise him so"; and she shuddered. "I used the supposed attentions of the Prince to put him off, and now you see the screw has been turned."

"The scoundrel," I muttered.

"Hard words will not solve my dilemma, my friend. I wish they would!" and she sighed heavily. "It is my turn to-day, to-morrow it will be Chalice's, and then my father's. I see only the one way out; but then there is this Jewess."

I sat thinking hard. "If there were a way out you would take it?"

Her face lighted eagerly for a second, and then fell again. "Of course; but there is none."

"I am not so sure of that. Will you let me try to find one?"

She thrust out her hand impulsively. "With all my heart," she said fervently.

Our eyes met as our hands were clasped. "Don't give up yet," I said as I rose. "We are a long way from being beaten yet. But you must let me take my own course, and promise to do nothing without first telling me."

"Why, of course. I promise that freely. But the power behind him is very strong."

My sister came in then, with a very official-looking letter for me.

"A very fussy individual gave me this for you, Paul, as I was coming in, and said it was urgent."

I opened it, and found it was a curt summons to an interview on the following morning with von Felsen's father. As I slipped it into my pocket I saw Althea's eyes fixed on me questioningly.

I told her what it was, and added with a smile: "I think it should be the first step to the way out."

"I have found the very place for us to go to, Althea," broke in Bessie.

"You may not have to go at all, Bess, and certainly not yet," I told her.

"What do you mean?"

"Fräulein Althea will explain everything," and with that I went off to think over the whole tangle.

CHAPTER VI

A STROKE OF LUCK

As soon as I reached my room I sat down to look the difficulties of the problem before me fairly in the face. And formidable enough they were.

The interview with Althea had shifted the axis of everything. What I had deemed the mere comedy of the Imperial marriage—a matter which a few words of explanation would set right instantly—had developed into a grave drama in which Althea's future was imperilled. And with that was intertwined my own happiness.

Her confidence in telling me everything so frankly, no less than the hundred little touches with which it had all been told, had at once raised my own hopes of being able to win her if only I could clear away the tangle, and at the same time had convinced me of her belief that the forces arrayed against us were too formidable to be overcome.

I did not make the mistake of underrating them. This summons to Count von Felsen was a proof that I must reckon with powerful Court influences; and that if I was not to be beaten, I must find some means of defeating not only von Felsen but his influential father also.

That meant that I must be able to secure the pardon for Althea's erratic father which was to be the price of her consent to the proposed marriage.

For such a purpose it would not be enough to rouse old Ziegler's fury against von Felsen on the score of the latter's contemplated refusal to marry Hagar. Even if that marriage took place and von Felsen were thus unable to marry Althea, the latter's case would not be helped. Her father would remain unpardoned, and she herself and Chalice would be in the same danger.

I must dig deeper than that. I had appreciated this when Althea had been telling me her story, and my thought had been to get von Felsen so completely into my power that I could make terms even with his father.

This would be difficult, of course; but not perhaps impossible. If I could but get proofs that he had been acting in collusion with the Polish party, and had actually used his position in his father's office to obtain information and sell it to them, I should have him surely enough.

That he had done it, and was going to do it again, my talk with Ziegler had made me pretty certain. But how was I to get the proof?

I spent several profitless hours wrestling with that puzzle, and sat far into the night endeavouring to hit on a scheme by which von Felsen might be trapped. Only to be utterly baffled, however.

If it could be done at all, it would have to be through Ziegler; but how to use him without rousing his suspicions of my purpose, I could not see.

On the following morning I was starting for the interview with the Minister, when a letter came from Ziegler asking me to see him on "very particular business." Glad of the opportunity to see him so soon without having appeared to seek the interview, I sent word I would call in the course of the morning; and I was not a little curious as to what the "very particular business" would prove to be. I could only hope it would give the opportunity I sought.

My reception at the Count's office was very different from what I had anticipated from the peremptory nature of the summons. I did not see the Minister himself but his secretary named Borsen, whom I knew to be closely in his confidence. He had moreover been friendly with me during my time as newspaper correspondent. He received me very pleasantly, and shook hands with a great show of cordiality. "I just want to have a little informal chat over matters with you, my dear Bastable, in a perfectly frank and friendly way," he said with a smile.

"The invitation was not exactly informal, Borsen," I replied.

"Ah well, you know we are sticklers for red tape. If I had been in London I should have dropped in on you without any invitation at all, but here——" and he flourished his hands as a finish to the sentence.

"I should have been pleased to see you in Berlin, also," I laughed, adapting my manner to his.

"But you have visitors and I might have been in the way, you see."

"Visitors?" I repeated with a lift of the brows. "Ah, let us be perfectly frank with one another."

"Certainly. Will you lead the way?"

"Well, we know that Fräulein Korper is in your house." He paused for me to make the admission.

"If she were there, I should certainly know it. My sister would scarcely——"

"Won't you admit it?" he interrupted. "And save time?"

"Hadn't you better tell me first why you think it?"

He laughed. "You were leaving Berlin and changed your plans at the last moment. At the station you were with your sister whose looks had so changed—she was dark, you know, not fair—that no one could recognize her. The dark young lady drove with you to your house. Your German servant, Gretchen, I think her name is, saw her on her arrival. You discharged that most worthy young woman suddenly. There is a lady in your house who sings the songs of the accomplished Chalice Mennerheim in a voice which is the counterpart of Fräulein Korper's. Need I say any more?"

"My dear Borsen, nobody knows better than you the absolute unreliability of merely circumstantial evidence. Herr Dormund came yesterday to see my sister, and would instantly have recognized her as the lady he saw at the station, but just as she was coming down to him, he had to leave the house."

"Very well, then we'll assume she is not there. But report says that you take a deep personal interest in her. Do you know who she is?" and he went on to tell me what Althea herself had already told me about the Baron von Ringheim, her father, his ill reputation as an irreconcilable, the desire to arrest him, and further that Althea herself was believed to have been helping him in his designs.

"All of which means?" I asked when he ended.

37

"That I am sure your knowledge of political matters and police methods here in Berlin will render you extremely unwilling to run counter to them in any way."

"I am much obliged to you for the warning, Borsen; and now suppose we get on to the real purport of this interview."

"As blunt as ever, eh?" he laughed.

"Well, my dear fellow, of course if she was in my house and your people knew it, you'd send straight away and arrest her; and then probably do something unpleasant to me for having helped her. Why don't you?"

"That may come, and be followed by the arrest of Fräulein Chalice Mennerheim as well. But we don't wish to involve you in any bother, you know. And if you were found to have helped her to escape, it might be very awkward for you. It might really."

"Oh, I think I have friends influential enough to see me through a little thing like that. Shall we get on? You spoke of frankness, remember."

"Well, in the first place I am bound to warn you; but we also wish to deal very confidentially with you. The fact is that a marriage has been arranged between her and Count von Felsen's son, young Hugo von Felsen, you know."

"I wish for his father's sake that I knew less about him, or rather that there was less to know. I know also that the Count is very anxious to see him settling down a bit; but what I am not so sure about is why a girl like Fräulein Korper should be sacrificed in the interest of a thorough-paced young scoundrel like Hugo von Felsen."

"You put it rather strongly; but he is not a very brilliant type, perhaps. Still, we can't talk of sacrifice. As a matter of fact such a marriage would be of the greatest advantage to the lady herself. His Majesty would pardon her father, and all the family estates and property, confiscated on his banishment, would be restored. You can see for yourself the advantages to her and her people."

"Another Imperial marriage, eh?" I said drily. "And the Prince von Graven?"

"That is another reason why she must really consent. If the Emperor were to get wind of that matter, well——" The consequences were too terrible to be told in words.

"It's a pretty mix up, anyhow," said I. It was clear that that secret about Chalice had been kept, at any rate. "And not particularly chivalrous to attack the girl in the case. But now suppose I had sufficient influence to induce her to abandon that Prince business?"

"Could you really do that?" he asked eagerly.

"Persuasion might succeed where force would certainly fail. Now, suppose she did give him up, would the Imperial clemency follow—for her father, I mean."

"That is the Emperor's matter. His Majesty does not make terms, he looks for submission to his wishes."

"The Prince would be a better match than von Felsen, even at the worst. Drive matters, and you may find some morning you have driven those two to the altar," I said meaningly as I got up. "Let me have a day or two to see what can be done."

He smiled, but not without some chagrin. "I sent for you to warn you, and here you are making terms, as if you were a delegate. My instructions are to tell you frankly that if you interfere in this matter, we shall ask you to return to England."

"That's better than gaol, anyway. But, seriously, don't you think it would be useful to have a delegate? Your own term. All said and done it isn't a pretty story—for the newspapers, say."

"Going to threaten us now, hanged if you're not. You ought to have gone in for diplomacy. Assurance like that would carry you far," he jested. "Well, come and see me again in a day or two and tell me that the Prince affair is at an end for a start."

I had gained two important things by the interview: delay, which was invaluable to me; and a confirmation of von Felsen's statement to Althea. I knew Borsen well enough to feel sure that, although he had referred in a tone of jest to his instructions to send me packing from Berlin, they were genuine; and I should have been under orders to leave, had he not managed to convince himself that more was to be gained by letting me remain "as a delegate."

As I had said, it was not a pretty story; and the affair was one which all concerned would be much more willing to settle secretly and peacefully than by force. He remembered no doubt that in a former matter I had won my way by means of suggestive paragraphs in the English papers. Publicity is a fairly sure card to play with the officials of his Imperial Majesty the Kaiser.

What I had to do was to make the best use of my time of grace, and I went straight from Borsen to old Ziegler.

"This is indeed an act of friendship to come so promptly, Herr Bastable," he declared with his customary effusiveness, as he placed a chair for me and put a box of cigars at my elbow.

"You said it was urgent, Ziegler. What's the matter?"

"There is nothing the matter; at least nothing that I should allow you to be disturbed about. But I want to have a little very confidential chat with you. You will smoke?"

I lighted a cigar. "Well?"

"I have been thinking over our talk of yesterday, and your

expressions of sympathy with us; and a curious thing has happened. I have not breathed a word to a soul about that talk; but last night one of our friends mentioned your name with a hint that some one had been talking to you of our plans."

"A curious coincidence," I replied drily.

"By my mother's memory, it is nothing more, Herr Bastable. I declare that most solemnly." He was very earnest and appeared to be telling the truth. "You were seen to leave here yesterday, and the question was asked whether you were ferreting out things, or whether you were likely to be in sympathy with our plans and objects."

"And what did you say?" I asked with a smile.

"I spoke of your expressions of sympathy."

"Yes?" I queried.

He smiled and rubbed his hands. "You see you have never before given me a hint."

"Intentionally."

"Yet I should like to know the extent of your sympathy."

"Why?"

"You are chary of your words, Herr Bastable."

"All the more time for you to talk, Ziegler. Out with it."

He rolled his eyes round his head and then let them rest on me. "You make it difficult; but at any rate you will not speak of what I may say?"

"You know that without my repeating it."

"Well, you English are like us Poles in one respect—you all love your country, Herr Bastable. What if I could get you news which closely concerns your country? You would not refuse to hear it, or to make use of it, eh? Merely because that course would prejudice the German Government?"

"I say nothing until I know more."

He lowered his voice and bent toward me. "England would like to know exactly the German policy in naval matters? This Government does not wish it known, because it would prejudice the Kaiser. If I had such information, Heir Bastable, could you get it published broadcast in England in such way as to prevent the source being known?"

"Easily and readily. But I must be convinced."

"If there were a naval scheme already in the pigeon-holes of the Government here formulated against England, and based upon knowledge of the strength of the English navy, its publication would make a blaze, eh?" His eyes were positively scintillating with cunning as he fixed them now upon me.

40

"You may gamble on that," I said. "But you'd have to be sure of your facts."

"If you were to have the secret papers themselves, eh?"

His eyes were off me so that he missed my start of intense satisfaction at this. To make a pause I took my cigar from my lips and pretended to relight it. "Von Felsen?" I asked then in a casual tone.

He was quick enough to detect that my calm tone was assumed and he shot a very keen glance at me. "Why do you ask that?"

"Because I don't trust him, and because he would not have anything to do with it if he thought I was in it."

"He will not know, and he will do what I tell him," was the terse reply.

"And why are you keen on it?"

"Do you think it would do this Government any good to be caught in double dealing with a power like England?" and he launched into a tirade against the Kaiser and his Government, all the venom and bitterness of his hatred apparent in every word.

This gave me time to think the thing round. It was just a lovely stroke of good fortune; and all I had to do was so to arrange matters that the proofs of von Felsen's treachery should come directly into my hands.

As soon as Ziegler's fury had exhausted itself, we set to work to discuss the details of the plan. He himself was not going to appear in it. That was his invariable practice, I knew. There was to be no jot or tittle of evidence in existence which would incriminate him, except only von Felsen's word; and as he would be the actual thief, his testimony would be entirely discredited. As soon as I perceived this, I offered to take the risk of receiving the papers direct from von Felsen the instant they were ready to be handed over. But I made it an absolute condition that he was not to know I was in the thing until the very last moment, when he had the papers actually in his possession and was ready to hand them over.

The hour and place were then to be communicated to me secretly, and I was to do the rest. That would fit in with my plans well enough, and I agreed readily.

"Then there remains only one little point," said Ziegler, after a pause. "There will be some money to be paid, of course. And this can only be in return for the papers themselves."

"Who is to find it?"

"My friends, naturally; but——" He paused with a gesture of doubt. "It is only equally natural that they would wish to have the papers first, and as you are to get them—— What do you think, eh?"

"How much?"

41

"Only twenty thousand marks," he replied lightly, as if a thousand pounds were a mere bagatelle.

Fortunately I was now in a position to be able to spare such a sum without inconvenience, and would willingly have paid a much larger sum to gain the end I had in view. "Not much difficulty there. You could give me the money and they could repay you."

"My dear Herr Bastable!" he cried, lifting his hands in horror at the idea. "Do you think I am made of money? Your country is going to gain."

"Oh, you want me to find it in the first instance. Very well."

"Oh, what a treat it is to do business with an English gentleman like you!" His relief at my ready agreement was comic and I smiled. "And now that settles the whole matter, except that one last little point. You must let me take you to one or two of our friends and let them know that you are in sympathy with our cause."

"Stop a moment. I can't turn Irreconcilable in that offhand manner."

"Let me explain. There are some of my friends who think that you are against us. Some hints have been dropped that you have been making inquiries, and not in our interest."

"That I am a spy, eh? You know better than that, Ziegler, don't you?"

"I would trust you with my life," he exclaimed grandiloquently. "But it would smooth things if you were to do as I suggest. Secrecy is everything to us; and there are some among us who would go to any extreme if they thought there was treachery anywhere."

I paused to take breath and think.

"This matter could not be arranged otherwise," he put in, seeing me hesitate.

"Very well. You can assure them I am in full sympathy in this particular matter anyhow, and I'll meet any one of them when you please. But von Felsen must know nothing."

It was a risk of course; but I could not let anything come in the way of my plans; and I left the house well pleased.

If matters went as they promised, I should have von Felsen so fast in my power that I could even dictate my terms to his father. For such an end, and all it meant to me, I would have faced twenty times the risk.

CHAPTER VII

PRELIMINARY STEPS

Of all the parts I had ever thought to play, that of a Polish Irreconcilable was about the last. But for the stake I had at issue—to save Althea and win her—I would have turned Russian Nihilist had it been necessary.

The risk I did not take seriously. So far as I had gone at present I could put up a pretty good fight in my defence. If old Ziegler was right, and the German Government were really contemplating some move against England, my old journalistic work would serve as a cover for my action. I could readily justify myself in running almost any risk to unearth and disclose such a thing.

But it was a case where nothing short of success would serve. If the Jew was wrong, I might easily find myself in an ugly fix. I must be careful also not to be drawn in too far. My investment in seditious intrigue must be strictly limited to this one affair.

A few days at most ought to see the issue; and then, I could leave Berlin and, as I now began to hope, take Althea with me.

In regard to her, indeed, my morning's work had imposed an extremely distasteful task upon me. Borsen had confirmed the statement von Felsen had made to her as to her father's pardon in the event of the projected marriage. And I must tell her so.

I had seen for myself on the previous day that even on his unsupported statement she had been very close to giving her consent. Self-sacrifice had become a sort of second nature with her, and she was ready to go to almost any lengths to secure her father's safety and ensure Chalice's future.

Keep the facts from her I could not; but there was something I could do before I told her—tackle von Felsen himself and endeavour to force on his marriage with Hagar Ziegler.

He went in deadly fear of Hagar's father; and I resolved to retract the promise I had given von Felsen on the previous day to hold my tongue about his intention to marry Althea. A word to Ziegler would set him to work at once.

Von Felsen's action in inducing his father to attempt to intimidate me was an ample justification for my taking back my promise; but I would fight him fairly, and give him notice of what I meant to do.

When I reached home I found von Bernhoff closeted with my sister, and they appeared to have had a pretty warm conversation.

"Here is Paul," cried Bessie, as I entered. "Tell him, Herr Bernhoff." She was very excited, and not far removed from tears.

"What is it?" I asked turning to him.

"I have been asking your sister to do me the honour to betroth herself to me," he replied, with rather a disconcerted air.

"She has no doubt given you your answer."

"You had better tell the rest, Herr Bernhoff," cried Bessie indignantly.

"I have merely been saying that if she would consent I should become to that extent a member of your family, and so concerned to help you in keeping secret any matters which you do not desire to have disclosed."

"Plainer, please," I said very curtly,

"There are certain things——"

"Mention them," I broke in.

"You have a guest here, Mr. Bastable," he said, lifting his hands and smiling significantly.

"You have already given this—this gentleman an answer, Bessie?"

"Oh yes, and he said——"

"Never mind that for a moment. Just let me have a word or two with him alone." She got up at once, and he rose at the same time as if to go.

"I do not wish to discuss it with you, Mr. Bastable," he said uneasily.

"But I mean to discuss it with you," I retorted; and I opened the door for her and prevented his leaving. "Now we'll have it out together, von Bernhoff."

He made no reply and stared at me sullenly.

"I've got the hang of the matter, I think. You have asked my sister to be your wife; she has not consented; and in reply you have hinted that you will tell certain suspicions you entertain if she does not retract her refusal. Did you say that as evidence of your overwhelming affection for her or as a proof of your high sense of honour?"

He continued to glare at me in silence.

"You find that an inconvenient question, eh?"

Still the same dogged silence.

"You can't brazen this out by just staring at me, von Bernhoff. Don't be under any mistake in regard to that. Nor can you bully me, as you have tried to bully my sister. You are an officer, and belong to a regiment in which the other officers at any rate are gentlemen. As for your suspicions, you can go and shout them at the top of your voice on parade, for all I care. But both you and I know well enough what your fellow-officers will think of your conduct."

This touched him. He winced and began to protest. "I did not mean anything of the sort."

"I don't care a beggar's shirt what you say you meant. It's what you have done. I know your Colonel pretty well, and he shall be the judge in this."

"I protest——"

"To the devil with your protests," I cried angrily. "It is your action which matters. That's all. We'll go straight to him together."

All his doggedness had vanished now, and he was as limp as a chewed cigar end.

"I beg you will not do anything of the kind. If you like to make this a personal matter between us two——"

"Not I," I broke in with a short angry laugh. "I'll have no duel as a way out for you. You can convince your Colonel that you did not mean what your acts suggest. Come to him with me now—if you dare."

But he dared not. I knew that; for I knew what the result would be, and so did he. "I am very sorry," he stammered. "I apologize. I—— What more can I do?"

"You can get out of the house," and I threw open the door. "As for your suspicions, tell them to whom you please—but don't let me hear of it."

Without another word, without a glance even, he slunk out with his tail well between his legs, like the beaten cur he was.

I could afford to laugh at his threats, after my interview with Borsen and my recognition as a sort of unofficial "delegate" in Althea's affairs. There was a tacit agreement that I was to have some little time in which to arrange things, and any chatter from von Bernhoff was not likely to do any harm.

I told Bessie the result of my talk to von Bernhoff, and then went out to lunch at my club and make some inquiries about the inner working of this Polish Irreconcilable movement. As I was to be one of them, I had better know all I could.

I got plenty of rumours and reports and gossip and a few facts. As England always has her Irish question with its disaffected Nationalists subject to occasional spurts of violence, so Germany will always have a Polish question. But her policy of drastic measures and sharp repression drives the trouble beneath the surface, where it festers like a national canker.

Openly the Irreconcilables were keeping within the law, and seeking an alliance with the powerful Socialist party and other sections, in the hope that eventually the combination would become strong enough to dictate the policy of the Empire, when it was hoped they would use their power to aid the renationalization of Poland.

At the same time, however, they were intriguing incessantly to throw discredit on the Government by worming out all sorts of official secrets the disclosure of which would tell to the disadvantage of the Kaiser. Mole work which was hateful to those in power.

In addition to this some very sinister hints were dropped to me in confidence by a Polish journalist whom I knew to have excellent channels of information, about certain mysterious happenings, classed as "accidents," to Government property. More than one warship had been suddenly disabled; machinery in Government works had been damaged; defects in arms and ammunition had developed, and so on.

"You may take it that the official explanation is never the right one. If the truth is known it is not told," he declared; "but it probably is not known. You can draw your own inferences. But some day a bigger accident will happen, and then you may recall my words."

The news was anything but cheering. I had no mind to be mixed up with men who were planning a policy of violence, and I resolved to speed matters all I could and put an end to the connexion.

As a first step I would force on von Felsen's marriage with Ziegler's daughter. I determined to go to von Felsen at once and tell him point-blank that I should let Ziegler know the truth. On my way to him I called to see Chalice. She had just returned from Herr Grumpel and was in high spirits, because the date had been fixed for her first appearance.

"Think of it, Herr Bastable. In a week's time! Oh, I am nearly beside myself with delight," she cried, clasping her hands ecstatically.

"A good many things can happen in a week," I said drily.

"Now you are going to be horrid and make me uncomfortable," she pouted. She had a hundred moods to be assumed at will.

"I don't wish to be horrid, as you call it, but I do wish to speak seriously to you about——"

"But I don't want to be serious to-day," she broke in. "I want to talk about the great concert. Just think of my immense stroke of luck. The Herr had arranged a State concert with the Ventura as his Prima. She can't come to it, or she won't or something, and he is actually going to put me in her place. In the place of the great Ventura! Oh, I am like a wild thing when I think of it. And if you were a little bit of a friend, you'd be just as excited as I am."

46

"I'm afraid I am not," I replied somewhat ungraciously. She had not a thought for Althea; had not even mentioned her name.

"If you have come only to say disagreeable things, I wish you'd choose another day for them. You'll make me ready to shed tears in a minute."

"What are you going to do about Prince von Graven?"

"Oh, bother the Prince. I have no time to think of him to-day, nor for the whole week. Think of all it means to me! To appear instead of the great Ventura!"

"I'm sorry to be a wet blanket, but I must tell you——"

"No, no, no. I won't listen," she cried vehemently, putting her fingers in her ears and shaking her head vigorously. "Herr Grumpel said I must not have anything to excite me between now and the concert."

"There will be no concert at all for you if you do not listen to me, Fräulein," I declared, as soon as I had a chance of getting a word in.

"Oh, I hate you, I hate you! Go away!" she cried like a child.

I sat on stolidly until she understood that I was really in earnest and that she could not get rid of me in that way, and then her manner changed suddenly. She became earnest and looked at me almost piteously.

"Of course I didn't mean that. If there is anything I ought to know which really does concern the concert, of course I will listen."

"You have not asked about Fräulein Althea," I reminded her.

"Of course I know she is all right or I should have heard. Has she sent you now to frighten me?"

"I have not come to frighten you at all, and she does not know that I have come. I wish only to warn you."

"It is very much the same thing," she said pettishly again.

"Not at all the same thing, I assure you. No one would be more pleased if you were to make a great hit than I should be. But the fact is that before a week passes you are much more likely to be in the same plight as Fräulein Althea than singing at a concert, unless you have cleared up this matter of the Prince."

"Do you mean they would try to arrest me? ME?"

"A great many things have happened since I saw you, and this morning I had it from a high authority that that step is under consideration. The one arrest has been decided on because Fräulein Althea is the daughter of Baron von Ringheim, you are his granddaughter and can judge whether in such a case you would be likely to be acceptable to the Kaiser as the chief performer at a State concert."

The colour left her face as she listened, and when I ended she

47

burst into a storm of tears. "You are cruel! It is infamous! Why persecute me in this way?" she cried over and over again. She was almost hysterical.

I said no more for the moment. If I tell the truth, I thought it only fair that she should be touched personally by some of the trouble which she had viewed with such philosophic indifference when it affected only Althea. With all her caprice and selfishness, however, she had plenty of shrewdness, and understood the gravity of what I had said.

Presently she choked down her emotion and seized my hand in both her own. "Forgive me for having spoken as I did. You are right, of course, and only acting as my friend in telling me this. But what shall I do?"

"Tell the truth, give up Prince von Graven, and let the Kaiser have his way in regard to this precious Imperial marriage."

"He would never forgive me," she wailed. "What does Althea advise?'"

Althea at last. I checked a smile. She could think of Althea when there was a difficulty to be solved. "I have not told her."

Suddenly she started as a fresh thought struck her. "You have quarrelled with the Prince, Herr Bastable."

"That is not the reason for my coming to you. I had some words with him because he would not be man enough to tell the truth and face the music."

"It was at my wish."

"I know that, but it does not make any difference to the fact that Fräulein Althea was being sacrificed for the sake of the secret. But if the truth is not told, you may depend on it you will never have the chance of appearing at that concert."

"I don't know what to do."

I got up. "The others will not let me decide for you, and you must do as you will; but you can now see all that hangs on the decision."

"Oh, don't leave me, Herr Bastable. Help me," she cried, catching and holding my hand and backing her words with appealing glances.

"Give up the Prince—you do not really care for him; write a renunciation grounding it on the fact that you do not wish to go counter to the Kaiser's wish and will do anything rather than injure the Prince's future; and let me have the document to get it to the Emperor."

"Help me to write it. You write so cleverly."

"No. Don't have it machine made. Let yourself go in writing it.

You have just heard of His Majesty's opposition, your heart is breaking, and so on."

"It is," she said, with a very piteous look.

"It will—if you don't get your chance at the concert. Think of all that means to you, and then persuade yourself that your emotion is for the loss of the Prince and not the sacrifice of your future."

It was rather brutal, but she only laughed. "I will try," she agreed; and saying that I would see her again on the following day, I left her to hurry to von Felsen.

I was convinced that she cared no more for the Prince than I did, and that she had merely kept him tied to her apron-strings as a possible means of advancing her interests. To me she stood for a type of calculating, callous selfishness; and yet to the Prince she appeared as a veritable queen among women. But then I was not in love with her, and he was; and he would certainly curse me heartily for the advice I had given her.

When I reached von Felsen's house a somewhat curious thing occurred. I was asked to wait a while; and as I stood thinking about the coming interview and staring out of the window into the now gloomy street, the electric lights of the room were switched on suddenly. I turned on the instant to find von Felsen in the act of closing the door which the servant must have left open.

He was not quite quick enough; for I caught sight of a man crossing the hall rapidly, and recognized him as a fellow named Dragen, one of the worst characters in Berlin, the bully and worse of a low gambling hell. I had come across him in my old newspaper work in connexion with a very unsavoury case.

"Who was that?" I asked sharply.

"Only my servant. What do you mean? And why do you come to me?" and von Felsen shut the door and stood before it.

Why the lie? Why had he been at such pains to let the man have a good sight of me? And how long had they been in the room before I knew of their presence?

CHAPTER VIII

TRAPPED

An instant's reflection convinced me that it would be prudent to accept von Felsen's statement and not to drop a hint that I had recognized the man who had stolen away so stealthily. If any trick were intended, I had better not let him think that I suspected it.

"I have come to talk to you seriously," I said in reply to his question.

"You do not suppose you are very welcome here?"

"It isn't intended to be exactly a friendly call."

"You had better come into my other room." He said this very curtly as he opened the door again and led me to a room across the hall. "Now what is it?"

I copied his blunt manner. "You broke the word you gave me yesterday, and I take back the pledge I gave you."

"What do you mean?"

"I was sent for to your father's office to-day."

"I know nothing of that."

"I don't believe you," I rapped out sharply.

"I'm not going to have you here to insult me," he blustered.

"Having failed in that trick of bringing Dormund to my house yesterday, you set your father's people on to me to see what they could do. You did this in the face of your promise to give up your attempt to find Fräulein Korper on condition that I said nothing to Herr Ziegler."

"They knew all about everything without me."

"What they are going to know next will be all about you and Hagar Ziegler. And Ziegler is going to know all about the other matter. It would have paid you better to run straight with me."

He appeared to be taken utterly by surprise by this, having been fool enough to believe that I should not see his hand behind that summons to his father's office. His bluster dropped away like an ill-fitting cloak. "I don't know why you want to hound me down in this way. What is Hagar Ziegler to you?"

"It's only my friendship for you—I wish to see you happily married," I replied with a grin.

He flung me a curse for my jibe and turned away to light a cigarette.

"Shall we send for old Ziegler, or will you come with me to him?" I asked in the same tone. It was a delight to rack him.

"It has nothing to do with you," he said sullenly.

"It has more to do with you, I admit; but I might be the best man and then——"

"Stop it," he growled. I laughed; and after a pause he glanced round at me. "Can't we come to terms?"

"We did, and you broke them."

"I tell you I have not said a word," he declared with an oath for emphasis.

I gave him a steady meaning look and replied significantly: "I saw Herr Borsen at the Count's office, and he happens to be an old friend of mine. He had no object in telling me anything but the truth."

He drew the inference I intended from this—that Borsen had given him away—and he made no further attempt at denial.

I turned to the door. "What are you going to do? Will you come with me to Ziegler's or shall I go alone?"

"Give me two or three days to settle things."

"Not an hour. I am going straight to Ziegler, and to-morrow Herr Borsen will know the other side." He made no reply and I left the house.

When I reached the Jew's I was amused to find how, in his petty short-sighted cunning, von Felsen had endeavoured to cut the ground from under me.

Ziegler and his daughter were together and were both in high spirits. He introduced me to her, and had evidently done all he could to impress her with the fact that I was one of his best friends.

"I have told her, Herr Bastable, that there is no man in Berlin whom I would trust as absolutely as I would you," he declared. "I wish her to think of you just as I do."

"Nothing would please me better; but I am afraid that some one who has great influence with her does not share your opinion, Herr Ziegler."

"You mean Herr von Felsen," she replied, with a frankness which I liked. "I should like you to be better friends, I confess, and would do anything in my power to secure that. My father's friends must always be mine."

"We were speaking of him as you entered," said the father. "He has just telephoned me asking that the date for Hagar's marriage may be fixed for a week to-day."

I could not restrain a smile at this, and Hagar, who was watching me closely while he spoke, saw the smile. "You are surprised at this, Herr Bastable?"

"I am pleased to be able to be the first to offer my congratulations."

51

"Your smile did not read quite like that," she returned with a shade of pique in her manner.

"I am surprised, I admit. The fact is I have just left Herr von Felsen, and, although he knew I was coming here, he did not drop a hint of the fact."

"Had you been as close a friend of his as you are of my father's, he would probably have told you." It was very neatly put.

But old Ziegler had read more in my words than Hagar. I saw that by the sharp look he shot at me. He began to talk quickly about the forthcoming marriage and the necessary preparations until an excuse offered to send his daughter out of the room.

"Now what is it, Herr Bastable. About Hugo, I mean, of course."

I told him at once precisely what had taken place in regard to Althea and von Felsen, and what I had heard from Herr Borsen.

I have never seen a greater frenzy of passion than that which took complete possession of him at the news. For some moments he was like a madman in his fury. His face went livid, his eyes gleamed, his lips worked spasmodically, he trembled violently, and with hands clenched tight he raved against von Felsen, and abused and cursed him with a voluble energy of rage that almost made me regret the tornado I had raised.

I stared at him, silent from sheer amazement until the first vehemence of his wrath had spent itself.

"He shall marry her to-morrow or at latest the day following," he cried; and with a hand that was shaking like that of one in a palsy, he went to the telephone to bid von Felsen come at once to the house. When the reply was that he was not at home, the old man's fury broke out again. "It is a lie!" he stormed. "He knows you are here and will not come. I will go to him. The scoundrel, to dare to lie to me in this way. But he shall pay the price"; and he was still in a furious rage when I left him.

Considering his opinion of von Felsen, I could not help marvelling that he was so set upon forcing him to marry Hagar. But analysis of other men's motives is not much in my way. Possibly he was eager that she should have a titled husband, and I recalled how he had appeared to gloat over that prospect in one of my interviews with him. I left it at that and returned to the consideration of my own affairs.

Now that I had drawn von Felsen's teeth, I did not shirk the task of telling Althea what I had heard from Herr Borsen in the morning. She could no longer be forced to make that hateful marriage. Ziegler would see to that.

But not for a second did I anticipate the effect of the news upon her. I had utterly failed to see the thing from her standpoint, and was blind enough to think she would be as glad as I myself was. I told her, therefore, in a somewhat jubilant tone.

The smile which my first words brought to her face gradually died away, and gave place to an expression first of perplexity and then of distress and dismay, as she heard me out in silence.

Then she looked up and sighed. "Oh, Mr. Bastable, don't you see?" she asked wistfully.

"I see that we take very different views of it," I replied gloomily.

She noticed my keen disappointment. "Please bear with me, and forgive me if I cannot see it as you do. But if Herr von Felsen marries this Jewess, it will make it impossible——" She paused and glanced at me nervously.

"Impossible for you to marry him, of course," I finished, smiling fatuously.

"Impossible for me to save my father, I mean. How else can I save him?"

I understood then and winced at the consciousness of my blundering. "But did you ever seriously contemplate such a sacrifice as that would have involved?"

"I thought I had made that quite plain to you. And now——." She broke off with a gesture of despair. "I would do anything to save him and Chalice."

"Fräulein Chalice is willing to give up the Prince von Graven," I replied, and went on to tell her of my interview with Chalice.

But she shook her head. "Please believe that I am convinced you have done everything with no thought but to help me. But nothing Chalice can do will save my father."

"I appear to have blundered all along the line," I exclaimed irritably.

She made no reply, and thus appeared to acquiesce in my verdict of self-condemnation. This was not soothing, to say the least. But after a moment's pause she laid her hand on my arm with a rueful smile. "You don't think I am blaming you because I am silent, Mr. Bastable, do you? I am only trying to think what to do. It is so difficult. It has all been my fault. I ought to have made it clearer to you that I was resolved to save my father at any cost."

"I think that will still be done."

"How?"

"I have a plan, and am pretty confident about it."

Her brows puckered in doubt, as if she were not disposed to trust my indiscretion any longer. "Had you not better tell me?" she asked nervously.

"For one thing I hope to go to Herr Borsen to-morrow with the news about Chalice's decision, and I shall tell him then about the Ziegler affair."

"No, no," she cried hastily. "You must not do that. That marriage may yet be prevented in some way."

"Not if the Jew has his way," I answered with a grim smile at the recollection of his frenzy of rage.

"You must not breathe a word to Herr Borsen. That would shut out all hope."

"Hope?" I echoed sharply, for the word jarred. "I did not know that hope was the feeling you entertained in regard to von Felsen."

She bit her lip and for an instant dropped her eyes, and I saw her fingers strain; then she looked up with a wistful smile. "Don't let me anger you, Mr. Bastable. I chose that word very unfortunately. It sounds as if I have done you so much less than justice after all the service you have rendered me. Forgive me, and do not punish me by thinking me ungrateful."

"I am a churlish brute," I answered, smiling in my turn. "My head was swollen with the thought of my own cleverness, and my temper suffered because my vanity was hurt. I admit I have blundered badly; now let us try and talk out some remedy together."

The bright look she gave me signalled absolution. "Let us start with this absolute condition—that my father's pardon must be obtained and Chalice's future made secure."

"I accept the conditions and still believe I can win." Her eyes flashed a question. "No, you need not doubt my discretion this time," I said in reply to the look. "I have learnt my lesson. But I cannot tell you all about it."

"I should like to know. I am very much of a woman in my curiosity. Besides, I should like to have firm ground for the hopes you raise."

"I shall know in a day or so."

"Suspense is not measured by hours, Mr. Bastable."

"I would lessen it if I could; but at any rate I can assure you my own suspense will not be less than yours," I said earnestly.

She let her eyes fall. Whether she guessed something of the feeling that lay behind my words I could not tell. But after a pause which was embarrassing to us both, she lifted her head and looked frankly into my eyes.

"I know I have your sympathy—as a friend, Mr. Bastable," she said simply, with a stress on the word.

"It is as a friend I speak. And because of that friendship I ask you not to take any step in regard to this monstrous proposal of your marriage with von Felsen until I have had time to see the result of this effort of mine."

"I will never take any step at all about it unless there is no other alternative, and not even then without telling you. I give you that promise freely."

"It is a bargain, and I can ask no more than that."

"Tell me again about Chalice," she said. I repeated all that had passed and we discussed the position fully. "I have never quite understood Chalice," she said slowly. "You think she does not care for the Prince?"

"If so, would she be willing to give him up to secure even such a first appearance as is offered to her?"

"That is incomprehensible to me."

"I think there are many reasons why she should do it. The Kaiser is only a man after all, and a very impulsive one at that. He is quite likely to be so charmed by the apparently spontaneous compliance with his wishes as well as delighted by the removal of the obstacle to this Imperial marriage project, as to promote her at once to the position of a Court favourite. And in that event you need have no fears about your father."

"There is the Count von Felsen to reckon with."

I smiled. "Unwittingly he has already done a great deal to help such an end. He must have explained to the Kaiser that your father is no longer capable of doing any real harm, or otherwise he could not have secured the promise of a pardon for him. Depend upon it, if Fräulein Chalice succeeds, there will be scarcely any favour she could ask which would not be granted readily."

"You almost make me hope," she said brightly. "You are so confident."

"If I can only succeed with my other plan at the same time there will no longer be the remotest reason even to doubt. Besides, Count von Felsen's plan will have been knocked on the head as well by his son's marriage."

But she frowned at this. "I wish that could have been postponed. It would have left us the other alternative as a last resource."

"God forbid that it should ever come to that," I cried fervently; and then fearing that if I remained longer with her I might betray myself, I went away.

I was not a little humiliated at the result of the interview. Althea had succeeded in making me appreciate not only her own point of view, but also my own motive. My motive in forcing von Felsen to marry Hagar had had much more concern with my own selfish desire to win Althea for myself than with any regard for her interests or wishes.

I had just fooled and flattered myself that I was acting for her, and so had blundered into this humiliating muddle. I had put it very lightly in saying that my vanity was hurt. I had made a big fool of myself; and what I had to do was to see whether I could repair the mischief.

I started off at once for Ziegler's house. In some way I must get him to agree to the postponement of the marriage. I owed that at least to Althea; and even if I had to break with him altogether, I must gain that end.

He was not at home, however, and after waiting a long time I went away leaving word that I must see him the first thing in the morning on very urgent business.

I had walked a very little distance from the house when a man overtook me.

"Herr Bastable, I think?" he said.

"Yes. What do you want with me?"

"I have to request you to come with me. I am a police officer."

"Do you mean I am arrested? On what charge?"

"It is possible you will not be detained. It is in regard to Fräulein Korper. It is desired to put some questions to you. I can say no more."

It was of course useless to resist, so I turned and walked with him. We passed through several streets, and presently he stopped at the door of a house in a side street.

"This is not a police station," I objected.

"You are to be confronted with another prisoner under arrest here—Ephraim Ziegler—who is being detained here."

"No. Take me to the station," I demanded.

He laid a powerful hand on my arm. "You will do as I tell you."

He was both taller and much stronger than I; but I knew that any such proceeding was quite against police rules, so I tried to wrest myself free.

The attempt was futile; and as the door was opened he seized me and thrust me inside into the arms of a couple of men, who gripped and held me, despite the struggle I made.

The man who had brought me shut the door quickly and, rushing forward, pressed a chloroformed cloth over my mouth and nose.

And then—unconsciousness.

CHAPTER IX

A PERILOUS CRISIS

My first sensation of returning consciousness was that of cold air being blown violently in my face as I was penned in between heavy bodies which crushed so closely against me that movement was impossible, while the throbbing noise of rapidly moving machinery sounded in my ears.

All was indistinct. My head was aching as if it had been split, my brain was dizzy, my senses dazed and chaotic. The ground under me appeared to have come to life and to be racing away from me at lightning speed.

Strange uncouth lights were flashing hither and thither, producing a medley of glare which was utterly bewildering and almost terrifying.

I was in total darkness, save for the eccentric flashes of light; and my first rational thought was the discovery that when I closed my eyes the flashes were still with me. I recognized then that they were caused by some sort of brain pressure.

Next I discovered that I was not bound in any way. I could not move, because I was hopelessly wedged between the heavy bodies. Moreover, I appeared to have no power of my own to stir either hand or foot.

Then my wits cleared very slowly, and I began to remember what had occurred. I had been drugged, and could do nothing until the effects of the drug had worn off.

And at last I realized that I was in the narrow tonneau of a small motor-car travelling at a rapid pace through the night. The heavy bodies which had so perplexed me were two men between whom I was half sitting, half lying in the narrow space.

The fearsome sense of terror abated with my understanding of the position. I lay back, indescribably weary and helpless, with a hazy feeling that rest would restore my faculties, and a half-awakened instinct that my safety might depend upon my appearing to be still under the influence of the drug.

I think I fell asleep, for my next conscious sensation was the pleasant discovery that the racking pain in the head had abated and the lights of my delirium ceased to flash in my brain.

The two men between whom I was jammed were bending over me, and I heard one say to the other: "It's all right. He's still dead off." It was probably their movement which had awakened me.

I lay as still as a drugged man would, and tried to collect my scattered wits. We were travelling at a good rate, some thirty miles an hour, I thought, and the car, a rather crazy vehicle, swayed and bumped and jolted to an extent that threatened a mishap. It was obviously not built for high speed.

Gradually I recalled all that had occurred in its proper sequence. My visit to Herr Ziegler's house; my stay there; my leaving; the encounter with the pretended police official; the scene at the house to which he had taken me; my futile struggle; and lastly the drugging.

When it had all occurred I could not of course tell. For aught I knew it might have been no more than an hour or two before I came to myself in the car, or it might have been as many days or weeks.

From my position between the men I could not see anything, but presently one of them put a question to his companion: "What place was that?"

"Glowen, I think," was the reply.

"How far from Wittenberge?"

"About twenty miles. Ask Dragen."

The man addressed leant forward and put a question to the chauffeur, who turned his head and flung back a reply over his shoulder. I could not catch what he said, however.

What I had heard told me a great deal. Wittenberge was a small place on the Elbe between Berlin and Hamburg, about a hundred miles from the capital. The man had spoken of it as if it were the end of the car's journey, and I wondered what could be the possible reason for my being taken there.

But the most important information was the mention of the man's name—Dragen. It sent my thoughts back at once to the time of my visit to von Felsen. Dragen was the man whom I had recognized there, and it was now clear that he had been brought into the room to be able to identify me.

Von Felsen was clearly behind my abduction, and it was with bitter self-reproach I saw how easily I had let myself be fooled. He had evidently had this plan to get rid of me in mind for some time, and my action in threatening to tell Ziegler the truth about Althea had brought matters to a crisis.

Dragen I believed to be a man capable of any villainy: murder at need, if it could be done safely; and I did not doubt that he had chosen as accomplices in the scheme scoundrels who were as reckless as himself. I should be lucky if I got out of the scrape with my life. I was being well punished for the blunder I had committed in trying to force on von Felsen's marriage with the Jew's daughter;

and it was the irony of the affair I had been caught in the toils at the very moment when I was about to try and undo that mistake.

But why were we running to Wittenberge? I asked myself the question over and over again, only to give it up in bewilderment. At the rate we were travelling I should soon know, of course; but my impatience and anxiety were only heated by that fact.

Presently the men bent down over me again.

"You must have given him a pretty strong dose," said one.

His companion laughed. "Do you suppose I measured it?"

"He's as fast off as ever. Look here." At this he shook me till the teeth all but rattled in my jaws, and then pinched me until I should think his fingers all but met in my flesh. He had a hand of iron.

"All the better. Saves trouble," growled the brute.

"Had we better give him another dose to get him on the boat? We don't want any noise there. It won't matter when he's once on board."

"If you want me to finish him, I will. Not else."

"Well, it's your look out that part of it, not mine."

"All right then, leave it to me. But I may as well make sure."

There was a pause, and I could tell that the man was feeling in his pockets. I wondered what was coming, and nerved myself for the ordeal.

"This'll touch him up if there's any return of sensibility," he said with another laugh. I remember wondering at the use of such a term and jumping to the conclusion that the fellow must have had some sort of training as a medical man, and had fallen to his present low position as the result of dissipation.

I had not more than a few seconds for this speculation, for he seized my hand roughly and plunged a needle into the back. I bore it without flinching.

"I told you so," he said. "But we'll have another experiment."

He took my thumb in his strong fingers then, and holding it up tried to thrust the needle down into the quick. Fortunately for me the lurching of the car interfered with his intention, and the needle entered the flesh some slight distance from the nail.

Again I succeeded in repressing even the slightest quiver at the pain it caused, although it made me almost sick. He loosened his grip of the thumb with the needle still in it, and I had the presence of mind enough to let the hand fall limp and flaccid.

He was satisfied with the test. He gripped my hand again and drew out the needle roughly. "He's good for hours yet, Marlen," he announced with an oath.

"You'd better tell Dragen," said the other; and he leant forward and spoke to Dragen, who was apparently the leader in the affair.

59

I was free once more to think. The mention of the boat had sufficed to give me a slight indication of their plans. I was being taken by car to Wittenberge in order to be transferred to a boat of some sort in which the journey was to be continued. Probably to Hamburg, I guessed.

That seaport had a very unenviable reputation for deeds of violence. If the intention was to take my life, no better place could have been chosen for the work than Hamburg. It would be a comparatively easy matter to knock me on the head, dress me in some disguise without a mark of any sort which would lead to my identification, and then either drop me into the river or carry me ashore to one of the low quarters of the town, where violent deaths were matters of no uncommon occurrence.

I am free to admit that I was intensely alarmed at the prospect. I was helplessly in their power. I was unarmed, and I knew enough of Dragen's reputation for cunning to be quite sure that he would so arrange matters that even if I succeeded in raising an alarm when they were taking me from the car to the boat, he would select a spot where no assistance would be available.

I had only one thing in my favour—their belief in my continued unconsciousness. How could I turn that to the best account?

For the rest of the time I remained in the car I thought over that point as strenuously as only a man can think who feels that his life will be the result of the thinking.

If I raised an alarm at Wittenberge and no help came, I was a doomed man. That was as certain as that the sun would rise on the following morning whether I saw it or not.

I could not fool them twice about being insensible. The perspiration stood thick on my forehead as I tried to come to some decision, and I was still undecided when the car began to slow down and turned away from the main road.

I guessed we were going down to the river, and perceived to my consternation that the place was absolutely deserted. Then the car came to a standstill, and I heard the sluggish wash of the water.

Dragen got out and walked away in the darkness.

"Is he going with us on the river trip?" asked the man who had drugged me.

"How the devil do I know?" was the response. "I know I'm going because I'll have to manage the launch, and you'll have to go, of course. We can't get on without the doctor. And somebody 'll have to take this rickety old puffer back."

"How are you going to get him on to the Stettin?"

"Why, go after her and pretend that we're passengers who have missed her at the landing-stage. He is going on the trip for his

60

health, and we are his valet and medical man looking after him on the voyage. She calls at Southampton for cargo; and you'll dope him a bit, and we shall slip off and leave him."

"It would be a deal easier to drop him in the river."

"Dragen has orders to do nothing of the sort. He's only wanted to be out of the way for a week or two."

"And then turn up and blow the gaff on the lot of us. I know which I'd rather risk," said the doctor.

"And lose half the plunder. The thing's as simple as it can be. Everything has been arranged."

The other man grunted his disapproval, and then they were silent.

I had heard the recital of the programme with infinite relief. Von Felsen had obviously been afraid to proceed to extreme measures, and for that at any rate I thanked him. If he could get me out of the way for a week or two, he would have ample time to complete the plans with which my presence had interfered, and this time he would gain by securing my presence on a liner which after it left Southampton would not touch land again until it reached the other side of the Atlantic.

I decided then not to make any attempt to escape or attract help for the present. And it was fortunate that I did so.

When Dragen returned to the car he told the two men that all was in readiness, and that they were to carry me down to the boat.

On the way I lolled in their arms as limp as a corpse. They handled me pretty roughly, and in getting on to the boat the doctor tripped and flung me on to the little deck in order to save himself from falling.

"Don't be a clumsy fool, doctor," called Dragen sharply, with an oath.

"He can't feel anything," was the growling response. "And you don't need to curse me, Dragen."

"I'll do worse than curse you if you drive me to it," came the sharp, angry retort, the threatening tone of which indicated Dragen's power over the other.

"This won't help us to get the boat under weigh, will it?" put in Marlen. "Come on, doc, let's put the passenger to bed."

But the other laughed sulkily. "You can finish the job by yourselves," and he turned back toward the car.

"Come back," called Dragen furiously, "or it'll be the worse for you."

The "doctor" turned on him with a fierce oath. "I've owed you something long enough, and this would be a mighty good place to

61

pay the debt in. I'm a better man than you, and if you use that tone to me again I'll prove it."

"What's the good of spitting at one another like two infernal tomcats?" put in Marlen.

"To hell with your tomcats," was the fierce retort. "Let him do the thing without me if he can. A dirty, low, sponging bully speak to me like that!" and, giving, a full rein to his temper, he let loose such flood of invective upon Dragen that I expected every instant to see the two come to blows.

I began to hope that I should find in the quarrel a chance of getting away, and I glanced round me stealthily in search of something with which I could arm myself for a struggle with the third man, Marlen.

But Dragen, perceiving that a quarrel at that juncture meant the failure of the whole adventure, kept his head and his temper. He let the "doctor" storm and rage without attempting a reply until the man's fury had spent itself in words.

Then he turned to Marlen and asked quietly: "And what are you going to do? Going through with me or back with the doc? You can have the car to run away in if you like."

"I'm going to see it through," was the reply.

"Then we must chance it and leave the car here. Good-night, doc. That's about the toughest speech you ever gave me, but I shan't take any notice of it. Maybe in the morning you'll see things differently."

He crossed the little landing-stage and came on to the launch.

"Can we do without him?" asked Marlen, rather nervously I thought.

"Of course we can. Oh, by the way, doc, you'd better let me have the drops," he said casually and went back to him. "I'm sorry I put your back up so, old man."

"Well, you should keep a better guard on that tongue of yours." The tone showed that his temper had passed.

"All right, we won't say any more about it. Give me the stuff."

The man laughed. "I'll go on with it if you like," he said half shamefacedly.

"Of course I'd like"; and thus to my infinite disappointment the quarrel ended there and the "doctor" came on to the launch.

"Let's get our passenger to bed," said Marlen. "We've lost time enough already, and more than we can spare."

With that they picked me up, carried me forward, and thrust me into a sort of forecastle, and closed and bolted the hatch upon me.

I heard the murmur of talk between the three men for a while, but could not distinguish what was said; and after a few minutes the launch started on her run down the river.

It was a roomy boat, and the place in which I had been thrust was almost large enough for me to stand upright in. There was a good deal of lumber stored in it, and my first effort was to hunt all round in the hope of finding some sort of weapon.

I had formed a rough idea of a plan. The hatch by which the place was entered was not large enough to allow of two persons entering at the same time, and my crude plan was to wait until one of them entered and then disable him.

I crawled all over the forecastle, feeling my way and fingering everything carefully as I crawled. For a long time I was unsuccessful, but when I had all but given up hope my fingers closed on a heavy broken cog-wheel. I could have shouted for joy at the lucky find. It was just the thing for the purpose.

I carried it back and lay down close to the hatch, choosing such a position as would enable me to attack any one who entered.

I knew enough of the plan in regard to me to feel confident that I should not be molested for some time. The "doctor" was under the impression that I should remain insensible for some hours yet, and I knew that every hour, almost every minute, of additional rest would be invaluable. I was still heavy and stupid from the effects of the drug, and would gladly have slept. But I was afraid to sleep lest he should come in to see me, and I should be thus unable to put up a fight for my freedom.

It was a fortunate fear, as it turned out.

I had not been long waiting before the bolt of the hatch was drawn back and the "doctor" thrust in his hand and raised one of mine to make sure that I was still unconscious.

"He's all right," he announced. "We'd better do it now. I'll bring him out."

"Wait a bit. Here's a boat of some sort ahead."

The "doctor" drew back quickly, but left the hatch open.

"I'm afraid of it, doc, and that's the truth," said Marlen.

"Don't be a fool, man. It's fifty times as safe as trusting our skins on the liner. The ship's doctor will want to know a heap of things. Dragen doesn't know that, but I do. There isn't a single mark of violence on him, and it'll look exactly a case of his having dropped into the river."

"Well, wait till we get past this boat."

A long silence followed.

So they were going to adopt the "doctor's" former suggestion and murder me rather than run the risk of taking me to the liner.

Instead of frightening me this roused all the fight there was in

63

me. I had to fight for my life, and I waited as tensely as they until the launch should have passed the boat, and settled myself in the best position I could choose for the attack when the moment came.

Minutes passed; they seemed like hours to me.

"It's all right now." It was the "doctor's" voice, and the next moment I heard him approach the forecastle. "I'll bring him out," he said; and his shadow came between me and the dim light glooming through the hatch opening.

CHAPTER X

IN THE HANDS OF THE POLICE

I had been afraid to shift my position lest the change should rouse any suspicions on the part of the "doctor," and his first attempt was to drag me out while he remained outside.

He seized my left arm and tried to pull me forward, but I had hitched my feet under a board of the flooring, and the attempt failed.

"Come here, Marlen. I'll hand him out to you," he said, turning his head for a moment. "He's got caught up in something or other."

"I can't leave the wheel."

"Stop the launch a minute then."

"It's your own job; do it yourself," was the surly reply.

Muttering an oath at his companion's cowardice, the "doctor" stooped down and, first pushing me roughly to one side out of his way, began to crawl head first into the forecastle.

"Curse the darkness," he murmured.

But my eyes had grown accustomed to it; and it helped me although it hindered him. I could watch him easily. The litter in the place hampered him also, and he stumbled and fell on his knees, and swore again volubly.

Taking advantage of the noise he made, I slipped back a yard or two and gripped my weapon in readiness.

"Where the devil is he?" he muttered, and began to feel about for me.

I was crouching in a corner waiting for a favourable chance to strike, and he could not see me.

64

The chance came an instant later, as he was stooping down in his hunt for me. Raising my hand I struck him two blows on the head with all my strength and at the same instant slammed the hatch to.

"What's the matter?" shouted Marlen, hearing the noise of the blows and coming forward quickly.

The "doctor" lay as still as a log. I had stunned him or killed him, and at the moment I did not much care which. I kept my hands on him, and if there had been the slightest movement I should have struck him again. I was fighting for my life.

When I was satisfied that he would give me no more trouble, I ran my hands quickly over him in the hope that he would have a revolver; but I could feel nothing of the sort; and as Marlen was fingering the hatch to get it open, I drew back into my corner again.

If he came in to see what had happened, I would serve him as I had served the "doctor." I hoped he would with all my heart.

He got the hatch open after some fumbling and peered in.

"Doctor!" he called, and paused. "Doctor!" A little louder this time. "What have you done? You haven't killed him, have you? Doctor!"

He put his head in a little way, but not far enough for me to make sure of disabling him, and then withdrew it again.

"What the devil does it mean?" He was evidently very frightened.

After a few seconds' pause he ran to the after-part of the launch and stopped her. He waited until the way was off her, and then came forward once more and called to his companion.

"The place is as dark as hell," he muttered and went off, as I guessed to get a light.

I used the time to make another search for a revolver in the stunned man's pockets, and failing to find one, I threw some of the litter over the head and shoulders, and went back to my corner and lay down as if still unconscious, but in such a position that I could spring on Marlen the instant he entered.

This time he brought not only a lantern but a revolver. He had little of the courage of the other fellow I soon saw, and he brought the weapon more because he feared the "doctor" than from any suspicion that I was the cause of the mysterious trouble.

"What fool's game are you playing, doc?" he said. "Don't try any pranks with me. What have you done to the man?"

He thrust in the lantern and peered all about him. I saw him take a long look at me, and the scrutiny apparently satisfied him that I was still of no account; and then he turned from me to the prostrate form of his companion.

65

He looked long and anxiously at him, and shook his head. "He must have had some sort of fit, if he hasn't got some devil's game on. Doctor!"

He appeared to be afraid to trust himself inside the place, and for some minutes remained in stolid thought.

Next he levelled the revolver at the other. "I'm covering you, doc. Get up or I shall fire." He shook his head again in dire perplexity when he received no reply, and at length made up his mind to risk entering.

He set the lantern down, fortunately on the side farther from me, and stooped to enter, holding the weapon all the time in readiness, and glueing his eyes on the still form of the unconscious man.

At that moment I changed my plan. I would have that revolver if it were in any way possible.

I let him enter, therefore, and crawl to the side of the "doctor." He moved very slowly and with intense caution, feeling the body as he approached the head. Then he pulled off the covering of the face and started violently.

For the instant he was entirely off his guard in his consternation, and I took advantage of that moment. I sprang forward, wrested the revolver from his grasp, thrust him violently down, seized the lantern and started out on to the deck, sliding to the hatch and shooting home the bolt.

I was now master of the situation, and with a profound sigh of relief and thankfulness I sank down on the deck.

I was still very shaky, and the reaction from the strain and suspense of my time in the forecastle tried me severely. My nerves were all to pieces, and when Marlen began hammering with his fists at the hatch, I started as if it were some fresh peril to be faced.

I let him hammer. So far as I was concerned he might have hammered all the skin off his knuckles before I would take any notice; and after my first start of alarmed surprise, I just lay still and rested until I had recovered strength and composure.

He grew tired of knocking presently, and began to whine to me to let him out. But I made no response. He was in a very ugly mess indeed, and a taste of the suspense I had had to undergo would do him good. He could spend the interval in thinking out some plausible explanation of his exceedingly compromising situation.

Meanwhile I had to think what I was to do. I did not understand the working of the launch, which was drifting at the will of the stream; and there appeared to be nothing for it but to let her drift until we met a boat, and I could get assistance.

But it then occurred to me that I myself might be hard put to it to give an account of myself. My clothes were in a filthy state as the result of my crawling hunt in the dirty forecastle, and when I examined them by the light of the lantern I found some ugly blood-stains on my sleeves.

These would go far to set up the presumption that I was responsible for the wound to the "doctor"; and as I was now outside and armed with a revolver and the two men were my prisoners, the German police would require a lot of persuasion that I was the innocent and they the guilty parties.

Any investigation would most certainly occupy a long time, moreover; and as my chief desire was to get back to Berlin with the least possible delay, I resolved not to run the risk of waiting for the police or any one else to come to my assistance.

There was only one way to accomplish this: I must swim ashore. I found much to my relief that my pockets had not been rifled, and that I had sufficient money for a ticket to Berlin. But I could not travel in a blood-stained coat; so I hunted through the boat and came across a rough reefer's jacket in the after-cabin, which I annexed. I then undressed, tore out the blood-stained portions of my own coat, made a bundle of my clothes, and managed to fasten it on my head.

Then I waited until the launch had drifted pretty close to the bank on the side where the railway ran, when I let myself carefully over the side and struck out.

Just as I was pushing off I heard Marlen start shouting and hammering again at the hatch, and the muffled sounds reached me across the water until I reached the shore.

They ceased as I finished dressing myself and started out to ascertain where I was and which was the nearest station to make for.

The swim in the cold water chilled me; but I set off at a brisk pace and soon had my blood circulating again.

I had not an idea where I was, except that I knew my way lay up stream; so I struck across country until I came to a road leading in the direction I had to go, and I set off to walk until I could ascertain where to find a station.

I knew I should have to be very cautious about asking any questions. German police methods were very different from English, and a man garbed as I was, without any papers of identification and carrying a loaded revolver, was pretty sure to be an object of suspicion. It would be exceedingly difficult for me to give any acceptable account of myself without telling all that had occurred; and that would certainly mean that I should be detained, and probably left to cool my heels in a police-cell while the cumbersome wheels of the law were put in motion to investigate my story.

I plodded along for an hour or two, keeping my ears at full strain for any footsteps ahead of me, and taking the greatest care to make as little noise in walking as possible.

In my weakened state, I found this extremely fatiguing, and more than once I had to sit down and rest. Eager as I was to reach the capital, I grudged every second of these intervals of inaction.

I was on fire with impatience to ascertain what had happened to Althea in my absence. How long I had been away from home I could not tell; and I tortured myself with a hundred fears on her account.

Von Felsen was not the man to lose a minute in getting to work, as soon as he knew I was out of his way; and of course his creature, Dragen, would have told him at once of the success of the attempt to kidnap me.

Until I had left the launch, the consideration for my own safety and the weighing of the chances of escape had kept me from fretting about matters in Berlin; but now that I was free and on the way back, every minute seemed to be of vital consequence, and the thought that I might be stopped by the police harassed and worried me into a positive fever of dread.

Fortune did me a good turn, however. I heard the rumble of a train as I was sitting by the roadside, and presently I saw it rush rapidly past a few hundred yards above the road where I was.

This did more to revive my strength than anything else could have done, and a moment later I was striding across the intervening fields to reach the line. I knew I should not meet any one there, and I pushed ahead with more confidence than I had yet felt.

Soon afterwards the gloom began to lift, and the sky grew grey in the east. Dawn was near; and as the light grew stronger, I saw a station not far ahead.

If all went well, an hour or two would see me out of my fix and speeding toward Berlin. But everything depended upon the "if." I was already committing an offence in walking on the line; and I knew that my greatest difficulties might easily come at the station itself.

I left the line, therefore, while still at a considerable distance from the station, and made my way back to the road again. In doing this I stumbled into a rather broad ditch and made myself in a pretty mess.

Under ordinary circumstances I should have laughed at this; but as so much might turn on my appearance, already dishevelled

68

enough, it irritated me and promised to prove an additional handicap, when the time came for questions to be asked.

I looked very much like a tramp, and the German law is not kindly disposed toward tramps at any time, and certainly not when they are found wandering about armed in the early dawn. Still, I had to make the best of things, so I plodded along until I reached the station.

But the door was locked and, although some one must have been attending to the signals, I could not see any one. The name on the end of the building was Wilden; but that did not help me much, as I had never heard of the place.

I was debating what to do when a very sleepy-looking official came lounging up to the door, unlocked it and entered, eyeing me with glances full of suspicion the while.

"When is the next train to Berlin?" I asked him.

He looked me up and down carefully and then grinned. "Do you want a first-class ticket?"

I took his impertinence lightly. "You needn't judge by my appearance," I said with a laugh. "I have money to pay for any ticket I want," and I repeated the question.

"Where did you get it from? And what are you doing hanging about here at this time in the morning?"

"I'm going to wait for the next train to Berlin."

"Well, you won't wait in here;" and with that he slammed the door in my face.

It is very little use to argue with a man who is on the right side of a locked door, so I turned away and walked a little distance along the road by which I had come, and sat down under a tree to wait.

I was cold, intensely weary, and famished with hunger; and although I fought against sleep, nature would not be denied, and I was soon off. The thunder of a train woke me, and jumping up I saw a train running into the station.

I hurried back to the station and the man I had seen before met me at the entrance. "Hullo, you again, is it?" he cried.

"I want a ticket for Berlin."

"That train doesn't go to Berlin. You'll have time to go and wash yourself first"; and he deliberately blocked my way.

As all railway officials were Government servants, I had to be cautious in dealing with him. "Where does that train go, then?" I asked very civilly.

He sneered. "Ah, I thought as much. Anywhere, eh, to get away from this place? But you're not going by it, my friend."

It was getting difficult to keep my temper, but I replied quietly:

"You are evidently making a great mistake about me."

"Oh no, I'm not," he laughed, with a knowing shake of the head. "Where did you sleep last night? And who are you?"

"I am going to Berlin," I said. But as the train started at that moment there was nothing to be gained by continuing to wrangle with the man, so I turned away.

Then he said in a less surly tone: "There's no train for two hours. You can wait in the station."

I was glad enough to have the chance, and sitting down on one of the benches in the waiting-room, was soon fast asleep again.

When I woke I saw the reason for his apparent concession. A police officer was with him and had roused me. I blinked at him confusedly.

"Come along with me," he ordered curtly.

"I want to go to Berlin. I must get there without delay."

"Come with me, I tell you," he repeated very sharply. "We must know something about you first."

With a shrug I rose, and he walked me off to the police station, the railway official accompanying us. I concealed my bitter irritation as best I could, and tried to think of the best story to tell. The railwayman said what he knew, and the officer in charge of the station questioned me. "Who are you?"

"There has been a great mistake made by this gentleman. I am an Englishman, Paul Bastable, 78, Miedenstrasse, Berlin, a newspaper correspondent. I have been away in search of information about some events I cannot tell you, and must return to Berlin at once."

"Where have you come from?"

"I am not at liberty to tell you; but you can send some one with me to Berlin if you wish, and I can satisfy him of the truth about me."

"Have you searched him?" he asked the man who had taken me there.

He did it at once without any ceremony, and together they examined the contents of my pockets. When they looked next at me, it was with obvious suspicion, and the constable turned back the collar of the reefer jacket at the back and then nodded to his superior.

"Paul Bastable, English, are you? Then how come you to have the papers of Johann Spackmann, engineer, with you, and to be wearing his coat?"

What a stroke of ill luck! I had seen the man take a paper from the inside pocket of the jacket I had annexed from the launch. I hesitated and then forced a laugh. "I suppose you know that

70

newspaper men have to be somebody else at times. I have told you the truth. Send some one with me to Berlin."

"I knew there was something wrong about him," put in the railwayman. "But I must be off, the Berlin train is due."

"For Heaven's sake don't let me miss that train," I cried earnestly.

A stolid stare and a shake of the head was the only reply.

"But I tell you I must get on at once."

"You will remain here while we make inquiries about you."

My heart sank. "Well, let me telegraph to my people and they will send some one out to identify me. Or wire the message yourself"; and I gave Bassett's name and the address of my former office.

"Well, good-morning," said the railwayman; and as he left the station I was led away and placed in a cell.

CHAPTER XI

MY RETURN

There is no need to dwell on the bitter mortification I endured in the first hour or so of my imprisonment, or to repeat my futile railings against the wooden methods and stupidity of the police.

I grew calmer after a time, and recognized that if I was to get out of the police grip before irreparable mischief was done in Berlin, it would not be by abusing the men who had detained me. My only chance would be to persuade them of the fact of my identity.

The thing that bothered me was the possession of the coat I had taken and papers they had found. What a fool I had been not to feel in the pockets. When it was too late I saw the blunder I had committed in the account I had given on the spur of the moment.

I considered long and earnestly whether I should out with the whole truth about the abduction. But I could not bring myself to believe that they would credit the story now. And if they did not, it would only serve to confirm and increase the suspicions already entertained.

Whether anything was being done to test the truth of what I had said, I could not ascertain. A man brought me some breakfast,

71

but he would not answer the questions I put to him; and when I asked to see the chief, I was curtly told that I should see him when he wished to see me, and not before.

Some hours passed in this galling suspense. I was eating my heart out in the desire to know what was being done, when two men entered the cell and ordered me to strip. They examined the marks on my linen carefully, and fortunately it had my name in full.

"How is it you are wearing these things?" asked one, looking at me with a very singular expression.

"Because they are my own, of course."

He grunted and exchanged looks with his companion. They whispered together and then took the shirt away, telling me to put on the rest of the clothes.

I did not understand the reason for this proceeding, but hoped that the marks would be regarded as confirmation of my identity.

Presently one of them returned and led me to the office, where the chief was examining my shirt and looking very grave and important.

"Will you now give an account of yourself during last night?" he demanded in a pistol-at-your-head tone.

"I can say what I wish to say when I get to Berlin."

"You had better be careful, and had better explain everything fully. There is a very serious charge against you. We have heard from Berlin."

I jumped to the conclusion, not unnaturally, that the charge referred to my actions in regard to Althea, and I recognized its seriousness as fully as did the man questioning me. "I would rather not say anything until I get to Berlin."

"I'll give you one more chance. We have heard that an Englishman, Paul Bastable, is mysteriously missing from Berlin, and you Johann Spackmann, are found here under these suspicious circumstances wearing his clothes. Account for that if you can."

Instead of accounting for anything I burst out laughing. "You mean that the charge against me is that of having murdered myself?"

"You will find it no laughing matter," he said sternly.

"My good man, I am Paul Bastable. How the devil could I murder myself?"

"The papers upon you prove you to be Johann Spackmann."

An entirely convincing proof to the German official mind, this. "Then you'd better behead me as Spackmann for the murder of Bastable," I said with a shrug of indifference. "Only for Heaven's sake whatever you are going to do, do quickly."

The affair had turned to a farce although the police did not yet see it. They put their heads together and whispered in solemn conference.

"Look here," I broke in. "If it will cause you to send me at once to Berlin, I will confess to the murder of Paul Bastable. And when I do get there, you will receive such praise for your zeal and cleverness that you will remember it all your life."

"Hold your tongue," cried the chief very angrily.

"I'll do nothing of the sort," I rapped out in reply. "This farce has gone too far already and lasted too long. Among the men who know me well in Berlin is the head of the police"; and I spun off a list of imposing names. "I demand to be allowed to go there, or to be taken there, at once; or to send word to my friends to come out and identify me. You refuse me if you dare."

The only immediate result of my protest was an order to take me back to my cell, but it bore good fruit. A very short time afterwards my shirt was returned to me; I was ordered to dress; and told that I was to go to Berlin in accordance with instructions which had been telegraphed from there.

They took me as a prisoner, but I did not care a rap for that. All I wished was to get there. I knew that five minutes' conversation with the police there would see me at liberty.

And so it turned out. I was ushered into the office of Herr Feldermann, who was very high up in the police administration; and the instant his eyes fell on me, he knew me of course, for we had had many a time together.

"This is Mr. Bastable, the Englishman," he said to my conductor. "You can return to Wilden and give my congratulations to your superior there for the zealous discharge of his duty. You may tell him at the same time," he added with a dry manner, "that although the criminal code is comprehensive, it does not yet demand the arrest of a man for the murder of himself."

The man flushed to the roots of his hair, laid down on the table the things which had been taken from my pockets, saluted, and withdrew without a word.

"And now tell me what it all means, Herr Bastable."

"Which ears have you on, official or private?"

"Do you want it kept secret? You've given us a lot of trouble, you know. We have wired your description all over the country. Let us talk it over privately first." He was one of the few men in the police administration who refused to be ruled by red tape, and I knew I could rely absolutely on his word.

"For your private ear only," I replied; and then gave him a fairly full account of all that had passed, withholding only von Felsen's name in connexion with the affair.

73

"I know that man they call the "doctor," and you may shake hands with yourself on your escape. And as for Dragen, every one of us knows about him. Who's behind it?"

"Don't ask me, even privately. Get Dragen first, and he'll tell you. Dragen hasn't a suspicion that I even know he was concerned in it."

He gave me a very shrewd sharp glance. "Nor Herr von Felsen either?"

"I mention no names. But tell me how did you hear about me?"

"Some one who took a considerable risk and came to me. We have had a hint to hold our hands for a while, or she would have remained as His Majesty's guest. I won't ask how she came to know so promptly that you were missing; but Herr Dormund is very sore about you."

It was Althea herself then. She had run this risk of imprisonment for me. The knowledge was worth all it had cost me.

"I don't want any fuss made about the affair at present if it can be avoided, but I should like to know if you get hold of the men," I said as I rose.

"Of course. You had better let me have that jacket and the papers. They may help us. Well, congratulations again. And by the way, don't run any more risks about the lady I referred to. She said she was at your house, and gave her word that if we had to do anything, she would either be found there or else would tell us where."

"Just one question, "When was I carried off?"

He smiled. "Why last night, of course."

I drove home and found my sister in the deepest distress on my account. She was overjoyed to see me, and declared that she and Althea had passed a night of terrible agitation and suspense.

I did not tell her what had occurred, but merely that I had been detained and unable to send word.

"We thought you had been arrested, Paul; and Althea insisted upon rushing off to the police this morning. Herr von Felsen came early, and again this evening, and is with her now in the drawing-room. I must run and tell her the good news;" and she was rushing out of the room when I stopped her.

"Don't tell her yet. I'll change and go into them. Von Felsen may be glad to know I'm back."

"Oh, how I loathe that man, Paul! Had he anything to do with this?"

"My dear child, how could he?" I replied as I hurried off to get into some decent clothes.

I was not more than a few minutes making the change, and I

went down to the room where the two were together. I paused a moment on the threshold in doubt whether I should not after all let Bessie announce my arrival.

"Yes, my solemn word on it. Bring him back and I will do all you wish."

It was Althea's voice and I could not help hearing. It decided me, and I opened the door and entered.

She sprang to her feet and cried out with astonishment and I hoped delight, while von Felsen turned as pale as death.

"Good evening, Fräulein Althea," I said quietly, holding out my hand. "I am afraid I have given you and Bessie a great fright. I am very sorry."

She could not speak for the moment and her hand shook as she laid it in mine. Then after a pause: "Oh, Mr. Bastable, I—I am so relieved."

Affecting not to notice her agitation I turned to von Felsen. "Good-evening; I suppose you know the fuss I have stupidly caused."

I did not wish him to think that I knew of his hand in the affair, and spoke much more courteously than I had ever addressed him before.

"Yes, I did hear of it," he replied uneasily. "The fact is I was just offering my services in the matter."

"Well, I'm afraid it's more than I should have done had you been the cause of the trouble. But then we don't hit it off very well, do we? But you could not have done anything. It was just a police blunder at the last. I had a little trip into the country, and they took me for a tramp, or something of the sort. Of course it was all put right easily enough."

"A trip into the country!" cried Althea.

"Well, not exactly a voluntary outing. The fact is I was robbed in the street here in Berlin, and the scoundrels took me off in a motor-car. I found myself early this morning miles and miles away—I suppose there must have been a smash up or something; I had been unconscious evidently—and when I reached a station the man sent for the police, who shoved me into a cell and kept me there all day." I laughed as if the thing were the merest joke.

"You are not hurt?" asked Althea.

"Not a scratch, thank goodness."

"I hope you would know the scoundrels, Herr Bastable?" said von Felsen.

"What a question!" I answered with another laugh. "Do you think you would, if you had been chloroformed to wake up on a lonely road in the dark miles away from anywhere. They knew their business too well for that."

"Well, I'm sure I congratulate you, Herr Bastable," said von Felsen, with well affected sincerity. "As you say, we don't exactly hit it in many ways, but a thing of this sort might happen to any of us. It's monstrous that it could occur. Of course you'll set the police to work."

I threw up my hands as if it were useless. "I've just been with Feldermann and his manner told me what to expect. Without a clue of any sort, what can they do?"

Althea had been watching him very closely, and now turned to him. "You said just now, that you had no doubt of your being able to get to the bottom of it all."

"I shall do everything in my power as it is," he replied uneasily.

"But you spoke of having knowledge that would lead to certain success."

"I made sure it was merely a case of arrest; in which event, of course, my influence would soon have enabled me to ascertain everything."

"I did not take it to be merely that," was the drily spoken reply.

"Well, it's very good of you, von Felsen," I interposed. "And if you can find the fellows, I'll prosecute them readily enough."

"You do not know all that has passed, Herr Bastable," said Althea with great deliberation. "And I think you should know."

Von Felsen took alarm at this and said: "As you have returned without my help, I suppose I can do no more. I'll go." I sauntered over as if to look at a letter lying on a table and got between him and the door.

"You should explain to Mr. Bastable, certainly. Herr von Felsen exacted a pledge from me to do a certain thing on the condition that he secured your return in safety," she added to me, speaking with some little hesitation.

"How could he possibly have done it?" I cried with a smile. "Anyhow, as I have returned in safety and without his help, the pledge may be considered as withdrawn, whatever its nature. That's quite clear."

He understood that I guessed what the pledge was, and turned at bay. "You may as well know what it was," he said with a scowl. "Fräulein Althea agreed to do what my father wishes—become my wife. You know well enough the many solid reasons there are for that marriage. Herr Borsen told you."

I laughed. "I thought you were going to marry old Ziegler's daughter. Is that off then?"

He shot at me a look of bitter hatred. "It's no concern of yours.

You have interfered a great deal too much as it is, Herr Bastable; and Fräulein Althea should know that your interference can only have serious consequences for her; unless, indeed"—and he turned to her—"she can see her way to comply with my father's wishes at once."

"Can't you bring some more relatives into it besides your papa?" I asked with a grin. "A baby brother or something equally influential?"

He let the jibe pass. "Now that your whereabouts are known," he continued to Althea, "the decision must be made immediately."

"If I may be allowed a suggestion," I said to Althea very gravely, "it might help matters if you were to meet Hagar Ziegler and arrange which marriage should take place first."

He all but swore at me for this. "You may think it a good subject for a jest, Herr Bastable; but Fräulein Althea and her father will find very little subject for laughter in it. If your decision is not made within three days, Fräulein, I will not answer for the consequences."

"Let me see, you named a week to Herr Ziegler, didn't you?" I said in the same tone of banter.

But Althea was alarmed by the threat. "Mr. Bastable!" she cried with a gesture of protest. It was a mistake. Von Felsen was quick to see the impression he had created, and the wisdom of not saying any more. If he was to win, it would be by playing on her fears.

"That is my last word," he said, as he turned to leave.

"But not Ziegler's," I retorted, as I shut the door behind him.

"I think I am frightened, Mr. Bastable," said Althea nervously. "Why did you provoke him so?"

"To make him take the buttons off the foils. But I am sorry you let him see that he had scared you. And there is less cause than ever now."

"Tell me."

"I have first to scold you. You did very wrong to go to the police about me and then give them that promise not to attempt to avoid arrest."

"Was I to sit still while I believed you were in danger?" she cried vehemently. "And after what you had done for me?"

"I am very angry," I replied with a smile.

"I should do the same thing again." And then her face lighted. "Oh, I think I was never so delighted in my life as when I saw you come into the room safe and unhurt!"

"If you had only had a little more patience you——"

"Patience? And you in peril!" She stopped with sudden embarrassment as the colour rushed in a crimson flood to her cheeks, and she lowered her head.

I was scarcely less embarrassed, and hot passionate words of love rushed to my lips only to be forced back with a resolute effort.

"Althea."

She looked up and our eyes met. I made a movement to take her hand when the door was opened and my sister came in hurriedly.

CHAPTER XII

MURDER

It was no doubt quite for the best that my sister interrupted us at such a moment. Althea's solicitude on my account; the sacrifice she had shown herself ready to make to secure my safety, and the emotion caused by my return, had filled me with stronger hopes than I had ever ventured to encourage before.

Yet to have spoken the words which Bessie's entrance had prevented, would only have complicated matters and have placed Althea in a position of supreme embarrassment. Whatever her feeling might be for me, she still held paramount what she believed to be her duty in regard to her father, and continued to look upon the marriage with von Felsen as a possible alternative.

There was another consideration, moreover. If I had blurted out the declaration of my love, it would make it very difficult, if not actually impossible, for her to remain longer in the same house with us.

Bessie was quick to understand that she had entered at an awkward moment, and paused for an instant by the door. "I could not wait any longer when I knew Herr von Felsen had gone," she said doubtfully.

"There is no reason why you should, Bess," I replied.

"Come and sit by me," said Althea, making room for her. "And now, Mr. Bastable, was I not right in thinking that Herr von Felsen was at the bottom of all your trouble? I read an absolute confirmation of it in his face when you came in; although I was sure of it before, of course, when I told Herr Feldermann."

"It is one thing to guess and another to have proof," I said, and went on to give them a general account of my adventure of the preceding night. They both plied me with a host of questions until at length I had to avoid the fusillade on the plea that I was both famished and worn out.

Bessie ran off at once to have something got ready for me, and again Althea and I were alone. But I had myself well in hand now. Besides, the conditions were changed; the moment of emotion had passed, and we were both cooler.

"It was on my account then that you got into this danger?" she said.

"If von Felsen was in it, probably; but then there has never been any love lost between us. He has always owed me a grudge." I had not admitted that I knew he had planned the thing.

"If you can prove it, you will have him punished?"

"I hope to deal with him in another way yet."

"Is it not all a terrible complication?"

"I think we shall unravel it," I said hopefully.

Bessie came back then to say that all was ready for me and I rose.

"How shall I ever be able to repay my obligation, Mr. Bastable?"

"I shall manage to get even with you some day, I expect. Bessie will tell you that whenever I do a little thing for her, she has to pay the price, eh Bess?"

"Bessie has already told me lots of things," was the reply.

"Ah, you mustn't believe half she says. She's a born gossip," I answered, and then went off.

The next morning I went early to the Jew's house and found him full of the news of my disappearance. I did not tell him what had occurred, merely that I had had to leave the city and had been detained.

"I came to see you that night because I wanted to know if your daughter's marriage could not be postponed for a time."

"It is fixed for to-morrow, Herr Bastable, and everything is arranged."

"I'm afraid you'll have to put it off, Ziegler." But he would not listen to this. He was deaf alike to arguments, persuasions and threats. And while we were in the midst of a heated discussion about it, Hagar herself came in.

He told her what I wished; but she added her protests to his and spoke with great passion. She was intensely agitated at the suggestion, and wound up a fierce tirade with the vehement declaration: "If it is put off, father, I will kill myself." And that ended the matter.

She was a strange girl; and the instant I said that I should urge it no more, she seized my hand and pressed her lips to it, not a little

79

to my embarrassment. "It is you I have to thank for its taking place so soon, Herr Bastable. I know that. Father has told me all: and I shall never cease to feel that you have been my best friend throughout."

"You see," said the Jew, lifting up his hands, when she had left the room.

"All right. Let us talk about something else. How goes the matter of the papers?"

"Just as we should wish; but I was sorry you did not come to me yesterday. I had arranged for you to see some of my friends."

"I can see them to-day. I am in earnest, and mean to go through with the thing. I am as eager as you yourself, I assure you."

He sat thinking a moment. "I ought to tell you, I think. There has been some rumour again of betrayal of our plans. Only vague, I give you my honour; but hints which I do not understand. You have not spoken to any one?"

"Not to a soul."

"I do not understand it. I do not understand it," he repeated. "Questions were even put to me about myself—to me, who have given so much to the cause and done so much, too. But if any questions are put to you to-day, you will understand the reason. Will you come here this afternoon?"

After some further conversation I agreed to return in the afternoon and left him. I attached little or no importance to his statements at the time, but they had a more than sinister look when I came to recall them in the light of after events.

I knew I was playing with double-edged tools in the affair. Suspicion of my good faith would bring on me the anger of men to whom treachery was the one unforgivable crime; while, on the other hand, the mere fact of my having any dealings at all with them might place me in jeopardy with the authorities.

It was for this reason that I had resolved to prevent von Felsen having any knowledge of the part I was playing until the very last moment. I should not be a free man for an hour after he got wind of the thing, unless I was in a position to call a halt by means of my knowledge of his own acts.

From Ziegler I went to Chalice, and found matters in a pretty muddle. Ever since I had seen her two days before she had been in a condition of excited indecision; and as I had not gone to her, she had sent for Prince von Graven. He was there when I arrived, and she had just told him all I had said to her.

His reception of me may be imagined. He looked as if it would have given him the pleasure of his life to run me through there and then, and his furiously indignant denunciation of my interference in the affair matched his looks.

A very warm altercation followed, in the course of which it came out that the Kaiser had heard the rumours in regard to the Prince and Althea. Chalice watched us both and appeared to side with each in turn. She evidently wished to be able both to marry a man of his high rank, and yet to secure the triumph of the promised Court patronage.

At length I began to find myself losing command of my temper under the fire of his invective, so I held my tongue and let him rage at will.

"If ill temper would solve the difficulty we should very soon settle it," I declared, when a pause gave me a chance to speak. "But we are not doing an atom of good by all this talk. The thing is perfectly simple: Fräulein Chalice can either give up this chance or give up you. One of the two sacrifices she must make, and if we stay here and talk till to-morrow morning we can't alter the position."

"You have no right to interfere, sir," he rapped back.

"My interference has consisted in telling her the plain truth."

"To attempt to come between us in this way is unjustifiable, monstrous. I will not allow it either. You shall answer to me, sir."

"I don't care a snap of my finger for your anger, Prince von Graven; and I certainly do not intend to have a personal quarrel over the thing. Can you deny that I have put the matter in its true light?"

"That is not the point. The point is your conduct."

I shrugged my shoulders and turned to Chalice. "It is for you to decide. I shall of course take your answer as final."

"But how can I decide? Is there no way out?"

"There is only one of the two ways. You can't have both. I will come for your decision in an hour," I replied and rose. I thought that it would be best for me to leave them together to discuss it alone.

But Chalice stopped me. "Don't go, Herr Bastable; but excuse us a moment"; and she took him into another room.

She was soon back again, smiling and carolling an air from one of her songs. "The Prince has gone," she announced. "He is in a tearing rage and vows he will never see me again if I do what you ask. But I shall do it. I wrote the letter yesterday, and it took me such a time. Here it is"; and she handed it to me.

"I may place this in hands which will give it to the Emperor?"

"Why, of course," she cried. "But you must make sure that it does get to him."

"I can promise that, I think."

"You don't know how I thank you, Herr Bastable," she said gaily, as we shook hands. "And if I tell the truth, I would really rather please the Kaiser than the Prince. I would indeed, although I didn't dare to say so while he was here. He is such a dear fellow. I hate to make him angry; but he is awfully handsome when he is in a rage, isn't he? And if he doesn't come round this time, I can't help it, can I? And now I must get to my practice. Good-bye."

In this way she settled it; and whether she did or did not care for the man who was willing to sacrifice all his prospects in life for her sake, I could not even then determine. Nor did I, in truth, very much care.

I went straight with the letter to Herr Borsen, who showed some surprise at seeing me. "I heard strange news about you, Herr Bastable. I am glad to see there was no truth in it. You were reported to have disappeared."

"I have reappeared, that's all; and I have news for you, which I think you will agree is of importance."

"You newspaper men have certainly the habit of rushing matters," he smiled. "What is it?"

"We must have a deal over it. It is something that the Emperor will be very glad to know; and if I tell you, will you give me an undertaking to get it direct to him?"

"Would you wish His Majesty to be also a party to the matter?" he asked with a very dry smile. "Or perhaps you would prefer an audience with him?"

I affected to take his jibe as earnest and replied very seriously: "Yes, that would be by far the simplest course."

"You could then force your own terms on him."

"Exactly. Do you think I had better just drop in on him in a friendly way?" I paused and then added: "Or shall we quit fooling and settle something?"

"What is the nature of your news?"

"I understand that at length the news about Prince von Graven and Fräulein Korper has reached His Majesty. Is that so?"

"Undoubtedly; and with results."

"Well, if I can hand you a statement as to the truth of the whole affair, together with a written renunciation on the lady's part, will you pledge me your word of honour that it shall go straight to the Kaiser?"

"You're a cool hand, Bastable," he said laughing.

"Well, my dear fellow, there are other ways of doing it; but I know enough of Court affairs to be aware that any one who could claim the credit of having obtained such a document would do himself a good turn. I would rather you had the credit than any one else; but you see you are Count von Felsen's secretary, and I have to reckon with him."

He sat thinking. He knew the advantage to be gained as well as I did. "Yes, I'll give you my word," he said after the pause.

I handed him the letter which Chalice had given me without a word, and watched his mounting surprise as he read it. "But this is not from Fräulein Korper at all."

"No. That's the mistake. The Prince cares no more for her than you do"; and I made the matter plain, taking good care to emphasize the sacrifice which Althea had made and her real motive.

"She is a singer, then?" he asked, referring to Chalice.

"She has one of the most beautiful voices you ever heard, Borsen. She is Grumpel's favourite pupil, and he is putting her into the programme for the State concert next week in the place of his Prima, who has disappointed him."

He looked at me, his eyes full of meaning and his lips drawn into a dry smile. "I think I see. And you don't wish to appear in it?"

"You can shut me clean out of the picture if you like"; and I rose.

"I hope she will make the sensation old Grumpel expects. She ought to, after this," he said as we shook hands.

"Oh, by the way," I said, turning at the door as if with an afterthought, "I expect to have some almost equally important news for you about the von Felsen marriage in a day or two. Matters are in train."

"Are you going to bring that off too?" he exclaimed. "Upon my word, I shall begin to have some real belief in you newspaper men."

"I only want a few days," I replied casually.

"After this, you can have a month, of course, or as long as you wish."

I returned home, speculating rather uneasily what Althea would say when I told her what had occurred; but she was not in the house, and my sister told me she had gone to see Chalice. I was not sorry that Chalice should tell her the news.

In the afternoon I spent an hour or two with Herr Ziegler, and was introduced to some of the men associated with him in the political schemes of the Polish party.

I could not see any real reason for me to meet them, and I said as little as possible, beyond expressing sympathy with their cause and a willingness to help in the manner arranged with the Jew.

They appeared to be equally on their guard with me; and the chief impression left on my mind was that the men were not going straight; that some of them distrusted Ziegler, and were disposed therefore to regard me with no little suspicion. There was an air of insincerity, a disposition to fence, and such a reluctance to do more than hint and insinuate and imply, that I felt anything but easy in mind.

I told the Jew my opinion when the rest had left us; but he explained it away as no more than the caution natural under the circumstances.

However, the main thing I cared about was the arrangement that I was to be the go-between with von Felsen in getting the papers; and as any hour might bring the news that he had obtained them, Ziegler and I were to keep in constant touch.

But the more I thought over the afternoon's interviews the less I liked the look of things, and the stronger grew the impression that there was something crooked. I began to worry myself with the fear that the plan on which so much depended would go wrong.

For the first time, also, there was something like a cloud between Althea and myself as the result of the news Chalice had told her. She said little more than that she knew what had been done; but added that, as there was no longer any reason for her to remain with us, she had decided to return home on the following morning.

I took this as a sign of her dissatisfaction at my action; and as I was in a fretful and rather irritable mood, I just held my tongue. The evening was thus passed with a feeling of restraint which all Bessie's efforts could not remove.

I sat worrying over matters for a few minutes after they had left me, and at length grew so uneasy that I resolved to go at once to Ziegler to thresh out with him my doubts about his friends. I could not rest quiet or shake off the sense of impending trouble; and I soon had a tragic and terrible confirmation of my fears.

I was close to his house when I met Hagar rushing along the street distraught with terror. She was bareheaded, her eyes wide and fright-stricken, and she was so absorbed by her agitation, that she did not see me and did not even hear me when I first called to her.

I turned and caught her up.

"What has happened?" I asked, seizing her arm.

She tried at first to break away from me with a cry of fear, as if not recognizing me.

"I am Mr. Bastable, your father's friend. Tell me what is the matter."

She looked at me with a dazed expression, trembling violently the while, and then, with a great effort as if her emotion were choking her, she told me.

"I was coming to you. Oh, Herr Bastable, my father is dead. He has been murdered. Oh God! Oh God!"

I caught my breath with the shock of the tidings, and in an instant all my suspicions of the afternoon recurred to me with startling force.

CHAPTER XIII

IN THE HOUSE OF DEATH

As soon as I had shaken off the first stunning effect of the news of the murder, I did what I could to calm Hagar, and then asked her to return with me to the house. But this induced a fresh paroxysm of alarm.

"No, no. They will take my life," she cried. "I dare not. I dare not."

"I will see that no one harms you," I assured her. "I am armed, and by this time they will have fled. There is no danger."

I prevailed in the end, and together we went back to the house. She shuddered violently as we entered, and clung to my arm, shrinking and shaking and glancing about her in terror at every step.

I knew where her father had kept his liquors, so I got her some brandy and made her drink a fairly stiff dose.

"Where are your servants?" I asked.

"One is ill, and the other has been away all the afternoon." Her lips trembled and her voice quivered as she replied.

"You must make an effort," I said sharply. "Tell me everything."

"I cannot think. I cannot think," she moaned distractedly, and laid her head on the table in an agony of wild grief.

I gave her some more of the spirit, and as soon as she had drunk it I said as impressively as I could: "If you would revenge your father's death, you must let me know everything at once. Revenge is still in your power, remember. Your father would have had you think of that."

The appeal had an immediate effect. She raised her head and her eyes flashed with a new light. "You are right," she cried in a strong vibrating tone. "I will never rest until he is revenged and his murderers are punished. That I swear to my God!"

She rose then and led me into the room where the body lay, just as it had fallen, huddled up on the floor close to the table at which most of the old man's life had been spent.

"You have had no doctor yet," I exclaimed, turning to the telephone.

"I ran for my life the instant I discovered what had occurred."

"What is your doctor's name?" I asked as I tried the telephone. She told me; but I could get no reply to my call. And then I discovered that the communication had been cut. A sinister and suggestive circumstance.

I knelt down by the body and made a rapid examination. He had been stabbed from behind, and was long past all human help. The eyes were fast glazing and the body beginning to stiffen.

As I was feeling the pulse a ring dropped from the hand, and intent on the work of examination, I put it without thinking into my pocket.

"When did it occur?"

"I do not know. I was in my room upstairs and came down to speak to him about—about my marriage to-morrow——" She paused and closed her eyes and clenched her hands for a moment, and then forced herself to continue. "I found him as you see. That was just before I ran out of the house in my panic and you met me. I remembered his warning to me and fled. I was mad for the time, I think."

"What was his warning?"

"It was after you left him this afternoon. Something you said made him speak to me. He had had a letter threatening his life, and charging him with treachery; and I was threatened also."

I had been kneeling all this time by the body and now rose. "You have no idea who can have done this?"

"None. He told me he had an important interview to-night, and must not be disturbed. That was why I did not come down earlier."

"We must find out with whom," I replied. "And now we must have the police. Have you nerve enough to fetch them or shall we go together?"

"Don't leave me."

At that instant as we turned to leave, I heard a sound somewhere in the house. Hagar heard it also, and clutched my arm shaking like a leaf.

"You say we are alone in the house?" I asked in a low tone.

She nodded, her eyes strained in the direction of the sound.

We stood listening intently.

"They have come back in search of me," she whispered.

"Then we shall find out who they are. Courage."

I glanced round the room and motioned to her to hide behind

the curtains which covered the deep window recess, and stood there with her.

Two or three minutes of tense silence followed. Then we heard footsteps stealthily approaching the room. A pause, and then three men entered. One a grey-haired, distinguished-looking man well on in years; the other two younger and of a commoner type, swarthy, determined-looking men.

From where they stood they could not see the body of the Jew, and judging by their start at finding the room empty, I judged that they had expected to see Ziegler at his desk.

Their words confirmed this.

"Not here, the old fox," growled one.

"Come away. Come away," said the elder man, laying his hand nervously on the arm of one of the others.

"Not till this thing is settled," he replied, shaking off the other's hand impatiently. "I mean to have the truth out of the old rat, or his life."

"And the girl's too," added the other. "You know what we were told about them both. I shall wait for him."

"No, no. No bloodshed, no bloodshed, for Heaven's sake," cried the old man with a gesture of protest and dismay.

"My God! Look here!" This was from one of the two who had moved forward and was pointing at the dead body.

The old man gave a cry of horror and sank into a chair covering his face in his clasped hands.

"What can this mean?"

His companions were standing by the body gazing at one another in blank wonderment and surprise. Then one of them stooped down and examined the corpse.

"Dead, sure enough; and murdered, too," he announced.

He rose and they both looked round at the elder man. "Do you know anything of this?" asked one.

Without a word the man they addressed sprang up and rushed out of the room.

The two stared at one another again in silence.

Then one of them laughed sneeringly.

His companion winced. His nerves were not so tough.

"What shall we do?" he asked rather huskily. He was beginning to shake.

"Do? Why, what we came to do, of course. Find the old rat's daughter and finish the thing," he said brutally, and with an oath.

Hagar was trembling like an aspen and her breath was so laboured and heavy that I made sure they would hear it.

I pressed her arm to try and reassure her.

"I think we'd better go," said the weaker fellow.

A muttered oath at his cowardice was the response. "I'm going to search the house," declared his companion, and he began to glance round the room.

But the other went toward the door. "I'm going."

At this moment Hagar could restrain her terror no longer, and a heavy half-sigh half-groan burst from her.

Both men turned at once toward the curtains, and the bolder one put his hand to draw a weapon, knife or pistol; but before he could get it out, I stepped forward and covered him with my revolver.

"The Englishman!" they both cried in a breath, and the man by the door darted out of the room.

His companion stood his ground and met my look steadily.

"So it's your work, eh?"

"Take your hand from that weapon of yours," I cried sternly.

"What quarrel have you with me?"

"Do as I say," I thundered.

He took his hand from his pocket, shrugged his shoulders, and deliberately turned his back on me and walked toward the door.

His consummate coolness placed me in a dilemma. Shoot him down in cold blood I could not.

Hagar's courage returned the instant she perceived that the advantage was on my side. "Don't let him go," she said, and stepped forward.

The fellow started at the sound of her voice and looked at her with an expression of the bitterest malignity.

"Stop, you," I cried.

He faced me, laughed again with his former deliberate coolness and paused as if about to return. "Very well," he said slowly, with a shrug of indifference; and then, before I could guess his purpose, he sprang backwards to the door and rushed out.

As a matter of fact I was much relieved by his departure; but Hagar flew into a passion and reproached me bitterly for having allowed him to escape. "He murdered my father and will kill me," she cried. "You should have shot him."

It was clear from this that her agitation had been too great to admit of her understanding the purport of what had passed while the three men were together in the room.

I did not stay to explain matters and let her reproaches pass without reply. "We must have the police here at once," I said. "You had better come with me."

We went out to the front door, and seeing a police officer at a little distance, I called him and told him what had occurred.

He came in with us and made a rapid examination of the dead man. "He has been dead some time. When did it occur?"

I told him all I knew of the affair: that Hagar had found her father dead; had fled from the house in fear; had taken me back; and the cause of our delay in telling the police, adding such a description as I could of the men.

Of course I quite expected him to suspect us of the deed, and was not therefore in the least surprised when he replied that we should be detained.

"You had better go for one of your superior officers," I told him. "We will remain in the next room."

"I'm not so sure of that," he replied knowingly.

"Then send for some one. You can easily get a messenger in the street."

I led Hagar into the next room, and he went out and did as I suggested. Then he came to us, and we waited for the arrival of the others. Hagar spoke to the officer, but I took no part in the conversation.

I was completely mystified by the affair. I recalled all the events of the afternoon. Ziegler's singular hints of treachery; the others' suspicion of me; the fact of the threatening letter of which Hagar had told me: and all these things pointed clearly to the conclusion that the murder had been done by some one who suspected the Jew, and that it was in revenge we should look for the motive.

But the arrival of the three men, obviously bent upon doing that which had already been down, negatived any such conclusion absolutely, or appeared to do so.

That they had expected to find the Jew still alive, there was not the shadow of a doubt. Their actions had shown this as plainly as their words had expressed it. They had come to obtain an explanation of the facts which they held to justify their suspicions; and in default of that explanation being satisfactory, they were resolved to take his life.

The words and acts of the eldest of the men had proved that.

The next question was whether their own thought was right— that some one of their number had anticipated them. It was a plausible supposition.

But there was another possible theory. The Jew was a man with many enemies. He had been a hard man, and had been threatened more than once by those who laid their ruin at his door. He carried many secrets, too; and it was easy to conceive that there were hundreds in Berlin who would welcome his death.

Had some such enemy dealt this secret stroke? It was a

89

question which could only be answered after a strict search into the hidden undercurrents of his life and business.

To me his death was little short of a calamity. It threatened to overthrow my whole plans. The suspicions of his good faith entertained by his companions were almost sure to fall upon me; and in that case I should assuredly find myself shut out from the scheme on which I had built so much.

It was this aspect of the affair which concerned me chiefly as we sat waiting for the arrival of the police, and I racked my wits in vain for a solution to the problems which it raised.

When they arrived, Hagar and I were subjected to a searching cross-examination at their hands: she in one room, I in another. I was questioned very closely as to my relations with Ziegler; and except that I did not say a word as to the Polish intrigue, I gave as full and complete an account as possible. I had indeed nothing to conceal.

I perceived that the questions were directed to elicit any possible motive on my part which could in any way connect me with the crime. My replies appeared to satisfy them, and I noticed that they were compared with the statements which had been obtained from Hagar.

After the comparison had been made, the manner of the men questioning me underwent a considerable change. Not a little to my relief.

"We accept your statement, Herr Bastable; but of course you will understand that we were compelled to interrogate you closely as you were found upon the scene of the murder. Now, I invite you to tell me frankly of any circumstance which you think will tend to throw light on the matter."

"I am utterly baffled," I replied. "The only guess I can make is that it may have been the work of some one whose hatred he has incurred as a money-lender. He must have had many enemies."

"His daughter believes it was the work of the men who came here afterwards when you were here."

"That is incredible"; and I gave my reasons, adding that Hagar had been much too agitated to understand what had passed.

"You know that he was associated with the Polish party of independence. She says so. Will you tell me all you know about that? Have you any reason to believe that he contemplated betraying them in any way?"

"None whatever. I knew that he was associated with them. I learnt that some time ago when I was on newspaper work here in Berlin."

"I will be frank with you. It has been suggested to us, before this

I mean, that you were associated with him in some such way, and that that was the cause of your recent visits to him. What do you say to that?"

This was getting near home with a vengeance. "The only foundation for such a statement lies in the fact that he had asked me as a newspaper man, if I could make use of political information of importance if he obtained it for me. That is of course my business— provided of course that the information is authentic."

"How was he to obtain it?"

"That I can't say." I used the equivocation intentionally. "I know I was to pay for it, and to judge of its worth when I knew it."

"How were you to receive it?"

"He was to tell me the time and place and means and everything. I should of course have used my own discretion in handling it."

"That lends itself to the fact that he did meditate some sort of betrayal. I presume the information related to his political associations."

"I scarcely think so in the sense you imply. More probably something that would have helped his party. I do not know, as I have told you, the exact nature of the news, but I gathered of course that it must affect my own country, seeing that it was as an English newspaper man he approached me."

"You have taken no other part in these Polish intrigues?"

I smiled. "I am an Englishman, not a Pole; and have no other feeling in their affairs beyond the natural English attitude toward any movement which has the liberty of the subject as its motive. But this was business, you understand."

"One other question. You owed him no money?"

"Not a mark. I never have. I am now a man of considerable means indeed."

He bowed and lifted his hands to signify that he had finished with me. "I can go?" I asked.

"Certainly."

"And Fräulein Ziegler? She is in need of a friend and I should like to help her if she wishes? It is the more terrible for her as she was to have been married to-morrow."

"Indeed? To whom?" he asked quickly.

I regretted my indiscretion, but it was too late. "To Herr Hugo von Felsen."

"Ah. That explains. She asked to see him."

"Can I see her?" I asked, and received a ready assent.

I went to her with the mere intention of offering assistance, the last thing in my thoughts being that a momentous discovery was to be the result of the interview.

CHAPTER XIV

THE MURDERER

It will be readily understood that at the moment of my leaving the police official to go to Hagar Ziegler I was in a very unusual mood. Within the past twenty-four hours I had been within an ace of losing my life; I had seriously wounded if not actually killed a fellow-creature in order to escape; I had endured the bitter mortification of police detention; and had returned to Berlin to take up the thread of an exciting struggle. And now on the top of all had come the murder of the Jew, with its consequences of personal hazard to myself and its disastrous menace to my plans. The examination by the police had, moreover, been a great strain, and when I rose from it I felt both nervous and unstrung.

I say this in order to account in some measure for an act which was altogether foreign to my customary habit, and a paltering and cowardly hesitation which I have never been quite able to understand.

I had been treading on very ticklish ground in that part of the questioning which had related to my connexion with Ziegler's political associates, and I had been most unpleasantly conscious that a very little thing would have induced the official to order my detention. At a time when in Althea's interests my freedom was so essential, such a result would have been fatal, and the relief with which I had heard that I could leave the house was indescribable.

This was the predominant feeling as I went to the room to see Hagar. It was my part to assume indifference, however, and I plunged my hands into my pockets with every appearance of casual assurance.

As I did so my heart seemed to stop suddenly; a shiver of dread chilled me to the marrow; every muscle grew instantly tense and set; and then with a bound the blood began to rush through my veins at a rate which set every pulse throbbing violently.

My fingers had touched the ring which I had taken from the

92

dead man's grasp, the existence of which until that moment I had forgotten.

In an instant the conviction rushed on me, that if I returned to the official and gave it him he would refuse to accept my explanation, would connect me in some way with the crime, and have me detained if not actually arrested.

The ring was certainly the most important clue; for it was virtually certain that the owner of it was the man who had done the deed, and it was my clear duty to hand it over to the police. To evade that duty would be a piece of paltry cowardice. I realized all that clearly, but at that moment I was a coward. I was afraid of being prevented from making any further efforts on Althea's behalf. And that fear prevailed.

Instead of returning with it to the official, I slipped it on to my finger and continued my way to see Hagar. It may appear like the language of exaggeration to say that the ring seemed to burn the flesh like a band of fire; but my nerves were so high-strung at the moment, that that was precisely the sensation, and my hand was trembling like that of a detected thief.

I was a little surprised to find that Hagar had almost entirely shaken off her former agitation. This had apparently been caused as much by her fears for her own life as by the horror at her father's fate; and now that she was safe, she had set herself to the task of helping the police to the utmost in the work of tracing the murderer.

The police were going to remain in the house, and she had readily expressed her willingness to stay there also. For this purpose she had sent for a relative to come and be with her. I concluded that the police were resolved to keep her under close observation; but she did not appreciate this fact.

My offers of help were therefore superfluous.

"You have been kindness itself, Herr Bastable. I shall never forget that I owe you my life. Those men would have killed me, as they had killed my poor father, had you not been here with me."

"Is there nothing more I can do for you?"

"No; unless you can help me to find those villains. I should know them again and so would you, I am sure."

"Yes. But I do not think they were guilty of this."

"I know they were. Why else were they here?" she cried. She was manifestly still holding to what I believed to be a quite mistaken belief; but I had already given my opinion to the police, and to argue with her was needless.

"I am going now, Fräulein. There is no message I can take for you anywhere? Nothing I can do?"

She hesitated, and after a pause said with some sign of anxiety:

"I sent to Herr von Felsen, but he has not come?" and she looked at me half doubtfully, half questioningly.

"Would you like me to see him?"

"You are not friendly."

"I am your friend, remember that. I will certainly go to him if you wish."

"Oh, if you would!" she cried, her face lighting with a smile of gratitude.

"Of course I will," I agreed, and held out my hand.

She was an emotional girl, and instead of merely shaking my hand she seized it, and was in the act of pressing her lips to it, when she paused and glanced up in my face with a smile.

"It is a coincidence," she said, still holding my hand.

"What is?"

"Your ring. It is a facsimile of one I gave Hugo."

For an instant the room seemed to reel about me. I knew that she put her lips to my hand and that it fell listlessly to my side as she released it. I knew that next she was looking fixedly and with alarm at some change in my face, and I heard her voice, faint and as if at a distance.

"You are ill, Herr Bastable. You are white as death. What is the matter?"

I must have staggered, too, for she put out her hands and held me.

But at that I made a strenuous effort. "I am all right. This—this has all tried my nerves. I shall be all right in the air"; and with that I walked none too steadily out of the house, dazed and thunderstruck by the sinister truth which her words had revealed with this stunning suddenness.

As soon as I reached the street I stood for a few moments breathing deep draughts of the cool air while I sought to steady my bewildered wits, and then plunged along at a rapid pace.

So it was von Felsen himself who was the murderer. It was all clear enough to me soon. I could see his wily hand throughout. It was he who had started the suspicion against Ziegler with hints and insinuations of treachery dropped stealthily in likely quarters. He had planned it all as a safe background for the deed he contemplated, and had probably written the threatening letter with his own hand.

Driven to bay by the old Jew's determination to force the marriage with Hagar and thus wreck his prospects in every other direction, he had seen that his only escape lay in Ziegler's death; and he had been callous enough to select the very eve of the marriage for the deed.

I recalled what Hagar had said about her father having told her that he had a very private and important interview that night, and must not be disturbed. Von Felsen had arranged that easily enough no doubt from his knowledge of his victim's affairs. He would have little difficulty, moreover, in getting into the Jew's house and to the Jew's room secretly; and the rest was easy to guess.

There had probably been a struggle of some sort in which the ring had been pulled off von Felsen's finger; but he had found his chance to deliver the death-thrust in the back, and in his unnerved confusion afterwards he had not missed the ring.

I believed him to be as great a coward as he was a scoundrel, and at such a moment of crisis his thoughts would be too intent upon escaping from the scene of his crime to think of anything else.

And now what ought I to do?

As I began to consider this, the thought flashed upon me that indirectly I had been the cause of the Jew's death. It was my action in forcing on the marriage which had led von Felsen to this desperate means of preventing it. I had thrust him into a comer from which he could see no other means of escape.

How often I had regretted that act of mine! Even Althea herself had deemed it a mistake.

Regrets were useless now, however. I had to decide what line to take in view of the fateful proof which had come into my possession. I had his life in my hands. Was I to use the power to further my own purposes or to help justice?

I had to a certain extent compromised myself by not disclosing the possession of the ring to the police before I left the Jew's house, and the fears which had operated to prevent my doing so had no doubt been well grounded. But this did not prevent me from seeing plainly that my duty was to return and state all I knew and give up the evidence I had.

It was a difficult problem. On the one side there was Althea's happiness and all I cared for in life; on the other, the satisfaction of the demands of abstract justice and the punishment of a murderer.

I do not know how another man placed as I was would have acted, but I could not bring myself to make the necessary sacrifice. Let those blame me who will, but let them first try to put themselves in my position.

I resolved to try and use the knowledge I had for my own ends.

There were many difficulties in the way. The deed was not one which I could use to force the hands of von Felsen's friends. It was too heinous. They would not dare to attempt to condone it. What I had sought to obtain was the proof of some act of his which, falling far short of such a crime as this, would drive them to agree to my terms in order to save him from exposure and disgrace.

But I could use the power with von Felsen himself to force him to the commission of such an act; and with this intention I resolved to go straight to him now, using the message from Hagar as the reason for my visit.

I should have to act very warily and use the utmost caution in choosing the moment for showing my power.

I did not find him at his house, and at first this rather surprised me; but I knew the clubs he belonged to, and set off to make a round of them. Then I guessed his object. On such a night he would not dare to be alone; cunning would lead him to do all he could to be able to account for his time, should suspicion ever point in his direction.

I found him at the second effort, and sent in my name, saying that my business was of the greatest importance.

"I must speak to you in private," I told him when he came out with an assumption of irritation at my interruption of his pleasure. But it was easy to see that under the surface he was intensely wrought and uneasy.

"I don't know what you can want with me," he said, as he led me to a room where we could be alone.

"I have very grave news for you and a message. Herr Ziegler has been murdered to-night, and his daughter wishes you to go to her at once."

He had schooled himself carefully to hear the news when it came. "Murdered? Old Ziegler? Do you mean that, Heir Bastable?" he exclaimed.

"Certainly. I have just come from there." I kept my eyes on him closely, watching every gesture and expression.

"Good God!" he cried next, throwing up his hands, as if the significance of the news were just breaking in upon him. He acted well, but could not meet my eyes. "Tell me all about it."

"The police will tell you. They are at the house."

"Of course they would be," he said, keeping his head bent. Then, after a slight pause: "Have they any clue to the thing?"

"Yes. They know who did it."

I spoke very sharply, and the unexpectedness of the reply startled him out of the part he was playing. He glanced up quickly, his face pale and his eyes full of fear. "Whom do they suspect?"

"They do not suspect. They know," I replied, emphasizing the last word.

Alarm robbed him of the power of speech for the instant, "I'm glad to hear that," he said quite huskily. "Who was it?"

"Some of Ziegler's shady political associates. They were seen at the house."

His sigh of relief was too deep to escape me; it came straight from his heart. Before he answered he took out his case and lighted a cigarette. "By Jove, the news has shaken me up; see how my hand trembles." Cool, to draw pointed attention to his own agitation.

"It couldn't shake much more if you had done the thing yourself."

The cigarette dropped from his fingers. "I don't know what the devil you mean. If it's a joke it's a devilish poor one."

"I was only wondering if you could have been more upset if you had done it," I replied, fixing him again with a steady stare.

Whether he had any suspicion of what lay behind the words I do not know, or whether some sense of danger nerved him to make an effort; but his manner underwent a sudden change, and he became callous and cynical. "I suppose you writing fellows affect that sort of experiment. If you can bring yourself down to plain facts perhaps you will give me some account of the affair."

"I should have thought you would be anxious to get to Fräulein Ziegler at once in such a case."

He laughed very unpleasantly. "Not if you knew how that girl bores me."

"You don't mean that you won't go to her?"

"What has it got to do with you?" He was fast recovering his self-composure. Voice and manner were steadier, as the belief strengthened that no suspicion would attach to him.

For a moment I hesitated whether to strike the blow which would bring him to my feet, and my fingers went to the ring in my pocket. But I resolved to wait. "It has nothing to do with me," I answered; "but as you are going to marry her to-morrow, and this blow has come at such a moment, you can understand how she needs the strength of your support."

"You don't suppose there can be any marriage to-morrow, surely! Of course the old man's death has altered everything—made that impossible, I mean."

"It would be like you to desert her at such a time; but she has all her father's papers, you know, and is not exactly the sort of girl to stand any fooling."

"She can do what she pleases, and so shall I," he answered with a shrug and a sneer. "Anyway, she can't be married on the day after such a thing."

I knew what he meant. He was not afraid of Hagar as he had been of her father. There would be no marriage if he could avoid it.

"Well, I have given you her message, and if you don't intend to go to her, it's your affair not mine"; and I turned on my heel.

"You haven't told me how it happened," he said quickly.

I turned for an instant. "You'll hear it all from the police and will get their theory; and perhaps when you do hear it, you'll take my view that they are all wrong. I told them so to-night."

I just caught his quick glance of consternation at this as I swung round and went off. As I was crossing the hall I looked back and saw him standing leaning against the table in moody thought.

I walked home thinking that the cool air would refresh me after the strain of the night's events. I was worn out and sorely in need of sleep.

My sister was waiting for me with a very worried expression in her eyes.

"I began to fear something had happened again, Paul," she said.

"Something has happened, Bess; but I can't talk to-night. I'm as tired out as a hound after a hard day across country. I must get straight to bed."

"You look awfully worried, dear. Eat something; I'm sure you need it."

"You girls always seem to think that if a man can only be got to eat, nothing else matters," I exclaimed fretfully.

"Well, try the prescription now at any rate," she replied with a bright smile. "And while you eat I have something to tell you."

"If it's anything in the shape of another worry keep it till the morning; if it will keep, that is."

"I'm afraid it won't, Paul," she said, with such a rueful air that I could not refrain from smiling.

"Well, I'll take your medicine, if only to please you"; and I sat down to the dainty little meal she had had prepared. "What is it?"

"Eat something first," she insisted; and began to talk about a number of insignificant matters.

"Now tell me," I said at length.

"We have another visitor, Paul."

"Another what?" I cried, looking up quickly.

"Althea's father, Paul. The Baron von Ringheim."

"The deuce!"

"I didn't know what to do. I couldn't send him away, and I did so wish you would come home. He said he was in great trouble, and begged to be allowed to stay here for to-night at any rate. And he is in trouble, evidently."

"Where is he?"

"With Althea. They both asked me to send you up to them the moment you came in."

A pretty complication in truth. A leader of the Polish Irreconcilables in the house at such a time.

"I'll go to them," I said.

I went upstairs slowly, thinking how on earth to deal with so unwelcome a crisis. For Althea's sake the thing must be faced and her father sheltered somehow. But how?

Althea's voice called to me to enter when I knocked.

I opened the door, and then started back in dismay as I recognized in her companion the eldest of the three men whom I had seen an hour or two before in the murdered man's house.

For a moment I was literally struck dumb with amazement.

CHAPTER XV

BARON VON RINGHEIM

Baron von Ringheim had been sitting by Althea, and rose at my entrance and bowed to me with old world courtesy.

"My father, Mr. Bastable," said Althea; and at this he advanced toward me with hand extended.

I was still under the thrall of astonishment caused by my recognition, and only the expression of mingled pain, alarm and surprise on Althea's face enabled me to take his hand and mumble some formal reply.

He did not appear to notice anything strange in my conduct, however.

"I have to return you many thanks, sir, for the assistance which you have rendered to my daughter. She has told me how you have helped her, and I beg you to believe that I am sincerely grateful."

He said this with an air of great dignity, of patronage, indeed; almost as if in his opinion the opportunity of helping a daughter of his was something upon which I might well congratulate myself.

I murmured some sort of reply about having done very little.

"I would not have you belittle your services, Herr Bastable," he continued in the same indulgent tone. "I and Althea—for she is entirely with me in expressing this sentiment—are your debtors, distinctly your debtors. Our family is one of the oldest and highest in the Empire, and although at the present time we are the subjects of cruel persecution and have suffered egregious wrongs and abominable robbery, it shall never be said that we are deficient in gratitude."

This long and curious speech gave me time to recover myself, while the look of growing embarrassment and concern with which Althea regarded him while he was making it recalled to my memory what she had said of him on a former occasion.

"I beg you to say no more," I replied.

"That is the modesty of an English gentleman, and I appreciate it," he answered with another elaborate flourish and bow. "I have heard of you, Herr Bastable, and was assured that I should find a welcome here. For that also we thank you."

"My father can remain to-night?" asked Althea, as a sort of aside.

He heard this, however. "To be frank with you, Herr Bastable, I am in a slight difficulty for the moment. It is some time since I was in Berlin; as a matter of fact, I am not supposed to be allowed to come here at all, and if my presence were discovered it might lead to very serious embarrassment. I shall therefore appreciate it very highly if you will permit me to ask your hospitality for a while."

"I shall esteem it an honour, Baron."

"Again I beg to assure you that I am extremely grateful."

I had still great difficulty in suppressing the signs of infinite amazement that this could possibly be the same man whom I had seen in the company of the two ruffians in the old Jew's house.

"You look very tired and worried, Mr. Bastable," said Althea. "Bessie has very kindly seen to a room being prepared for my father."

"I am worn out, and shall ask the Baron to excuse me"; and we bowed gravely to one another. "But there is a question I should wish to put before retiring—who spoke so highly of me to you as to induce you to put this confidence in me to-night?"

"I knew that my daughter was here, Herr Bastable. The information came from a highly confidential source. But I was absolutely sure of you."

A glance of appeal from Althea accompanied this courteously worded roundabout refusal to tell me anything more, so I bade them good-night and went away. I was indeed so fatigued that even this strange development, with all the awkward and indeed perilous complications it threatened, could not keep me awake. I slept soundly for many hours, and did not awake until late in the morning.

Over my breakfast Bessie gave me her views of the Baron.

"He is a very strange old gentleman, Paul. His room is next to mine, you know; and I heard him moving about very early, hours before I got up. And when I saw him afterwards he had forgotten who I was, and spoke to me as if I were a servant. What do you make of him?"

"I am probably more puzzled than you are, Bess."

"How did he come here? Did Althea tell him of us?"

"I don't think so. Has she ever said anything to you about him?"

"Has she said anything to you? She did to me, but I don't know whether she meant me to tell you."

"About the effect of his troubles upon him, you mean?"

"Yes," she nodded rather eagerly. "I suppose he is harmless."

"Oh yes," I said with a smile. "He'll be all right in that respect. You needn't be scared."

"He has a loaded revolver. He left it under his pillow. Ellen was nearly frightened out of her life when she fetched me to see it."

"Where is it?"

"He came in for it just as we were both there. He was really very odd. He had that little bag of his with him and——"

"What little bag? Did he bring any luggage with him, then?"

"Nothing except the little leather bag. Well, he apologized to us, taking me for one of the servants, as I told you, and declared that the thing was not loaded—although I am sure it was—and made up a story that he was accustomed to have it with him just for practice, and said that we were not to say anything to any one about it; and then he offered us some money."

"What did you do?" I asked with a grin.

"It's no laughing matter, Paul. Ellen declares she can't stay in the house if he stops here."

"I'll see to it. But what did you do?"

"You don't suppose we took his money. I told him pretty sharply he had made a mistake; but he was so polite and seemed so sorry, that I couldn't be angry. But you'll have to do something, or we shall lose Ellen."

"Oh, I'll do something. You need not be frightened, nor Ellen either. So far as I can see, his brain has been affected by his troubles and persecution, and he is just a mixture of dignified gentleman and something else; and I'll see that when he is something else, he will not be able to do any harm."

"Poor Althea is in an awful state about it all. She almost broke down this morning when speaking to me about it, and you know what wonderful strength she has. She believes that he will be arrested here, that some one has betrayed us, and that he has been sent here merely to get us all into trouble. She intends to take him away somewhere to-day, I think."

"Well, it is a bit of a mix up, Bess, and that's the truth; but I'll find a way to straighten things out. You talk to Ellen and put her right, and if you can't, I'll see her. In the meantime, I'll go and talk things over with Althea and her father. I was too tired last night."

"Althea wants to see you. She told me so."

"All right. I'll go up to her room as soon as I have thought matters over."

It was of course quite on the cards that Althea's guess at the reason for her father's coming to my house was the right one; and it was certainly a disquieting suggestion. I remembered Feldermann's hints about my connexion with the Polish party and the questions put to me on the previous night by the police. If we were found harbouring a man who was held to be so dangerous as the Baron, the consequences to Althea and to us all might be really serious.

As to his object in Berlin at such a time, I myself could make a pretty fair guess. Ziegler had more than once suggested that a stroke of some sort was to be attempted soon, and the mysterious hints dropped to me that day in the club by the Polish journalist prompted the exceedingly disquieting thought that the attempt might take the form of some kind of violence.

That Baron von Ringheim was in league with the more desperate section of the party was shown plainly by his having been with two of them on the previous night at the Jew's house on a mission of violence. Yet he had obviously gone to the house to attempt to prevent violence. His protests had proved as much.

So far as I could judge, he had gone there to investigate some charges of treachery which had been made against the murdered man; and that von Felsen had intentionally started those suspicions, and had in some way been instrumental in sending the men to the house, I was convinced. But why send such a man as the Baron? Did von Felsen know that he was actually in Berlin—and then a light seemed to break in upon everything.

It must have been through von Felsen that the news of Althea's whereabouts had been conveyed to her father, and he had deliberately contrived that he should arrive at a moment when the murder had just been committed—apparently by Ziegler's associates. The moment of all others when the Baron would be in the greatest need of shelter.

But one of the most perplexing parts of the puzzle still remained to be solved. What was the precise character of the relationship between the Baron and the rest of this Polish party? Althea had suggested that although formerly he had been a real power amongst them, in later years his authority and influence had ceased.

102

There had been ample ground in the conduct of the two men toward him on the preceding night to confirm this, but I must satisfy myself completely on the point. I was ready, for Althea's sake, to run the risk of harbouring him; but I was certainly not going to allow him to use the house for the furtherance of any schemes of his party, whether violent or not.

I went upstairs, resolved to find this out from himself. I was fortunate to find him alone in his room. I could talk more plainly to him alone than when Althea was present.

He had the little bag of which my sister had spoken, and he gave a little start of surprise and hurriedly shut and locked it. I think he was rather offended at the abrupt manner in which I entered the room, and with much the same outward show of old-fashioned courtesy which he had displayed on the previous night there was a nervous restlessness which was fresh.

He greeted me with a bow and words of thanks, and for a moment we played at just being guest and host. But I kept my eyes fixed steadily on him all the time, and he began to grow exceedingly uncomfortable under the scrutiny, and at length found himself quite unable to meet my eyes.

"You must excuse me now, Herr Bastable," he said at length; and hugging his bag as if it contained all he had in the world, he made as if to leave the room.

For a second or two I did not reply, but just stared hard first at him and then very pointedly at the bag.

"I must first ask you one or two questions, Baron von Ringheim." I dropped the courteous tone and put a spice of sharpness into my tone.

He noticed it at once and drew himself up, but could not meet my eyes. "I don't understand by what right you adopt that tone, sir."

"And you will please to answer me quite frankly. Nothing else will satisfy me or meet the needs of the case."

"This is quite extraordinary."

I pointed at the bag. "You have a revolver there. Why?"

"I decline to be questioned in this tone by you or any one, sir. I am under an obligation to you for what you have done for my daughter and now for myself, but this gives you no right——"

"I take the right, Baron. In the first place, believe that I am wishful to be your friend in every sense of the term, and you may safely give me your fullest confidence. Your daughter will have told you that, I am sure."

"My private affairs——"

"Are precisely those which I am determined to know, Baron," I broke in pretty sternly. I felt that I must dominate him. "This is as

103

much for your own sake as for your daughter's. Now, please, an answer."

But he would not answer, and made an attempt to avoid doing so by a show of anger.

"Tell me then the object of your presence in Berlin?" I said next.

"This is insufferable conduct, sir. Insufferable," he cried.

I should have to hit him harder if I was to do anything with him. "Tell me then what you were doing at the house of Herr Ziegler just after he had been assassinated last night?"

The effect was instantaneous. He turned very white, stared at me for a second and began to tremble violently.

"What do you mean?" he faltered after a pause.

"I was there and saw you, Baron."

He clasped his hands to his face and fell back into a chair.

"Remember, please, that I speak only as a friend. I declare to you on my honour that I have no motive but to help you. But I must be told everything. Put yourself unreservedly into my hands, and I can and will save you; but there must be no half measures. I repeat, you must tell me everything."

For a long time he was unable to speak a word, and I made no attempt to force matters. I wished him to recover some measure of self-control.

"I had nothing to do with that—that deed," he said presently, speaking in a slow broken tone.

"I know that. I know that the man was dead before you arrived; but your companions came prepared to do it, and but for my presence, there would have been a second murder."

"No, no, no," he protested.

"I know what I say to be true, Baron; just as I am convinced that you went there to protest against any violence at all."

"Ah, you know that. Yes, that is true. I swear that," he cried eagerly. "I should have prevented it. My authority as leader would have prevented it. Would to Heaven I had been in time!"

"You have great influence with your associates, then?"

"I am the leader of the whole movement. My word is absolute."

The declaration was made with a singular mixture of pride and simpleness. It was obvious that he believed it. "You think those men last night would have obeyed you?"

"They would not have dared to disobey," he replied in the same tone. "I went there to inquire into a charge of treachery against Ziegler—that he had betrayed some of our plans to an Englishman—— Why it was to you, of course." He said this with a little start as if he had just recalled it. "I was called to Berlin on that very matter."

I began to see light now. Althea was right in one respect—his mind was so affected and his memory so clouded that consecutive reasoning was impossible. He was not responsible for either words or deeds. But there was more behind. Some one was using him as a stalking horse for very sinister purposes.

"You arrived in the capital yesterday and were told to come to the house of a man believed to be about to betray your schemes?"

"Yes," he said simply, almost pathetically.

"Can you think of any reason for that?"

"No. I didn't understand it. I forgot until this moment, indeed, that you were the suspected Englishman."

It was obviously useless to question him any more about that. "Now, as to this other purpose—the bigger plan of your associates?"

"You know that too?"

"Have I not proved to you that I know things? But I am not a traitor, Baron."

He smiled childishly. He had become almost like a child, indeed, now. "It will be a grand stroke against the Government. We shall destroy the vessel, of course; but there will be no loss of life. I will not sanction the taking of lives, Herr Bastable."

So this was the scheme. To blow up one of the Kaiser's warships. I repressed all signs of astonishment and tried to look as if I had expected the reply. "But you cannot avoid loss of life, Baron."

It proved a very fortunate remark. With a very cunning smile he looked up and nodded his head knowingly. "I shall not allow it to be done until I am sure of that. I keep the bomb in my own possession till then"; and he hugged the little bag closer than ever to his side.

Here was a complication indeed. A lunatic in the house with a bomb in his possession capable of blowing a warship to fragments.

And this was the man I had described to Bessie as harmless!

CHAPTER XVI

MY RÔLE AS A CONSPIRATOR

Baron von Ringheim did not observe my profound consternation at hearing that he had a bomb in his possession, and he appeared to regard it only as a useful thing to carry about in a dressing-bag. He was indeed engrossed by his own shrewdness in keeping it by him so as to prevent its use at the wrong moment.

I believe that he interpreted my dismay rather as a tribute to his admirable caution. That I should object to have such a thing in my house did not occur to him.

For some moments I was at a loss what line to take. Of course I had to get possession of the bomb at any cost. If he were arrested and it were to be found there, we should all find ourselves in prison and called on to face a charge involving heavy punishment.

"I have done you an injustice, Baron," I said, changing my tone for one of profound admiration. "You are a wonderful leader."

He accepted this with something of a return to his former dignified bearing. "You have greatly wronged me, Herr Bastable," he said with dignity.

I played up to this at once. "For the future you will have no more devoted follower than myself. I crave your pardon for my bluntness; but you shall know the truth. I was told that you had ceased to lead the movement, and it was essential that I should satisfy myself. My life is at stake in this cause. But I shall doubt no more."

"Then you are with us?"

"With you, Baron, heart and soul. I raised my voice against it all at the time; I protested against the shame of doubting you; I used every means in my power to convince the others. But all was in vain. They insisted; and I was but one against all the rest."

He was as much bewildered at this as I had intended. "I don't understand," he said.

I replied with a passionate harangue against the wickedness of any attempt to undermine his authority, and talked until his poor half-crazed wits were in a whirl of perplexity. Then with dramatic earnestness I cried: "You have been shamefully betrayed and deceived."

"What do you mean?" he stammered.

"That," I exclaimed indignantly, pointing at the bag. "But I will see that all is made right. The bomb you have there is a sham, a fraud, a trick. The real one is in the hands of those who mean to use it when and how they please. Your counsels of humanity have been set at naught, and the lives of hundreds are in peril."

"It is impossible," he protested weakly.

"Show it to me and I will prove my words; aye, and do more than that. I will see that the real one is placed in your possession."

The look he cast at me was almost piteous in its appealing trustfulness; and after a second's pause, he unfastened the bag, and with fingers which trembled so violently that I feared he would drop it, he handed me the bomb.

That I took it with intense relief may well be imagined, and I handled it with the utmost caution and no little dread. Whether it was really the terrible engine of destruction that he believed, I did not know; but with an assumption of confidence I was very far from feeling, I pointed to some mark on it. "I knew it," I cried. "See that. The proof of the betrayal; shame! shame!" and with that I slipped it into a large inner pocket of my jacket.

"What are you going to do?" he asked as I turned to the door.

"I am on fire until this has been righted. When I return I shall have something to tell you. From this moment you, and you only, are my leader."

He was going to protest, but I gave him no time. My one thought was to get rid of the thing at once. But how to do so perplexed me sorely.

I was consumedly uncomfortable and intensely scared. I felt that my life was in danger every second the confounded thing was in my possession. Every time it moved ever so slightly as I walked I feared that it would explode, and I drew my first deep breath of relief the instant I was out of the house.

But the streets had even more potential terrors. When any one approached me on the side where I was carrying it, I was afraid they would knock against it and blow me and half Berlin with me into eternity.

Every policeman I met was an object of dread; and when one turned to gaze after me, I jumped to the conclusion that he knew what I was carrying and was about to arrest me.

I left the house with no definite purpose or plan for getting rid of it, and I walked on at first aimlessly, wondering vaguely whether I should hide it or bury it somewhere without being observed.

With this thought I made for the Thiergarten, and I had reached the west end of Unter den Linden when it occurred to me that the best and simplest course would be to drop it over the Marschall Bridge into the river.

I walked down North Wilhelmsstrasse with much the sort of feeling a thief might have who had the proceeds of his theft upon him and knew that the police were close on his track. Every harmless citizen I met became a detective, told off especially to watch me; and when I reached the bridge and loitered along, gazing enviously at the water below and waiting for a chance to drop the thing over unseen, I was convinced that everybody there could tell from my manner that I was intent upon the commission of some ill deed and had slackened their pace to watch me.

My fingers trembled so violently as I held it in readiness that I wonder I did not drop it on the pavement; and when a chance did come at last, and I was alone close to the middle of the bridge and took it out of my pocket, glancing furtively all round me the while, the perspiration stood in great beads on my forehead.

At the last moment even I had a horrible and almost paralysing fear that when dropped from such a height it might be exploded by contact with the water; and when at last I did succeed in letting it go, I watched its fall with bated breath and a sort of dread that the end of all things for me was at hand.

But it disappeared from sight and nothing happened, and I drew one deep, deep breath of fierce exultant joy, and then leaned against the parapet with the helpless inertness of a drunken man.

It was some time before I could rally myself sufficiently to set about finding something which I could take back with me to the Baron as the real bomb. How to manage this puzzled me not a little.

I searched the shop windows for some kind of hollow metal ball; my intention being to fill it with shot and other things so as to be of about the same weight as the thing I had thrown into the river. I hunted in vain for this until a man in an ironmonger's shop suggested a ball-cock.

I had invented a little story about wanting it for some private theatricals. He was an ingenious fellow and became quite interested in helping me. He hunted up one of the size I wished, filed off the long handle, drilled a hole and stuffed in some cotton waste and enough shot to give it the required weight, and succeeded in making up a very passable counterfeit of an actual bomb.

At a gunsmith's I bought some blank revolver cartridges for the Baron's revolver, in case he should object to hand that over to me; and thus prepared I turned homewards very much easier in mind.

Close to the house I met Herr Feldermann, and he stopped me. "I have just come from your house, Herr Bastable—about the Ziegler murder, you know."

"Have you found the men, then?" I asked as unconcernedly as I could.

"Not yet; but of course we shall find them. We have such a close description."

"I shall certainly know them again."

"There is a somewhat curious thing about it," he said slowly, and then with a sudden penetrating glance: "Have you ever seen the Baron von Ringheim?"

There was nothing for it but a lie, so I lied. "No. You don't mean that he has anything to do with this?"

"Dormund swears that your description fits him like a glove."

I managed to smile. "Isn't the Baron something of a red rag to Dormund? He gave me that impression that day at the station."

"There's something in that, perhaps. But he's a very shrewd fellow. You don't think there's anything in the idea, then?"

"My dear Feldermann, how on earth should I know? If I had seen him I could tell in a second."

"His daughter is with your sister; do you happen to know if the father is really in Berlin?"

"I can ask her if you like."

"Of course if you find out anything about his movements you'll tell us?"

"Of course. It would make a rattling good newspaper story, wouldn't it? By the way, I suppose you'll want my evidence. Don't bother me unless it's necessary."

"I came to tell you that we shall not have to trouble you yet, and perhaps not at all if you can help us in the way I've suggested. And I think you'll be able to, if you wish."

With this uncomfortably suggestive hint he left me.

Did he know already that the Baron was with me? One never could get to the bottom of his thoughts. If he did know anything, why had he not arrested the man whom the description appeared to fit so exactly?

Ah well, it was no use to seek trouble. Plenty of complications were coming my way unsought. I was fast getting into the mood of a fatalist. If everything was destined to go smash, smash it would go; and nothing I could do could prevent it.

As soon as I reached home I had a long interview with the Baron. It was very much of a burlesque. I made up a story about the manner in which I had secured the deadly bomb which I placed in his hands; succeeded in substituting blank cartridges for those in his weapon; and, what was of even more importance, got from him the particulars of the contemplated destruction of the war-ship.

This was after I had thoroughly convinced him that I was heart and hand in the cause of which he believed himself to be the leader, and had told him that Althea should be taken fully into our confidence.

I saw her alone first, however, and gave her an account of all that had passed. She was deeply moved by the story.

"They are merely making a tool of him, Mr. Bastable; and they must have given him that awful thing because they were afraid of the results to themselves should it be discovered in their possession. My poor father!"

"If you will take the line I have already taken with him, I think it may be possible to stop any further mischief at least," I said. "But he must be made to feel that unless he trusts to me he can do nothing. Then we can see about getting him away from the city."

"But the danger to you. We have no right to place you in such a position. I intended to take him away somewhere to-day."

"Bessie told me something about that. But it is impracticable. You had better remain here. You forget that you promised Herr Feldermann to let him know wherever you were," I reminded her.

"What can we do then?"

"I am still confident that all will come right if we can only get time enough. And time we must have at any risk and cost."

"There is always one way open," she said hesitatingly. "At least I presume so. Do you think if I were to agree to do what Herr von Felsen requires, that he could still obtain my father's pardon?"

"Would you do it, if I did think so?"

"What else can I do?" she cried distractedly.

"For one thing—keep a stout heart and have patience. I do not pretend that your father's arrival here and his visit to the Jew's house has not seriously complicated matters; but you may still have a little grain of trust in me."

"As if I had not! But the thought of the danger you are——" She broke off as if she had been about to say something that might have been embarrassing. "Of course I trust you," she added after the pause.

"That is all I ask—at present, at all events, until that last resource you spoke of need no longer be contemplated. And now, let us have this talk with your father."

She put out her hand impulsively, and as I pressed it our eyes met. No other word was spoken, but I think she understood much of what I should have said had not my lips been sealed.

The interview with the Baron was a curious mixture of pathos and burlesque. The pain which I could see Althea was suffering cut me to the quick, and I sought to shorten the conversation as much as possible. But her father was so full of his own importance, so talkative about his wrongs, so insistent upon my complete obedience to his orders, so obviously unable to take a rational view of any part of the subject, and so incapable of understanding the risks and dangers of the position, that it was a long time before we could drive it home upon him that the only hope of success lay in his leaving everything to me.

"But your very presence in Berlin is a danger," said Althea more than once when we were attempting to persuade him to leave the city.

"No one knows of it, child. And I have not done anything if they

110

did. Beside, would you have me, the leader of the whole movement, shirk the danger now that the hour has come?"

"It may get to be known that you were at Herr Ziegler's house last night."

"I went to prevent violence, child. That is surely no crime."

"And you are placing Herr Bastable in danger by remaining here."

"Is it not his duty to run risks in the cause? Is he to be the only man to venture nothing for our country? Danger, indeed," he cried indignantly. "Have we not all suffered? What of my own sufferings?" and he was off again on his favourite topic when I interrupted him.

"Have you any commands in regard to the forthcoming attack?"

"Ah, that will be a stroke; and it is my own conception"; and as the wind will turn a straw, he went off to the fresh subject and spoke at length about it.

It appeared that a new cruiser, the Wundervoll, had just been launched; and the intention was to wreck her as she lay waiting to be taken to be fitted up. The bomb which, thank Heaven, lay at the bottom of the Spree was to do the mischief, and the exact details of the plan as to time and means were to be discussed and settled at a forthcoming meeting of some of the more reckless men of the party.

A very little ingenuity succeeded in extracting from him the place of the meeting—a house on the riverside which had been taken by them, ostensibly for some business purposes. But the time of the meeting he did not appear to know.

"I shall learn that in due course. They cannot move without me; for I trust no one but myself with the means. But it will not be yet for some days."

"Do you mean then, father, that some one else knows you are here?" asked Althea in a tone of alarm, with a glance in my direction.

"Could I lead them without their being able to communicate with me? You are foolish, Althea. Did they not prepare this shelter for me?"

"Oh, it is terrible," she murmured with a deep sigh.

"It will be glorious, you should say rather, child," he replied, with a wild look in his eyes. "The greatest blow which we have yet been able to strike at the oppressors of our country!"

"I will go and see what is doing," I put in as I rose. "I will report to you the results of my inquiries, and you will of course do nothing without first hearing them, and without my aid. You would not rob me of my share in the coming victory?"

"Bring me word instantly," he said in a tone of sharp command.

111

"And I wish to see Sudermann and Bolinsk to consult with them. See them and bring them here to me at once."

"It would not be safe for them to be seen coming here. My house is too well known for them to take such a risk."

"See them then and tell them—— Wait, I will write you a letter." He turned aside and wrote rapidly, and in the meantime Althea looked at me with an expression of such pain and concern that I was almost ashamed of the deception I was practising.

"Here is the note. 'The bearer, Herr Bastable, has my fullest confidence and knows my wishes. Consult with him freely.' That will satisfy them, if they should have any doubt about speaking frankly to you."

"Oh, but they will not," I answered confidently; and with that I left the room.

As I went downstairs I was about to tear up the letter, when it occurred to me as a possibility that it might be of use in any future case of emergency, so I put it carefully away.

Then I set to work to think out some means of inducing the Baron to leave Berlin, by using my supposed influence in the party. If I could tell him a plausible story to the effect that the attempt had had to be postponed for a few weeks and that the authorities had got wind of it, he might go. And for Althea's sake, as well as for our own, I was intensely anxious to get him away.

As I sat planning this a letter was brought to me from Herr Borsen.

"MY DEAR BASTABLE,—

"Can you come and see me? I understand that you have another visitor in your house, and it is about that I should like a few words with you. I wish to be able to contradict a strange report which has reached me concerning him; since, if uncontradictcd, it might be a somewhat serious matter for you. Any time to-morrow will do, but not later.

"Yours as ever."

If I had been wishful for the Baron to go before, the letter turned the wish into a strenuous anxiety.

It looked very much like the beginning of the end.

CHAPTER XVII

"W. MISCHEN'S" WAREHOUSE

When I read Borsen's letter through the second time, I thought I could detect a little more in it than appeared on the surface. "Any time to-morrow will do, but not later," he wrote; and he had dated his note "midday."

I judged therefore that he was really stretching a point in order to give me time to get my visitor away, and so be able to "contradict the report." There was plenty of time for him to have seen me that afternoon: the obvious course in the case of a matter so really serious. But he had given me the interval to afford me the time to free myself from suspicion.

He was a very good fellow, and had at one time been very friendly with me; but there was something besides friendship behind his present step. I had convinced him in Chalice's matter that I was likely to succeed as well with Althea; and being a negotiator with a preference for the path of least resistance, he preferred that I should have the time to pull that chestnut out of the fire for him rather than that he should have to do it himself.

There was a still further reason. The presence of Baron von Ringheim in Berlin was likely to be more than a little embarrassing to Count von Felsen's scheme for his son. They knew perfectly well that he would only venture to come to the capital for some such purpose as that which had actually brought him; and if he were to be taken at such a juncture and under such suspicious circumstances, the Kaiser's promise of a pardon was pretty sure to be withdrawn.

Borsen was thus turning the screw on me to force me to take the steps which they greatly desired and could not take for themselves.

I determined to put this to the test at once, therefore, with a little bluff, I scribbled a hasty line to the effect that I could go round immediately, if he wished; but that on the following day I should probably be going on a journey with a friend.

I intended him to infer that I should be taking the Baron out of the city. He read the letter in that light; and sent back word that he was going away at once, and that under the circumstances the next day but one would do well enough for the purpose.

I had a respite of twenty-four hours. I told Althea what had passed, and that I could not possibly face Borsen unless in the meanwhile we could prevail upon her father to leave the city, and I described my rough idea of getting him away by a fairy-tale about the discovery of the plot.

Partly with the object of being able to give colour to the story, and partly out of a desire to ascertain something more about the doings of the Baron's associates, I went down to the riverside to have a look at their headquarters.

I was extremely anxious about his account of the intended attempt to wreck the Wundervoll, and resolved of course to prevent it. The whole Empire was in one of those flushes of feeling about the navy which the Emperor's policy had created; and I knew that such an outrage would incense the authorities, and that the punishment meted out would be in proportion to their wrath.

Directly or indirectly, some of that demand for vengeance would fall on Althea as well as on myself—if it became generally known that I had sheltered one of the chief perpetrators—and I had to find the means of secretly preventing so disastrous a result.

The riverside premises looked harmless enough. The name, "W. Mischen," had been newly painted up, and a suggestion that a corn business was being carried on there was evidenced by some sacks of grain.

The office was open, and I could see one man inside, lounging idly at a desk, obviously with nothing to do. But the moment he heard my step and caught sight of me, he began to work on a big ledger with over-acted activity.

I resolved to risk going in. The adjoining premises were to let, so I used that as an excuse and asked him if he could tell me anything about them. A very few questions convinced me that he was a Berliner who had probably been engaged as a clerk to give a cover to the fictitious business.

Under the pretext of a desire to see whether the water front would suit my purposes—I was a wharfinger for the moment—I got him to show me over the premises. I found, of course, that the place would not suit me.

"Some one appears to be very busy over there," I said, pointing a little way down the river where a number of men in boats were at work.

"They are dockyard men laying down moorings. They have all but finished now. I believe the Wundervoll is to be moored there for a while. Have you seen her? A splendid ship she'll be when she's fitted. I am a big navy man. We shall never be safe until we have a fleet as big as England's."

"It will come in time," I replied; and we went inside again. I saw

114

the reason for the wharf now; and wondered how they had succeeded in getting wind of the Government's intention so early.

"I am really very much obliged to you," I said as we stood again in the office. "You seem rather short-handed too, so I mustn't take up your time."

"Oh, I haven't much to do yet. The firm is only just starting here. This is to be only the Berlin branch; the business is at Hamburg, you know. I wish I had more to do; but of course it takes a lot of time to get things going."

I thanked him again and left. I was well repaid for the visit. The scheme had been shrewdly planned. When the vessel lay within so short a distance of the wharf, the attack would be comparatively easy, and success quite attainable. A bomb with a time fuse attached could easily be thrown on board her.

How could I prevent it? That was the rub. I went up to the Press Club thinking this out.

If I could have been certain that the bomb which I had thrown into the river was really that which was to be used, I should almost have been willing to let the matter rest where it was, for I had already prevented disaster.

But a little further consideration almost made my flesh creep. The bomb I had given the Baron would do no harm to the vessel, but it might very well blow me into prison. It would be found, of course; inquiries would follow, and the obliging young man who had made it for me, "for private theatricals," would give a description of me and an account of the transaction which I should be unable to explain away; while the agreeable fellow at the wharf would be able to tell how I had gone down to "inquire about the untenanted premises."

That wouldn't do; so with a curse at the Baron and all his works—except paternity of Althea—I turned to think of some other plan.

There was only one way. I must get such information to the authorities as would induce them to choose some other moorings for the warship. And I must do it at once.

My old press connexions must find the means. There were plenty of German newspaper men who would have given their ears for such a story as I could tell them; but I could not trust them to hold their tongues as to the source of the information. And that was of course essential.

The story must come from London, or better, from Paris; and the only man I dared to trust in the matter was Bassett—the correspondent who had taken my place. I telephoned him to come to me at the club, and when he arrived I told him as much of the case as was necessary.

I explained that I had stumbled on the information by chance, but in a manner which rendered it impossible for my name to be mentioned. He was anxious enough to get a "scoop," and readily promised to keep my connexion absolutely secret. Together we drew up such a paragraph as would set the ball rolling, and he agreed to warn the naval authorities in his own name that the object of attack was the Wundervoll, and that her safety depended upon her not being taken to the proposed moorings.

It was a common enough thing for newspaper men to get hold of information a long way ahead of the authorities, and for the sources of it to be kept secret.

"I'll hold my tongue about you, of course," he said as we were parting. "And I'm awfully obliged to you. It's just what I want, as a matter of fact. The navy people here have been awfully close with me and standoffish, and this will put matters on just the footing I need."

I went home in a well satisfied mood. One of the many tangles was unravelled. There would be no outrage of any sort; and for my own protection I must get that bogus bomb back into my own hands as soon as possible. That was almost as essential as getting the Baron away.

But I found trouble waiting for me at home. The Baron had gone to bed ill, and Althea was at her wits-end to know whether she dared call in a doctor. I went up with her to his room, and found him apparently very bad indeed. He looked very ill, and had been complaining of intense pain.

To move him was clearly impossible, even if he had been willing to go away.

"For his own sake we must do without a doctor if we can," I told her.

"I thought he was going to die a little time ago, but he appears to be easier now. I did not know what to do for the best," she replied as she bent over him and smoothed his pillows and kissed him.

"After Borsen's letter I meant to get him to leave the city. Every hour after to-morrow will be one of danger for him."

Unfortunately he heard this, and between his gasps and groans of pain he abused me for a traitor and ordered me out of the room. I did not pay any heed at first, but it soon became evident that my presence excited him so much that Althea begged me to go.

His illness was checkmate so far as getting him out of the house for the present was concerned; and as that was all important, I

116

deemed it best to take the additional risk of having a doctor to get him well enough to travel.

While I was still considering this, Althea came down, and I told her.

"Not yet," she said decidedly. "I think he is better again. He raved almost deliriously after you had left the room; that you and all of us in fact were bent upon betraying the cause, and that if any attempt were made to get him out of the city he would—— Oh, he talked most wildly. What can we do, Mr. Bastable? I am so grieved that I have brought all this on you."

"I told you before that we would not go out to look for trouble. After all, it may end in nothing serious. We have all to-morrow; and it will be quite time enough if he goes then."

"You try to make so light of it, but——" She broke off and threw up her hands.

"We shall have plenty of time to worry when the need comes, if it is to come," I answered with a smile. "You will be ill yourself if you are not more careful."

"The excitement has worn him out so that he is sleeping a little now," she said. "I dare not leave him for long; but I felt I must come down to you for a minute."

"It may be the beginning of an improvement. Of course there is one way in which we might venture to move him."

"How?"

"A sleeping draught, and take him away as an invalid."

But she shook her head vigorously at the suggestion.

"I dare not. His heart is so weak, he might die under it."

"That closes that door then"; and I endeavoured to make her feel that I refused to take things too seriously.

There was a slight pause during which she glanced at me twice nervously and said hesitatingly: "There is another way if you will take it."

"Not the last resource, yet. It has not come to that by a long way."

"No. I—I mean—you ought to think of Bessie. I wish that. You must."

"Do you mean she should go away? I am afraid she would not care to go. I wish she would."

"But you—you might take her."

"Althea!" The Christian name slipped from me unwittingly in my quick protest against the suggestion that I should desert her. I stopped in confusion, and the colour rushed to her face. We were both embarrassed by the blunder.

117

Presently she raised her eyes to mine. "Please do it. I wish it," she urged in a low, intensely earnest tone.

"Do you believe it possible?"

"If you care at all for what I say or wish, you will do it."

"Then I am afraid we must take it that I do not," I answered, smiling.

"But if Bessie were only safely away, I should not mind so much."

"She is not in any serious danger. They would not do anything to her."

"You know what I mean," she cried quickly. "Why force me to say it? I cannot bear the thought of bringing you into this danger. The fear of what may happen haunts me every moment, day and night. You must go."

"You are letting your fears exaggerate the danger. I cannot go."

"You must. I insist." Quite vehemently uttered, this.

"Don't force me to the discourtesy of a flat refusal."

Her earnestness was only magnified. "You shall go. I am quite determined. You shall go or——" Her eyes were flashing and her features set with resolve.

"I am just as determined as you."

She paused and then said very deliberately, but with lips that quivered: "If you do not, I shall go to Herr von Felsen and accept his terms. I will not accept the sacrifice which you are intent on making for me."

There was a pause while we looked one at the other, every line of her lovely face eloquent of her purpose; and before I could reply, we were face to face with another crisis that drove everything else out of our thoughts for the moment.

Believing that I was alone, Ellen opened the door and announced Herr Dormund.

I had just time to whisper to Althea, "You had better be Bessie, remember," when he came in bristling with importance. He paused on seeing that I was not alone, and I went forward and offered him my hand. "Come in, Herr Dormund. It is only my sister. Then you'll see to that for me, Bessie; and don't let me have to bother again about it."

Dormund had bowed when I referred to her and then turned to me with a very significant look. "I have not yet had the pleasure of being presented to—your sister."

"I clean forgot. Pardon. Bessie, Herr Dormund. You have often heard me speak of him."

She was close to the door and turned to give him a gracious bow. Would he let her go? I watched him very anxiously.

"I have had the pleasure of meeting you once before, Fräulein—at the station a day or two ago," he said. "I am delighted to see you again."

She was at a loss for a reply, so I cut in: "Run and see to that at once, Bess; and then perhaps when Herr Dormund has finished his business you can return."

He did let her go; so I gathered that Feldermann had passed on to him the instructions from Borsen.

And very fortunate it was. For just as the door closed behind her, I heard Bessie's voice calling loudly and with some alarm: "Althea! Althea!" followed by the voices of the two as they met.

"Then you have two sisters, Herr Bastable?" said Dormund very drily as he turned with a very meaning look. "It is a coincidence that the name of one of them should be Althea."

"'Tis odd, isn't it?" and forcing a smile, as though it was a coincidence and nothing more, I motioned him to a chair, sat down, and pushed the cigar-box across to him.

It should be his move first at any rate.

CHAPTER XVIII

THE LUCK TURNS

My assumption of indifference appealed to what little sense of humour the German police routine training had allowed Dormund to retain, for he burst into a quite human laugh as he lighted a cigar. "Need we pretend any longer, Herr Bastable?" he asked.

"Not unless you like," I replied, as grave as a judge. "But what about?"

"The very charming young lady who has just left us."

"Bessie? My sister, I mean," I said, as if genuinely perplexed.

He waved his hand impatiently. "Ah, her name is von Ringheim. We know that."

I clapped my hands to the arms of my chair and started forward as if intensely surprised. "Do you mean that my sister has got married without my knowledge? For Heaven's sake, what are you saying?"

He gave me a dry look. "You are overdoing it, Herr Bastable. I mean that the lady who has just gone out is Fräulein Korper, otherwise von Ringheim. Is that clear?"

"Oh," I said with a sigh of relief. "Is that all? Then why the devil didn't you arrest her?"

The blunt question drew another laugh out of him. "I need not tell you, for you know. So long as we are certain where to find her— — But Herr Feldermann told you. I have not come on her affairs, however; nor to refer to what happened the other day at the station."

"I am always delighted to see you—provided of course you don't come to arrest me."

"I trust I shall never have to do that, but you will do well to be cautious in your hospitality."

"Not with you, I hope," I laughed. "At all events unofficially."

"I am here unofficially now, and will go so far as to warn you that an official visit from one of us has been very seriously considered. Berlin, and indeed the whole of Germany, is considered very unhealthy for some foreigners at this season, you know."

"I appreciate your friendship, Dormund; but I shan't bolt. I shall be found here whenever I'm wanted. I shall stick it out."

"It is more serious than you think perhaps; but it is of course for you to decide. Well, now, I have come to-day to act the part of a mutual friend, Heir Bastable; from Lieutenant von Bernhoff. He feels very deeply the breach that has occurred."

"I think I would rather you did not say any more about that," I broke in.

"Bear with me a moment. He is devotedly attached to your sister and he has a genuine regard for you yourself; he has empowered me to offer you an unqualified apology for what passed when he was last here, and to assure you that you placed quite the wrong interpretation on what he said. He is very unhappy."

"Do you know what passed?"

"It was very unfortunate," he replied with a gesture of regret. "But remember, please, the feelings of a man who sees himself about to lose what he prizes more than anything else on earth. A man in love, you know!"

"But my sister does not return his regard."

"He wishes only to be allowed to call and make his apologies for himself. I can assure you, of my own knowledge, that his regret is abject."

"There is good ground for it," I said drily. "And his coming here would do no good. I don't believe he ever had a ghost of a chance of getting my sister to care for him and am dead certain that whatever chance he had was absolutely ruined by his conduct that day."

"Well, may he come? Let me put it as a personal favour to me?"

I hesitated a second. "I can't refuse you; but it is for your sake not for his that I consent; and he had better not come for a few days."

"In the meantime you will speak to your sister and tell her of his regrets and perhaps say a word——"

"No, no," I interrupted, shaking my head. "In England we let our girls settle these matters entirely for themselves. But I'll tell her what you have told me."

"Well, I have not failed entirely at any rate," he said as he rose. "And now will you accept a last word of caution, and get rid of your visitors."

Plural number, this time. He apparently knew all about the presence of Althea's father. "I am going to," I answered with a smile.

"I am unfeignedly glad. You have many friends among us, you know."

"I am seeing Herr Borsen about it the day after to-morrow."

"Good; but don't forget that even his hands may be forced"; and with this parting caution he went away to leave me pondering very uneasily what could be behind the words.

Was his warning genuine or was it a veiled threat? Had he come as von Bernhoff's friend to force the reconciliation with this as his weapon? The events of the last few days had so tried me, that I was suspicious of almost every one with whom I came in contact who had any concern with the affair. It was possible that he meant von Bernhoff could make such a to do as to force the police to act despite Borsen's promise. Yet he had seemed genuine enough.

There was of course another interpretation—that some influence could be brought to bear strong enough to force even Borsen. Whose? The Emperor's? No. I had made that right with Chalice's letter. Could it be the Prince von Graven in his rage at my interference? No. He might have the intention but he lacked the power.

There was only one man left—von Felsen himself. He could do it through his father, if he could persuade him that I was blocking the scheme and not, as Borsen believed, seeking to carry it through.

But Dormund would know nothing about this unless—and at that moment the light began to break in—unless certain steps had already been taken of which Dormund's colleagues had spoken to him.

If it was only that, I had little reason for fear. A word or two from me and von Felsen would come crawling to heel at my beck. The sooner that word was spoken the better, perhaps; and I decided to speak it at once.

I told Althea and Bessie the result of Dormund's visit and then went straight off to interview von Felsen. I did not find him, however; he was at his father's house, the servant told me, and would not return until very late.

I was very disappointed. So much depended upon the result of the interview, and Dormund had made me feel what danger there was in delay, that I was exceedingly anxious to bring the fellow to his knees at once.

There was, moreover, the almost equally critical matter of the papers he was to secure—the act which I believed would put the card I needed into my hand—and I was at my wits' end to think of some means by which I could discover what was being done in the matter.

When I had reduced him to a proper condition of terror by the threat of charging him with the Jew's murder, I intended to force from him the necessary information. But I could not do anything with him in that matter at his father's house. If he had the papers already, they would be at his own house; and thus for my purposes the interview must take place there.

I could not do anything more that night, however, and I turned homewards in none too amiable a mood. The luck had appeared to go so dead against me, and I was trying to hit on some way to change it, when I blundered into a man hurrying in the direction from which I had come. I looked up with a growl on my lips at his carelessness, when I recognized the young clerk I had seen at the wharf.

"I am sure I beg your pardon," I said. "I was thinking. It was my fault."

He had a very pleasant smile. "Really I'm afraid it was mine. I was looking about for the name of the street. I don't know this part of the city at all well. This is the Coursenstrasse, isn't it?"

"Yes. What number do you want?"

"268d," he replied looking at an adjoining house door.

It was the number of von Felsen's house! What did "W. Mischen" want with him? I became very friendly at once. "I'll show it you"; and I turned with him. "I have nothing to do; and it's very curious, I wanted to have a chat with you."

I would not risk going up with him to the door, lest the servant should report the fact to von Felsen; but I waited for him, standing near enough to observe that he delivered a message and not a letter.

What that message was I would learn before the night was out by hook or crook; and when he rejoined me I led the way to a restaurant, and insisted on his joining me at supper. I did him well; a good meal, plenty of the best wine, and a cigar such as he rarely

122

smoked. While we were eating I spun him a yarn about my intention to start a big wharfinger's business, asked his advice about a heap of things, flattered his judgment, and worked him into a properly loquacious mood.

I then sounded him as to whether he would care to enter my employ, and named a salary about three times as big as he had any reason to expect, with light hours and so on, and in this way worked round to an expression of surprise that he should have to stop so late at work.

It was very plain sailing then. He did not always work so late, he said; but he had been asked to stay that night until one of the heads of his present firm arrived from the lawyers', where he had been engaged in regard to the lease of the wharf.

"There was really no reason why they should have kept me; but I am never afraid of an extra hour or two, of course." This was for my benefit as his future employer.

"Of course they will pay you. When I detain one of my clerks I always do what is proper, especially when the business is important."

"This wasn't. Only a trifle about the lease of the wharf. Herr von Felsen is the owner of it, you know, and he was to have delivered it to-night; but something came in the way. All I had to do after all, was to take a message that they would call for it to-morrow night at eight o'clock."

"Well, I am glad they did detain you as it turns out"; and I poured him out a last glass of wine. I was indeed glad, but the reason was not quite so much on the surface as his smile showed me he thought.

"I suppose the gentleman you have been to is a very wealthy man, then?"

"Oh yes, they tell me he owns no end of property. What luck some people have!"

As I knew that von Felsen hadn't a single brick or plank to call his own, I put my own construction on the story about the "lease"; and as I had got all I wanted from the clerk, I brought the interview to a close soon afterwards, having taken his address and given him to understand that he would hear more from me soon.

The incident was a piece of such stupendous luck that I could scarcely believe in my good fortune. If all went well, I should be too firmly seated in saddle within twenty-four hours for any one to be able to unhorse me. That "lease" meant the stolen papers; and with them in my hands I could laugh at every other difficulty. And that I could drag then from von Felsen by my knowledge of his guilt I was certain.

And the vein of good luck was not exhausted with that one precious nugget.

Althea came to me the first thing in the morning looking so white and troubled that I was full of concern. "Your father is not worse?" I asked quickly.

"No. He is better, much better; but he will not think of leaving the city. He will not listen to me when I urge it."

"It does not matter so much now," I said cheerfully.

"Ah, but it does. The trouble is greater than ever. Read this. It was brought to the house this morning"; and she handed me a letter.

"Addressed to you in your own name," I exclaimed, glancing at the envelope. Then I read the letter. It was from von Felsen. He said that he knew the Baron was in the house; that my arrest had been decided upon for having sheltered him; and that her father's presence with others at the Jew's house on the night of the murder was known. He concluded: "You must give me your decision to-day, and upon your decision every one of the steps I have mentioned will depend. If you are not my wife by to-night, the word will be spoken, and everything will be too late. Meanwhile Herr Bastable's house is being watched closely. I shall come this afternoon for your answer."

"You see now?" cried Althea in dismay, as I stood thinking over the letter. "I shall do it, Mr. Bastable. It is the only way."

"It depends upon when and where he means the marriage to take place," I answered, speaking out of my thoughts rather than in reply to her words.

"You agree that I should do it?" she asked almost piteously.

We were standing at the moment opposite a large mirror, and as I looked by chance at our reflections a thought struck me. I turned to her with a smile. "I think, perhaps, you will have to agree to his terms."

"You smile at this?" she cried, not without a touch of indignation.

"God forbid that I should smile at anything threatening your whole life as this would do. I must think; but if you can bring yourself to consent, you must make your own conditions as to the time and place of the marriage."

"And this is all you have to say?"

"No. The marriage will not take place, because he dare do nothing against my will. Don't lose heart for an instant."

"Tell me. You must see what it means to me, this suspense. You are in such danger—and Bessie."

"We were never safer. That I assure you. But trust me and have patience."

124

"You know I trust you"; and she laid her hand on my arm.

"Yes, I do know it. And bear this in mind. I am absolutely confident that we shall win. Remember that, and if you see me appear to be alarmed, and even panic-stricken, don't believe what you see."

She let her eyes rest on mine. "I should never believe that," she said.

At that moment Bessie said her father was calling for her, and we parted.

I took my sister to my room and had a long talk with her, and in the end sent her out to make one or two purchases for the plan that had occurred to me, telling her to be very careful that she was not followed. I should have gone myself, but after von Felsen's statement that the house was being carefully watched, she could do what had to be done better than I could.

When she returned, we two were busy together for two or three hours, at the end of which we had a little rehearsal.

"It is positively wonderful, Paul! Wonderful!"

"It will do in the dark, anyhow," I replied, quite satisfied with the result. "Say nothing to Althea about it; but if you can manage it, drop her a hint that I have had very bad news. It is so essential she should act naturally when von Felsen comes, that I must even venture to frighten her a little."

I would not trust myself to see Althea herself again before von Felsen's visit, lest I should be led to tell her everything in my desire to relieve her anxiety. So much depended upon his being entirely deceived, that I dared not take the risk of her not being able to appear completely sincere in what she had to promise.

It was a hard task to mislead her even for so short a time; and twenty times I started off to relieve the suspense I knew was torturing her. But I did not go.

Then von Felsen arrived. He asked openly for Fräulein von Ringheim, and by my orders Ellen showed him into my room. He was a very different man from the shaken reed he had been when I had interviewed him at the club on the night of the Jew's murder. He was now self-confident, resolved, and sure of himself on the strength of the cards he held.

On the other hand I endeavoured to express alarm and genuine apprehension.

"It is no use your denying that Fräulein Althea is here, Herr Bastable. I know it and the police know it. I shan't go without seeing her."

"What are you going to do?" I asked, letting my eyes fall before his.

125

"That all depends on what she does. You have made a holy mess of things in your cleverness. Your house is watched by the police, and you can't escape. If things go wrong, you'll have to answer for having had the Baron here. I know he's here, too."

"You are not going to play on a woman's fears about her father, are you?" A spice of mild indignation in this. "As for me, you can't harm me."

"Harm you? Can't I?" he cried with a snort of anger. "Perhaps you'll change your tone when I tell you, on my honour——"

"Never mind your honour," I cut in with a sneer which had the intended effect of adding anger to his bluster.

"When I leave this house I shall only have to hold up my finger and the lot of you will be inside the nearest gaol as quickly as you can be taken there by the police—you and Althea and her father and your sister too. You are all in this, you know. And if you provoke me, by Heaven I'll do it at once."

I did not reply but sat looking down at the table in intense dismay.

"Now are you going to deny that she is in the house?" he cried triumphantly after a pause.

"No, I don't deny it." The words seemed to be wrung from me, and I continued my stare of dismay at the table.

"I thought that would bring you to your senses. Where is she?"

"I'll take you up to her;" and I rose.

"No, thank you. I don't want you," he declared with a short laugh.

I sat down again. "I must think all this over," I murmured with a sigh of concern. "She's in the drawing-room, the room at the top of the stairs."

"I'll find it right enough, you bet." He went to the door and then turned for a last shot. "You understand, Bastable, if she says no, you'll all sleep in gaol to-night."

I let my head sink on my hand, and with a last leer of satisfaction he went out.

My only fear was lest I had overdone it; but he was anything but a keen observer, and was himself a man of exaggerated gesture.

I waited a few minutes to give him time to put his cowardly proposition to Althea and then, having rumpled my hair a bit to give the appearance of intense perturbation, I followed to add my plea to his—that Althea should agree to marry him.

It was, as she had said, the only way; but in furtherance of my plans instead of his.

CHAPTER XIX

VON FELSEN GAINS HIS END

I entered the room just when matters had reached the crisis. Althea, very pale and troubled, was sitting near the window and von Felsen stood over her dictating his terms. He had wrought upon her fears until she was on the point of yielding.

He resented my interference, therefore, fearing lest I should cause her to change her mind, and he turned on me angrily. "There is no need for you to come here, Herr Bastable. You can do no good."

"I could not keep away. So much depends upon Fräulein Althea's decision that I must know it at once." I spoke like one distracted with doubt.

A gloating, boastful, confident smile, for which I could have kicked him, was his reply.

Althea shuddered at it and then turned to me. "What else can I do, Mr. Bastable?"

I flung up my hands and sighed distractedly. "This cannot be necessary. Herr von Felsen must give us a little time in which to think. I have still influence, and I must go and see what I can do."

"If you leave the house it will be to go straight to prison," he declared with a sneer.

Althea winced again at this. "You see, I must do it."

"You coward," I cried to him. Then I started as if an idea had just occurred to me. "I can stop you. I had forgotten. You are pledged to marry Fräulein Ziegler. She shall know of this at once"; and I turned as if to hurry from the room.

"Stop," he shouted. "Leave this room and that instant I will call in those outside."

I stopped obediently, as if baffled and frightened. Then I gave another little start and shot a furtive, cunning glance at him.

"You said just now you didn't want me in the room," I said slowly.

He looked at me very searchingly. "You stop here. I can read your thought easily enough, but you won't fool me. Neither you nor any one here will leave this house until Fräulein Althea is my wife. Understand that."

I did not reply, but sat down and began to finger my moustache, moving my eyes about as if thinking of some means to outwit him. "We shall see," I said with a repetition of the cunning smile.

"Mr. Bastable!" said Althea, in a tone of appeal.

"No, no, no. There must be some other way. I am not afraid for myself." Then I laughed. "If we are not to leave the house then, there shall be no marriage. There shall be none here, that I swear. Let come what may, there shall not. You are driving me to bay, von Felsen. Have a care, man, what you do." I spoke without passion, but the suggestion of threat in my tone drew his eyes upon me and started his suspicions.

Althea was completely puzzled by my conduct, and I was glad to see that. If I could mislead her, after what I had said that morning, I was sure to be successful with the grosser wits of von Felsen.

"Herr von Felsen has proposed that the marriage shall take place here this evening, and it—it must be so," she said after a pause.

"No, no, it shall not," I cried quickly; and then as quickly, and with apparent inconsistency, changed my note. I clenched my hands and shot a glance of intense malevolence at him. "Wait. I agree. Yes. Come here this evening then. On second thoughts it will be best so. I'll see that everything is ready for you then. Yes, yes, this evening and—here."

He read this as I wished. "No, thank you," he answered with a knowing shake of the head. "I'm glad you reminded me in time. We'll have it where it will be a little safer. I shall have to trouble you to come to my house, Althea. I've no intention to have the marriage wind up with a funeral"; and he nodded again at me with a chuckle at having so cleverly read my thought.

I endeavoured to portray the picture of outwitted cunning. "Oh, you needn't be afraid of coming here; and it will be much more convenient."

"You mind your own business," he blurted out.

"If the thing has to be done at all, it should at least be done with the least trouble to Fräulein Althea. That means here," I protested.

"There will be plenty of trouble if it isn't done," came the retort with a bullying smile. "Now, please, Althea, your answer?"

Her face was a mask of troubled perplexity as she pressed her hands tightly together. She shot a look of appeal at me.

"You needn't look at him. He can't help you."

I jumped up with a heavy sigh, made as if to rush out of the room, remembered myself, and went to the window and stared out. Von Felsen laughed.

"I agree," said Althea in a low, trembling tone.

I groaned, and von Felsen laughed again. As if stung by the

128

laugh to a last protest, I turned round. "How do you know that this man will keep his word?" I cried desperately to Althea. "He hates me, and his first step when all is too late may be to betray me."

"I thought you didn't care about yourself," he sneered. That I should be in a condition of abject fear about myself appeared natural enough to him, no doubt.

"Fräulein Althea!" I exclaimed, as she did not reply at once.

"He has pledged his word, Herr Bastable."

"His word! what is that worth?"

"You needn't let yourself be scared out of your wits, at any rate," he said with another sneer. He was enjoying his triumph intensely, and the sight of my fear was the best part of it, apparently. "If the Baron and Althea are pardoned, who's going to hurt you? You'll be all right," he declared contemptuously.

"I'm not thinking of myself," I replied vaingloriously, but putting a note of relief into my voice. "But there's the rest of his promise."

"Are you a fool? Do you think I am likely to let my wife be prosecuted as a traitor? You know what Herr Borsen told you. You are only trying to deceive Althea by this rot."

"Your wife? But she will not be your wife when she leaves here. Have the marriage here, as you proposed at first. There will be some guarantee then that you mean to run straight."

"The marriage will be where I say," he answered angrily.

"It must be as he wishes, Mr. Bastable. What do you wish?" she asked him.

"I shall come for you at seven o'clock." I gave a start at this, and he turned on me sharply. "No, I shan't be fool enough to enter the house, thank you. I shall wait for you in the carriage, Althea; and if a single soul except you attempts to leave at the same time, there'll be trouble. That's all."

"A very gallant groom," I sneered. But Althea interposed with a gesture of protest. "There are some hours of grace yet," I muttered.

"And the house will be carefully watched all through those hours. Don't forget that. I shan't run any risks. I shall be here at seven then," he added to Althea, and moved toward the door.

I started as if to follow him, but he stopped me. I believe he was afraid I should shoot him.

"You stop here, thank you. I can find my way out as I found it in."

I fell back a step as if frightened, and he left us.

"Oh, Mr. Bastable," cried Althea, the instant his back was turned, almost overcome by the scene.

129

I put my fingers to my lips, I thought he might linger a while to listen.

"He has us at every turn. My God, I shall go mad, I believe," I cried in a voice loud enough to reach him if he were there; and I thought I could catch the sound of a chuckle outside.

A minute afterwards we heard the front door slammed, and I went out to be sure that he had really gone. Then I hurried back to Althea.

"Wasn't that just lovely?" I asked with a smile. "Don't look so frightened. I was afraid to tell you my plan for fear that if you had it in your thoughts you might not have been able to prevent his suspicions being aroused. You must forgive me that. Everything has gone splendidly."

"I don't understand in the least," she cried, in her infinite perplexity. "You agreed to it all."

"Did I not tell you not to believe your eyes if you saw me agree?"

"Tell me now, everything."

"Of course I will. Stand up here a moment." She came to me and we stood before the mirror. "Once before, this morning, we were standing together just as we are now and I happened to look in that glass. It suggested a thought. See if anything is suggested to you."

She looked and turned to me as she shook her head. "I don't understand in the least."

"You are a tall girl and I am not a very tall man, so that our height is nearly the same. You are broad-shouldered for a girl; I am the reverse for a man. If I were dressed as you are, the difference would be imperceptible."

"But I am dark and you are fair—and your moustache!"

"Any sort of dark wig will alter the hair. Bessie bought one this morning. A razor will deal with the moustache. A touch or two on the eyebrows and a veil, fairly thick, will do the rest. I am going to borrow your dress for the evening's entertainment."

"Oh, Paul!" she cried, catching my arm, the name slipping out in her agitation.

I laid my hand on hers and took it gently into mine. She left it there.

"Did you really believe I would let you marry that brute? My dear, I would take his life first. This was all make-believe just now. I frightened him from having the marriage here—he thought I should kill him if he did—because it is necessary that I should be at his house to-night."

"But the danger to you?" she murmured.

130

"Is as straw to iron compared with the danger to him. To-day I could have spoken a word which would have brought him cringing to heel like the cur he is."

"Why didn't you?"

"Almost I spoke it, when he was blustering here. But I have a still better plan. Put away all your fears, and let me see a smile in place of all that pain and agitation. I tell you surely that by to-morrow all the clouds will have passed."

"I am only afraid for you," she whispered.

"And I—well, I will tell you when I have succeeded what other feeling than fear I have had about you in all this time."

Her answer was a smile, almost as if she knew.

For the moment the words trembled on my lips, but I pressed them back. We stood the while in silence.

"It has been so terrible that I can scarcely dare to hope," she murmured, her voice unsteady.

"Hope! For what, Althea?" I whispered.

She raised her head and our eyes met. All was clear to us both then.

"You may hope, Althea. I am sure."

Instinctively I stretched out my arm, and of herself she came to me and laid her head on my shoulder.

"You know what I have hoped, then?"

"Paul!" Just a sigh of happiness and full content.

"You love me? Ah, Althea!"

I lifted her head from my shoulders and took the sweet face between my hands, and then our lips met in the lingering ecstasy of love's first kiss.

"My dearest!" I whispered.

A little fluttering sigh of delight escaped her as her head was again pillowed on my shoulder; and in that realm of love's entrancing bliss we remained oblivious of all save our own rapture, and heedless each of everything except that together we had come into our own kingdom of happiness and perfect understanding.

We were roused by the sound of footsteps approaching the room. Althea drew away from me in tremulous confusion, her eyes shining radiantly, her colour mantling her cheeks.

It was my sister. "I was just coming for you, Bess," I said hurriedly, meeting her as she entered.

"I couldn't think where you were. You were awfully quiet"; and she looked from one to the other doubtfully, and then went toward Althea.

Althea turned quickly on her approach, and kissed her very

lovingly, and put her arms round her waist. And seeing her eyes, Bessie understood.

"Oh!"

Her glance at me was an eloquent substitute for anything more. And then in her turn she put her arms round Althea and hugged her.

"I'm going to my room, Bess; come to me presently," I exclaimed, and left them together.

At first the sense of the rapturous happiness which had come to me filled my thoughts to the exclusion of all else, and it was only Bessie's arrival that called me down from the clouds.

She was a good chum but not usually demonstrative. Now, however, she came straight up to me and kissed me. "It's just lovely, Paul; but of course I've been expecting it; and you two have been a long time coming to an understanding."

I laughed. I was in the mood to laugh at anything. "All right," I said inanely.

"Ah, you don't understand women, Paul, or you'd have seen as plainly as I have that Althea has cared for you ever so long," she said sententiously.

"Where is she?"

"Gone upstairs to her father. That's the only part I don't like in it. But poor Althea can't help that. And now, haven't we a lot to do yet? One of the three must be practical and think of things; and Althea can't. Oh, Paul, I never saw anything like her delight."

"Yes, I suppose one must be practical even at such a time"; and then we plunged into the discussion of my make-up for the evening's business.

She had brought Althea's dress down with her, and she fitted on the skirt and made such alterations as were needed. I kept it on, in order to accustom myself to it and be able to walk without tumbling over it. I should wear it over my own things of course as I knew that I must be able to get it off when the need arose.

The bodice proved impossible, however; so Bessie cleverly improvised a substitute; and we arranged that I should wear a short cloak of hers which would come just below my waist. And she so contrived everything that I could readily reassume my own garb.

When all was finished I went up to my room to shave off my moustache, and we laughed long and heartily together at my clumsy efforts to follow her instructions about holding up the skirt in getting upstairs.

It might have been a sort of mad frolic we were planning instead of the grim business which I knew that night would see.

Then came the face make-up and the arrangement of the wig,

hat and veil; and while Bessie was intent upon this, I slipped a loaded revolver into the pocket of my jacket, to which I had arranged ready access.

"I declare, you make quite a pretty girl, Paul; but you're dreadfully awkward. You must take shorter steps or you'll be found out the instant you leave the house," said Bessie, turning to survey the effect a moment later.

"Thank goodness there are only a few steps to walk in any event. The only tough part will be in the carriage with the beggar. By Jove, it's close to the time. I'd better be ready in the drawing-room."

Just as we reached the room, Ellen met us. She took me for Althea, and was so astonished at seeing her dressed for the street that she exclaimed: "Are you going out, miss?"

I did not open my mouth and went on, but Bessie replied: "Yes, Ellen. A carriage is coming directly for Fräulein von Ringheim"—since Althea's visit to the police when I had been taken away, we had dropped all attempt at concealing her name—"and when it arrives you will just come to this room and tell her."

"I could scarcely keep a straight face with Ellen," she said as she joined me.

"It took her in anyhow, and that's hopeful; and now I'll spend the last few minutes in practising this infernal walk."

I managed it better after a time, and I was in the middle of the practice when Althea came down. For the moment she mistook me for a friend of Bessie's, and was going out quickly when she recognized her own dress.

"I declare I shouldn't have known you, Paul."

I walked up to her with the little mincing gait and held out a gloved hand. "I hope you are well," I said in a falsetto voice. I saw how really anxious she was about the thing and was resolved to treat it as a joke.

But Althea was too overwrought to see any but the dangerous side of the affair. "I hope no harm will come to you," she exclaimed fervently.

"There is not the slightest fear of anything of the sort. But there mustn't be three of us in the room when Ellen comes in or she'll take one of us for a ghost. And the time's up."

She came very close to me and I saw she was trembling. "I pray to Heaven all will be well," she cried earnestly.

"Within five minutes of our reaching his house I shall have that fellow on his knees. And now, you must go, or I shall be tempted to upset all these beastly arrangements on my head and—well, you know," I laughed.

At that moment we heard the sound of the carriage and she hurried away upstairs.

Then I saw how my sister had been hiding her real apprehension under a light laughing humour. "It will be all right, Paul? You are sure?" she asked, her lip trembling.

I replied in the same light vein as to Althea. "Unless the fool tries to kiss me in the carriage, or I give myself away, I cannot fail. I shall be back again in a very short time; and remember what I told you—you may have to rush off by the mail to-night. Be ready."

Ellen opened the door then and announced that the carriage had come.

"Good-bye then, Althea," exclaimed Bessie, most naturally. "And with all my heart good luck."

She walked with me as far as the front door to cover my burlesque of a girl's gait, and I tiptoed quickly across the pavement, entered the carriage, and leaned forward to wave my hand to her.

The next moment the door was shut and we started.

CHAPTER XX

A BRIDE ELECT

My first inclination on taking my seat in the carriage with von Felsen was to laugh. His face wore such an expression of self-satisfaction and triumph that the absurdity of it appealed almost irresistibly to my sense of humour.

The whole thing was like a little farcical curtain-raiser at a theatre which prefaces the real drama.

That he did not discover the deception at once was a cause of wonderment to me. If my feelings were any indication of my appearance, I must have looked as awkward a creature as ever wore a petticoat. The skirt of the dress was "anyhow." That is to say, it hung in awkward creases and folds as I sat with my legs doubled close under me for fear he should see my very ungirlish feet.

I had to keep my hands out of sight, pulled uncomfortably up under my short cloak; and I had to sit bolt upright, because, when I had tried to appear overcome and had leant back against the side of the carriage, I was within an ace of dislodging the whole of my headgear, hat, veil, wig and everything.

But of all the troubles of that terrible costume, I think the veil was the worst. It tickled my nose; it irritated my freshly shaven upper lip; it caught my eyelashes and brought the tears to my eyes; it interfered with my sight; and it made me twitch my lips, and chin and nose as if I had St. Vitus' dance, until I could have sworn aloud at it in all the languages I knew.

I presume that von Felsen took my extraordinary attitude for sullenness, and he appeared quite undecided as to the correct manner in which to behave to a girl he was forcing to marry him. He made very little effort to speak to me during the journey, and the attempts he did make were of course unsuccessful in eliciting anything from me but a gesture of indignation or anger.

"I am sorry to have had to do this, Althea," he said after one of these gestures of mine. I had just turned my back on him as he had sought to get hold of my hand in a spoony way.

I shrugged my shoulders and gave a little toss of the head— none too energetic of course, for fear of consequences.

"I'll make it up to you. You know that, dearest. You know that I worship the very ground you tread on, and all my life shall be devoted to make you happy."

It was a queer sensation to have a man making love to me, and if I could have counterfeited Althea's voice, I'd have led him on a bit. Although, how any girl could feel romantic with a thing tickling her face, as that infernal veil was tickling mine, beat me. My chief sensation was an almost overpowering desire to rub my nose.

My silence and my attitude of resentful disbelief annoyed him. "You let me make love to you before that infernal Englishman came in the way," he said, only he used a stronger epithet for me. "I suppose he has done his best to set you against me. But I'm even with him now."

I maintained the same stolid coldness.

"Aren't you going to speak a word to me?" he cried after a long pause; and he bent forward and tried to look into my face.

It was fortunately a very dull evening, and the light inside the carriage was so dim that even at close quarters he could not have made out my features; but I took care he should not get too close, and twisted away from him.

Then he commenced to claw for my hand again. I was afraid he would put his arm round my waist, for I knew that the dimensions of it would give him something of a shock. As it was he fooled about with my arm; and that he did not at once discover that no girl, except an athlete, was likely to have an arm as hard as mine, was

135

amazing. However, he got hold of my fingers—I was sitting with arms crossed—and when I found that the size of them did not rouse his suspicions, I let him retain his hold.

This appeared to satisfy him, and he kept hold, squeezing them now and again as if he found great pleasure in the business.

I could not refrain from speculating whether a girl in such circumstances would have thought a man such an awful ass as I thought him. I suppose she would.

He appeared to regard this hand-fumbling business as a sign of relenting on my part, for we were quite close to his house before he said any more.

"The mere touch of your hand is a delight to me, Althea," he murmured, like the fatuous idiot he was making of himself.

I drew my hand away and turned my back squarely upon him. The sigh he gave might have come right from the pit of his stomach and been gathering weigh all the journey.

"I will make you love me, yet, Althea. You are the only woman in the world to me." Not a very original sentiment, perhaps; but apparently quite earnest; and before he could make any further headway with his love-making, the carriage drew up at his door.

He got out and held his hand to help me. But I disdained his assistance, and grabbing hold of my dress in the way in which Bessie had carefully instructed me, I stepped out and hurried up the steps and into the hall.

Seated there was the clerk from "W. Mischen"; and he rose at my entrance and gave me a long curious stare. In his eyes I was, of course, a lady of quality; and he scanned me from head to foot. I had presence of mind enough to let my dress fall well over my boots, however.

When von Felsen saw him he started and was for hurrying me into his room; but the clerk stepped forward.

"I came for the lease and papers, sir, from W. Mischen," he said respectfully.

"You are before your time; but I'll see you in a minute," replied von Felsen changing colour and speaking nervously. "This way, Althea"; and he pushed the door open for me to enter.

I had feared to find in the room the priest and any others who were to be present at the marriage and I hesitated a second on the threshold. The hesitation was really no more than an involuntary start of surprise and pleasure at seeing it empty. It was his private room, as I knew.

But he mistook the gesture for one of doubt of him. "The rest are in the room opposite," he hastened to explain. "I wish to speak to you first. We must have an understanding before we go to the others," he added when we were inside and he had closed the door behind us. "There must be no tricks before the priest. You must promise me not to make a scene of any sort."

The moment had come for undeceiving him; but as he was standing between me and the door I tried to put it off for a while longer. I shrugged my shoulders, and then, as if seized with a sudden frenzy of despair, I clapped my hands to my face and flopped down on a chair. My back was to him, of course, for the electric lights were full on.

He came to me and laid a hand on my shoulder; but I shook it off, got up and rushed to another chair nearer the door, and gave such a back view of a girl's agitation as I could manage to portray.

It was sufficient for the purpose. "You must compose yourself, Althea," he said, following me.

I glanced round and shuddered as if at his approach, and ventured to grunt out a little moan of pain.

He stopped and looked at me, half in anger and half in dire perplexity. "I won't come near you then," he growled, and down he plumped into a chair to watch for any signs of my return to self-control.

I was now between him and the door and was much easier in mind; and began to prepare stealthily to throw off the disguise. I had taken off my gloves when it occurred to me to try to continue the scene long enough to induce him to get out the papers for which the clerk was waiting. I had no doubt they were in the room somewhere.

I remained inconsolable, therefore, until his patience waned. He sat for some time tapping his fingers restlessly on the table and staring at me; and then with a sign of vexation, rose and crossed to an old bureau desk.

"For Heaven's sake calm yourself, Althea. The thing has got to go through if you mean to save your father," he said; "and I pledge you my honour that afterwards I will do everything in my power to make you happy. I will, on my soul."

I responded to this with a gesture sufficient to enable me to turn and see what he was doing, and let out a sigh.

I saw that he was watching me furtively while he opened some secret recess in the bureau and took out a carefully sealed envelope.

I sighed again—this time with a genuine feeling of relief—and rose.

He put the envelope quickly into his pocket and turned. "I have one little thing to do first," he said, and was coming toward the door when I gave him the first of his surprises.

I stepped forward quickly, locked the door and took out the key.

"What are you doing, Althea?" he cried.

I put my back to the door and slipping my hand through the opening in my skirt got my revolver in readiness. With the other hand I took hold of the string with which we had tied on the skirt. All the top hamper of hat and so on would come off with one vigorous tug.

Thus prepared I waited to see what he would do next.

His first attempt was bluster. "How dare you lock that door? If you think to try and cheat me at the last moment, it will not help you. I have only to send word and your father will be in gaol." He was afraid to speak too loudly for fear that those outside should hear him; but his temper was rising quickly.

On my side I was absolutely indifferent who heard us, and I stood stock still with my back against the door staring at him as hard as I could stare through the meshes of the thick veil.

"Open that door, or give me the key at once. Do you hear, Althea? This is all foolishness. Then I shall take it from you," he continued, when he got no reply. He came up to me and I thrust him away.

Even then he did not suspect the trick I had played him. Presumably he could not believe any one could have made such a fool of him.

He was at a loss what to do next. He was but a weakly fellow, and the strength with which I had pushed him away had startled him.

"What is it you want, Althea? I'll do anything you wish."

I chose that moment to end the farce. I drew the tape which held up the skirt, and with a vigorous tug got rid of the hat and wig and threw it all aside as I disentangled my legs from the skirt.

He started back as though I were the devil himself. I must have looked a curious figure. I had had to roll up my trousers to prevent their being seen underneath the dress; I still had on Bessie's short cloak and was thus still garbed on top partly as a man and partly as a woman, while my drawers showed as high as my knees.

But it was not the humour of the change which appealed to him now. His wide eyes were fixed first on my face and then on the revolver which I took good care should attract a full share of his attention.

"Sit down and hold your tongue till I tell you to speak," I said.

He was ashen white and trembled violently. But he was obedient enough. He sat down, or rather fell into a chair, and glared helplessly at me.

I got rid of the rest of the disguise and then rolled down my trousers. I had to free myself from the sense of the ridiculous figure I cut.

He watched every movement like a lynx. I bundled the things into a heap. "You can send them back to my house presently," I said with a grim laugh. "And now we can talk. First, give me that paper which you were to send by that fellow in the hall."

He tried to force some sort of lie in response, but his lips were trembling so that he could not frame the words.

"I'm glad to see you are suffering from a touch of the agitation you were quite ready to inflict on Althea. Now don't make any mistake. You have to do exactly what I order you. It's a matter of life or death to you."

I gave him time to digest this so that it might sink right into his inmost convictions, and saturate his little soul with terror. He had enjoyed the sensation that afternoon of riding rough-shod over me; and he should learn now how it felt to have some one else in the saddle. Judging by his looks he found the experience mightily depressing.

In the pause some one knocked at the door. A passing gleam of hope flashed into his eyes and he half rose. But I lifted my weapon just the fraction of an inch and gestured to him to keep his seat. He obeyed and crouched back in the chair like a whipped hound.

In this way we waited while the knock was twice repeated.

"Tell them to go away," I ordered.

And then he gave me a surprise in my turn. "Break the door open," he called in as loud a tone as he could master. But fear had clogged his utterance, so that they could not hear his words distinctly.

"What did you say, sir?" called some one in response.

Before he could reply to this I sprang on him and tore the coveted packet from his pocket, ripped off the seals and glanced at the contents. The glance was enough to satisfy me of the prize I had secured.

"You can call them in now, if you dare. I don't want your life now."

He stood a few seconds staring at me, quivering with rage and fear; and then the question was repeated from outside.

"Don't try that trick again, mind," I said.

"Go away till I call," he answered.

"Good," I said with a grim smile. "Now listen to me. Do what I tell you and you shall have a chance to get out of the mess. Go to your desk there and make up a dummy packet like this in appearance and give it to the man who is waiting."

For the moment he was incapable of movement. The failure of

139

his little attempt to outwit me and the result had unnerved him utterly.

"You are going to kill me?" he murmured, wiping the sweat from his forehead.

"Not if you do as I bid you. I don't lie, and I have passed my word."

It was necessary to steady his nerves in some degree for what I meant him to do; so I waited while he fought down some of his paralysing terror.

Presently he rose and shambled across to the desk, steadying himself as he went by holding to the furniture. He fell into the chair before it and buried his head in his hands and groaned.

"Come. Make an effort." He started at the sound of my voice and glanced round at me. I think he was the most despicable coward I had ever seen. With another deep sigh he picked out an envelope like that I had taken from him and then with shaking fingers folded some sheets of paper, placed them in it and addressed it.

"Seal it," I ordered as he held it out to me. This occupied a longish time; and in his agitation he burnt his fingers badly with the wax. "So far so good," I said. "Now a note to the priest that the ceremony cannot take place. It can't very well, unless you wish to marry me," I added with a short unpleasant laugh.

With a great effort he succeeded in writing the note; and again held it out for me to read. "Now, take these to the door and tell your servant to give the one to the priest and the other to the messenger from W. Mischen. Not a syllable more. I shall be behind you with this"; and I held up the revolver.

I rang the bell and we crossed the room together. I unlocked the door and stood close behind him with the muzzle of my weapon pressed close to his ribs.

"My finger is on the trigger," I whispered, as the servant knocked and he opened the door. He was too abjectly frightened to try any tricks this time, and delivered the message just as I had told him. The next instant the door was safely locked once more, and he tottered back to his seat.

"You can take your own time now to recover; but you have a good deal more writing to do, so you had better pull yourself together."

A silence, lasting some minutes followed; and I used the time to read the paper which I had secured and to make a rough précis of it. He glanced up once or twice at me the while, and when I put the paper back into the envelope, he asked: "What are you going to do with that?"

I paid no heed to his question.

140

"Are you ready? Then go over to your desk again and write me a true account of how you got this."

This threw him again into a condition of trembling fear. "What do you want it for?" he stammered.

"I'll give you two minutes to make a start in"; and I drew out my watch.

He got up and fumbled his way to the desk again, and after a pause began to write, with many delays and hesitation.

Presently I crossed and over his shoulder read what he had written. A silly lie about having found the paper. I tore the sheet from the desk and crumpled it up.

"Don't think to palm off that lie to me. I know how you got it. Write the truth, or I send for Herr Borsen." The threat had little effect however.

"I swear on my soul that that is the truth," he muttered, looking round.

"You are playing with your life, man. Your only chance of getting me to hold my tongue is to make a clean breast of it, not only about your theft but another thing."

"What do you mean?" Just a whisper of terror. No more.

"Your loss of this."

I took out the ring which I had found on the night of Ziegler's murder.

It was the breaking point. He stared at it a second like a man bereft of his wits, gave one glance up into my stern, set face, and with a groan let his head fall on the desk before it.

"Come," I said, shaking him roughly.

But he had swooned; and when I released my grip of him, he slipped from the chair to the ground and lay a huddled heap on the floor.

CHAPTER XXI

LIKE A DOG AT HEEL

As soon as I realized that von Felsen had fainted, I laid him on his back and hunted round for some spirits. I found some brandy, and after having poured about half a wineglass down his throat, left him to recover his senses.

He was in a desperate plight when he came to; and at one time I was so alarmed by his looks and his feeble flickering pulse, that I was on the point of calling assistance. If his heart failed while he and I were alone together, it might be awkward for me.

For him I had no sort of feeling but loathing and contempt; and whether he lived or died was a matter of indifference so long as he lived long enough to do what I required.

When he was looking his worst, he rallied a bit, however, and another dose of the spirit set his pulse beating again with less irregularity and some strength.

After a while he sat up and looked about him vacantly.

"I fainted?" he said, in a weak shaky voice.

"Yes," I nodded. "I found your brandy and gave you some."

"Give me some more. Oh, my God, I remember now," he cried wildly, and clapped both his hands to his face.

I gave him the spirit and the glass rattled as he placed it to his chattering teeth. "You'd better get on that sofa and lie down for a while."

He glanced at me like a dog at his master, crawled across the floor to the couch and dragged himself up slowly on to it. He was shivering violently, so I threw over him the skirt of the dress I had worn, and left him to himself for a long time: half an hour probably.

I took out again the paper he had stolen from his father's office and re-read it carefully, fixing all the main points in my memory.

Old Ziegler had known well what he was about in forcing von Felsen to steal such a document, and in getting me to agree to publish it in London.

It was nothing less than a complete statement of the Kaiser's shipbuilding policy for the future; the strength of the future navy, a full list of the ships which were to be built; their tonnage, equipment and armament; the number of the crews needed; everything given with scrupulous detail.

Against every vessel indicated there was the name of a British vessel with the same detail of its size and armament. In each case the German vessel was to be of superior strength. It told its own story with a clearness of inference that no one could mistake.

That it was an authentic document, I could not doubt. It was full of interlineations and corrections in different handwritings. I recognized one or two of them, and the whole appearance of the thing convinced me that it would have been practically impossible for von Felsen or any one else to have forged it.

That its disclosure would have raised a storm all over Europe was as certain as that day follows night; and that it would injure the

Imperial Government immensely was equally clear, in view of the then excited condition of public feeling.

It might even have provoked a war with England. Already the relations between the two countries had been strained almost to a breaking point by the Kaiser's hot-headed telegram to the Boer President and the belief of his desire to intervene in the war in South Africa.

Even had I been still a newspaper man I should have hesitated to take the responsibility of publication; and as it was, I did not contemplate such a step for an instant. I had obtained possession of it for my own private ends, and for those I would use it. For such a purpose it was precisely what I needed.

But the instant the theft was discovered there would be such a hue and cry raised that the mere possession of it would be a source of danger. Luckily I had foreseen something of this; and it was my plan to get it out of the country with the least possible loss of time. It was for this I had told my sister to be ready to leave by the mail.

Time was getting on too; so I roused von Felsen. "Come, you must get to work," I said. "I can't wait any longer."

With a heavy sigh he sat up. "What do you want?"

"Write me the truth as to how you came by this paper. Where it was kept; in whose charge it was; how you knew of its existence; why you stole it; and precisely the steps you took to obtain it. As short as you like; but in such detail that your story can be tested."

"I daren't. It's more than my life's worth," he protested.

"You can choose between that and standing your trial for Ziegler's murder. Without this ring I have enough evidence to convict you—what you did before the crime; where you went from; how you gained admittance to the house; when you left; where you went; and, mark this, what you did with the weapon."

The greater part of all that was, of course, mere bluff; and I put it only in general terms. But he was in such fear of me, that it was safe bluff. Not for a second did he doubt that I could make every syllable good. I could tell that by his looks.

After another groan of anguish he rose and crossed to the desk. "What do you mean to do with it?" he asked, looking round with the pen in his hand.

"Hush it all up, if you go straight. Use it, if you don't."

After a pause he began to write; and the scratch, scratch of his pen was the only sound in the room for many minutes.

I took each half sheet as he finished it; and had no doubt he was writing the truth. He was completely in the toils of the old Jew, and the latter had forced him to do this under threats of ruin and exposure. He had been drawn into the toils of the Polish party and they had threatened to tell of the information which he had sold to them on former occasions. This was to be the price of his complete emancipation from them; and in dire fear of them he had consented.

"You were to receive twenty thousand marks. Put that in," I interrupted.

It was an excellent stroke. He was overwhelmed by the fact that I knew so much; and it settled all thought of any doubts about the rest of my knowledge.

"Let me leave that out," he whined.

"Do as I say," I rapped back sternly; and he obeyed. Then he went on to describe the means by which he had committed the theft. He had duplicate keys of all the locks in his father's office.

When he had finished the confession and signed it, I made him hand over those keys to me. With such a piece of evidence as they constituted in my hands, I cared comparatively little whether his statement were true or false. They would speak for themselves.

The writing of the confession with the breaks and pauses occupied nearly an hour, and I could see that he was nearly collapsing; so I told him to make the statement about Ziegler's murder very short.

"I have enough evidence without this at all," I declared; and he believed me. But I made him give such an account of his doings on the night, and particularly about the dagger he had used, where he had obtained it, and what he had done with it, as would enable me at need to find the proofs of his guilt.

When the ordeal was over he tottered back to the couch and lay down exhausted; and I gave him a few minutes while I ran through both his statements. Then I was ready to leave.

"Now about your future. I'll keep my word to you. The stolen paper and your keys shall be returned to your father's office as the price of Baron von Ringheim's pardon. I shall see your father and show him what you have written about it all; and you know well enough that no harm will come to you through him as the result. Are you listening?"

A feeble gesture of the hand was his only response.

"You'd better, for your life hangs on your understanding all I say and doing what I tell you. Your admission of the murder I shall keep a dead secret"—he started at that, raised himself on his elbow and looked across at me—"on one condition. You must be out of the country within twenty-four hours. If I find you here at the end of that time I shall hand it to the police."

With a deep breath of relief he sank back. "I'll go; but I've—I've no money."

"I'll find you enough to get away with"; and I laid a sum on the table; "and as soon as you are across the frontier you can communicate with your friends."

The assurance that he was to have a chance to save his worthless skin had a surprisingly invigorating effect upon him. Now that the suspense was over and he knew the worst which could befall him, he was greatly relieved. He got up and lighted a cigarette. "Don't go yet," he said.

I was at the door and turned.

"I've made an awful mess of things," he went on.

"I don't want to discuss the ethics of your conduct," I retorted.

"I'll go straight now. I'll prove it to you in a minute. But I want you to know that I didn't go to Ziegler's with any intention of killing him. I went to get off that marriage with the daughter; and it was only when we quarrelled and he made me mad that I did it. He threatened me."

"Anyhow you had arranged that some one else should do it, because you had secretly accused him of treachery to his associates. And there isn't much difference between the two."

"How the devil do you get to know so much? Yes, I did that. I'll admit it to you after all this. But I'll go straight, as I said. And here's the proof, so far as you are concerned. The police are still round your house, and if you were to go back without a sign from me you'd all be arrested."

I had not thought of that. "You'd better give me something then."

He went again to the desk and wrote a line or two. "You are to withdraw your men. Hugo von Felsen," I read when he handed it to me.

"Perhaps that will convince you that I am in earnest," he said. "Give it to the fellow in charge there. I shall leave for Austria to-night"; and with that we parted.

On my way home I found myself speculating whether he had been sincere in that last act of his, or whether he could possibly have some other kind of motive at the back of his head. It was uncommonly like a Greek gift.

And then a possible solution occurred to me. My arrest at that moment with the papers I was carrying would have betrayed everything. He had had wit enough to remember that, although I had overlooked it. That sudden return to comparative self-possession took a fresh light in this connexion.

Could he, even now, when I had possession of such damning proofs of his guilt in both affairs, be contemplating some further treachery? Would he dare such a step? He had been reduced to the

145

lowest depths of abject terror when I had confronted him with the proofs and extracted the confessions from him, that it was difficult to credit it was all shamming.

What could he do? His life lay in the hollow of my hand, and he knew me well enough to be certain that at the first glimpse of a trick I should act.

But he was such a slippery devil I could not be sure; and a dozen suggestions flashed into my thoughts. Had that parade of his about the police surrounding the house been no more than a bluff? There were men there, because I had taken care to see them for myself. But were they really the police?

If it had been no more than a lie, it had at any rate resulted disastrously for him. That was a consolation, anyway. But if they were only his creatures and not police, why had he given me the letter to order them to withdraw?

He might be afraid of the papers falling into their hands, of course, and so constituting a source of practically inexhaustible blackmail for them. But, on the other hand, he might be just laying a trap for me to fall into their hands.

Whatever view I took of it, I should have to be on the alert; and when I reached the house I kept my hand on the revolver which had already done me such service that night.

The men were still there, and as I approached one of them stopped me. He was dressed in the uniform of the police, but he lacked the military bearing of that remarkably fine set of men.

"I am from Herr von Felsen, and have this note for one of you," I said as I drew it out.

We went to a lamp close at hand, where another man not in uniform joined us. They read it, put their heads together in a whispered conference, and then favoured me with a searching stare.

"It's right enough," said one of them. "Good-night, sir"; and with that they turned away, spoke to some others who appeared mysteriously from I didn't know where, and all walked away in a body.

I waited until they were out of sight before I let myself into the house; and as I closed the door, my sister and Althea came running downstairs.

"Is that you, Paul?" asked Bessie.

"Yes. Everything is as well as we could wish."

Althea laid both her hands in mine. "It has been like a nightmare," she said.

"Von Felsen thought so too, I can assure you. But with a little luck now a few hours will see all righted. Get ready to start, Bess. You must go right through to Brussels. Sew these papers into your

146

dress; or hide them in any way you like, so long as you get them through safely."

"I shall be ready in a few minutes"; and she ran off with the packet.

"Tell me how you have managed it, Paul. It seems like a miracle," said Althea.

I put my arm about her. "I found out things that beat him, and you will have no more trouble through him."

"What things?"

"Ah, there you must have patience. I am pledged not to speak for twenty-tour hours, in order to give him time to leave the country."

"He will not go," she answered instantly, shaking her head vigorously.

"He dare not stay. If you love me, nothing now can come between us."

"If? Paul!" and she put her arms round my neck; and what followed concerned nobody but ourselves. But when she drew away it was to shake her head doubtingly. "I do not trust him."

"Him? No; but his fear, yes. I tell you he dare not play me false."

"Pray Heaven it will all be right; but I still fear for you, Paul."

"It will be as surely as I kiss you now," I whispered. "And now can you get your father to leave? There is no absolute need now, thank Heaven; but while I am doing what I have to do, it would be best for him to be out of the city."

"And you?" she asked with quick solicitude.

"I shall be all right. I hold all the winning cards, whatever happens."

Her dear face clouded and her brows puckered with a frown as she shook her head. "I could not go if you were to remain. I will not, at least until I know that all is right with you. Nor indeed could I if I would. My father has been in a terrible state for some hours. I told him what you suggested—that the scheme had failed, you know— and he wanted to rush out of the house on the instant. I only stopped him by pointing out the police to him."

"They are gone, I am glad to say. Von Felsen himself gave me a note calling them away. What's that?" I broke off, as a sound upstairs reached us, followed a moment afterwards by the shutting of a door.

"Bessie probably," suggested Althea.

"Of course. I forgot; but I have been a bit strung up by the night's business. I was going to say that you had better not tell your father the police have been removed. If he will not leave the city, he is safest here." I hurried away then to put von Felsen's confessions and the keys I had taken from him in safe hiding, and soon after that Bessie came down and we started for the station.

After what Dormund had told me that day at the station about the passports, I had some doubt whether some demur might be raised about Bessie's departure; but no questions were asked, and she was soon seated in the ladies' compartment with two other Englishwomen who, I was glad to hear, were going through to Brussels. In the bustle of the preparations and in giving her full instructions about the packet she was carrying, I had thought no more of the little incident while I was with Althea; but at the last moment I remembered it.

"By the way, Bess, did you come out of your room and go back again while I was talking to Althea?"

"No. Why?"

"I thought I heard some one run upstairs and shut a door."

"It must have been Baron von Ringheim. He passed my room while I was secreting the papers, and went into his own room. I wondered at the time what had taken him downstairs."

"By Jove, I hope he didn't hear any thing about the police having left the house. I must get back. Wire me the instant you arrive, Bess. Good-bye."

The train was signalled out then, and with a last wave of the hand to her I left the station. I was eager to be home again. If the Baron had been anxious to leave the house and had really heard me tell Althea the road was clear, it was quite likely he might take advantage of my absence to carry out his purpose.

Anxious as this thought made me, I was not too preoccupied to keep my eyes about me; and it was not without a start of concern that I observed one of the men whom I had seen a short while before at my house. It was the man in plain clothes who joined his uniformed companion to read the letter.

He was apparently absorbed in reading a timetable, but I saw that he followed me as I went out.

I got into a cab therefore and promised a liberal fare for a quick journey. But the night horses of Berlin are not more brilliant than those of London, and we had gone a very short distance before the horse fell.

I jumped out, and found myself in a by thoroughfare which the man had taken for a short cut.

I knew my way well enough, however, and set off homewards at a brisk pace; but as I turned into a narrow street I tripped and fell, just as a man rushed round the corner after me and fired a pistol at very short range, and then bolted like a rabbit.

My fall probably saved my life; and I jumped up and rushed after him, like a fool, instead of resting content with my narrow escape. But he disappeared round a corner and, as I darted after him, I ran into a couple of policemen who had heard the shot fired. As no one else was to be seen, they thought I had fired the shot and was running away; and despite all I could say, they insisted upon arresting me.

Fortune could not have served me a more scurvy trick at such a moment.

CHAPTER XXII

IN SEARCH OF THE BARON

Anyone who has ever lived in the capital of the German Empire, or indeed in any German town of size, knows the absolute futility of arguing with the police. Definite regulations are laid down for them, as the sand of the sea in number and an auctioneer's catalogue in precision of detail; and unless you are a person of infinite leisure and unruffled temper, you will do what they tell you and do it without remonstrance.

When they insisted upon detaining me upon suspicion of having fired the shot which had attracted their notice, I could not restrain a heated protest or two; but I soon ceased to remonstrate.

I chafed and fretted at the detention; and all the more so, because while one of them took charge of me, his companion made a long search for my assailant. He must have been an extremely conscientious fellow, for he showed more than German thoroughness in the search. They are very rarely quick in their methods, but they claim to be sure; and when he returned after nearly an hour, he had quite convinced himself that the man was not hidden anywhere near us.

"You must have fired the shot," he said, with an air of satisfied conviction, "or I should have found the man. There was no one else about." He then ran his hands down outside my coat, felt my revolver and drew it out. "Ah, I knew it," he exclaimed triumphantly.

"Do let us go to the station," I said impatiently.

"You'll have enough of that before this is settled. Who are you, and where do you live?"

I said I would explain everything at the police quarters, and to my relief we set off for them then.

As a matter of fact, I was not a little bothered how to reply to the questions. If I gave my address, I knew that it was quite in accordance with the regulation methods for some one to be sent to search my house; and apart altogether from the alarm which such a proceeding would cause Althea following upon the news of my arrest, there was the awkward fact of the Baron's presence there.

Again, the ordinary process of interrogation would be directed to extracting from me a detailed account of my movements during the hours prior to the act with which I was to be charged. Police inquiries under such circumstances are inspired with as much minuteness as the average Teutonic biblical criticism.

The inquisitor at such times always presses his questions under the belief that at the bottom of the charge there is some heinous crime which he will be able to unearth if only he is clever enough.

The moment I was inside the building, therefore, I made haste to get out my version of the affair, and ended with a request for a communication to be made at once to Dormund or Feldermann.

The officer in charge listened with a frown of impatience, and then turned to the men who had taken me in charge. He was a surly individual; and when my revolver was produced, he gathered it in with a sort of cluck, such as a broody hen might give on discovering a titbit for her chicks.

"You will see that it is loaded in every barrel," I said.

He did not even take the trouble to look. The fact that a shot had been fired, and that I had been found running away and in the possession of a weapon, was obviously proof enough for him. "Well, your name and address?" he grunted as he took up his pen very deliberately.

"Paul Bastable."

"Where do you live. Answer."

I replied that I had been a newspaper correspondent and gave him the name of the paper, adding that both Dormund and Feldermann were my friends.

"Where do you live?" he repeated.

"They know me perfectly well, and I desire to communicate with them."

"Address refused," he murmured as if to himself, and wrote that down. It was the preface to just such a list of questions as I had anticipated. What I was doing in the streets at that time of night;

150

where I had been; where I was going; why I carried a revolver; why I had fired the shot; what I had done all the evening, and so on.

I returned much the same answer to all the questions—that I wished to be allowed to communicate with either Dormund or Feldermann; and we reached a deadlock, and he was ordering me to the cells, when it occurred to me to play the "British subject" card.

"Wait a moment, please. You have ignored my statement and are going to charge me with a serious, offence. I am a British subject and demand to be allowed to communicate with the British consul."

I knew he dared not refuse, and was pleased to see his shaggy brows knit more closely than ever as he thought it over.

"How do I know that?" he asked after a pause.

"Both Herr Dormund and Herr Feldermann know it." I was resolved to rub their names into him at every available chance. "Let me assure you that I have told you the absolute truth in regard to that shot. The mistake which your men made was quite intelligible under the circumstances, but it was a mistake. The shot was fired by a man whom I think I could identify; it was fired at me; and I was pursuing him when I was arrested."

His face might have been a barber's dummy for all the effect this appeared to produce. A long pause followed while he thought over the position, and then he told the others to take me off to the cells.

"You will enter the fact that I have demanded to see my consul, please," I said as I was led away; but like the rest, this elicited no notice.

I was left to cool my heels there for about an hour. I did not care two straws about the charge which had been preferred against me; but the delay fretted me almost into a fever, and had I been left much longer I believe I should have even ventured to make some attempt to escape.

But to my intense relief when the cell door was opened, Dormund was there. He favoured me with one of his driest smiles as he held out his hand. "You have a rare capacity for getting into trouble, Herr Bastable. Surely you know that revolver practice in the streets of Berlin is illegal."

"You have some really sharp fellows under you," I retorted with a grin. "Last time they accused me of having murdered myself, and now they think I tried to do it again."

He led me off to a room where we were alone. "Now tell me all about it."

I told him succinctly what had occurred. He accepted my story at once and together we smiled at the mistake of the others. "But you had no right to have this thing with you at all," he said, referring to the pistol. "You know the law. We shall have to keep it, and I'm afraid you must be prepared to answer for its possession."

"Anyhow, you can see that it hasn't been fired since it was cleaned. Get that quite clear, and I don't mind admitting that I often carry such a thing for my own protection."

"Do you still wish to communicate with your consul, or to make any fuss about the mistake these men made?"

"I want to get home and get to bed. All the rest can go hang."

"We can manage that, but you'll hear about the revolver from us in a day or so. Here are the rest of your things"; and soon afterwards we left the place together.

"Have you taken the advice I gave you yet?" he asked as we walked toward my house.

"What was that?"

"You were at the station to-night, you said. Have your friends gone?"

"No," I replied after a pause. "But I can assure you that all that bother is over and done with. I've been very anxious, but I've won all along the line."

"I am very glad to hear it. How?"

"You'll hear all about it to-morrow or the next day at latest."

"Well, we're schooled to patience, you know. I hope you are right. And I'm heartily glad you were not detained to-night; it might not have been so easy to get you out to-morrow, if a singular rumour running round our place has any foundation—about that old Jew's murder. Fortunately, I don't know anything officially, or I couldn't tell you. But I should advise you to be careful. Good-night"; and without waiting for any reply he turned away and left me.

I attached no importance to his words at the time. It was not probable that anything could have leaked out yet about von Felsen or the fact that I had got a confession from him; and having that, I cared not a jot for anything else.

My one anxiety was to get home and assure myself that Althea's father was still in the house.

Althea met me as I entered, and her looks showed me in a second that something was wrong.

"Thank Heaven, you have come, Paul. I have been tortured with the fear that something must have happened to you."

"Your father?" I asked.

She threw up her hands. "You have guessed it then?"

"Tell me. I have been haunted by the fear that he heard us speaking about the house being clear of the police."

"He has gone, Paul. What do you think can have happened?"

152

At the sight of her agitation I blamed myself for having let her see by my eager question how grave a view I took of the matter.

"I was half afraid of something of the sort," I replied in a much lighter tone, as we went into the drawing-room; "but no doubt I can put it all right. Bessie told me at the station that he had been downstairs; and that noise you and I heard when we were talking about the police was probably when he heard what we said. It is unfortunate, of course; but it will be all right."

"You are only saying that to ease my mind, Paul."

"No, on my word. I am quite sure of being able to secure his pardon, and no trouble can come of this unless he meets with it from any other source. No police trouble, I mean. As for the rest I believe I know where to look for him, and of course I must be off at once. But tell me first all what led up to his going."

She described his conduct during the day. He had been possessed by the thought that there had been some treachery to the cause; our story of the failure of the scheme had intensely excited him, and in this respect he suspected me of treachery; he had been fretting to get away to consult with others, and had only been kept in the house through fear of the police surrounding it.

"I went straight up to my room the moment you left with Bessie," she concluded, "and not finding him there went to his room. He was not there either. I called to him, but he did not reply; and thinking he might have been taken ill again, I made a thorough search of the house. He must have hidden somewhere and slipped out without my knowledge."

While she was telling me this the thought of the bomb I had given to him flashed across my thoughts, and only with the greatest difficulty could I repress the consternation it caused. Had he taken it with him? Was he mad enough to make the attempt to wreck the cruiser alone? If so, and he were found with that in his possession, or if he made any such mad attempt, the discovery of my part in the affair was all but certain.

"I'll go and have a look at his room, Althea," I said quietly when she had told me all she knew, and we went upstairs together. "Thank the Lord he has left his bag here," I cried with a sigh of satisfaction as I saw it. I had never felt such a flush of infinite relief in my life before.

But it was only for a moment, until I had forced the bag open.

The bomb was gone!

Althea saw then how the discovery affected me. The sudden rush from fear to relief, and back to fear.

"Paul!" Her face was white and strained.

I shook myself together and forced a smile. "Thank goodness he can do no harm with it at any rate. And he might have taken this too." He had left the revolver behind, and I slipped it into my pocket. "He cannot get into any very serious trouble before I find him. I'll go at once."

I went first to my own room to get some cartridges for the revolver in place of the blank ones with which I had before loaded it, and as we were going downstairs Althea asked me what had kept me so long away.

"I was arrested, but had no difficulty in explaining matters." I did not say anything about the attempt on my life, not wishing to alarm her.

"I was sure there was trouble," she cried in distress. "I have brought so much to you already."

"To-morrow we shall just smile at it all. I am absolutely confident, Althea."

"I cannot smile yet, Paul, nor be confident either. I could almost wish——"

I gathered her in my arms. "You must never harbour that thought again, dearest. Never if you love me."

"You would at least be safe; and the thought of your danger chills me with dread every minute you are away."

"But the mere fact that I have been in the hands of the police within the last hour and am here now at your side may tell you there is no such danger as you fear. You do but frighten yourself with shadows. If there had been any real trouble such as you fear, they would have detained me."

"I cannot help it, Paul. If it were only myself I should not care," she said with a heavy sigh.

"Keep this in your thoughts then. Bessie has taken with her something which would cut the knot of our difficulties were it twenty times worse than it is. But now what of yourself? Will you stay here alone, or go to Chalice?"

"Stay here. My father may return. I shall wait up all night for him."

"I shall bring him back in an hour or so. You will see," I said cheerfully.

"I pray with all my heart you will. But where are you going?"

"I think I know where to find him; but I must not stay to tell you any more. Keep a stout heart for that hour or so, and all will be well."

I put all the cheering confidence I could into my tone and manner, but it was of little avail. "I wish I could go with you," she cried wistfully. "If you do not return soon I shall be fit to do something desperate. I cannot tell you how this suspense tortures

154

me. It was all I could do to prevent myself from coming after you just now."

"You cannot do anything but wait, dearest. Wait and trust. It will all come right."

But although I had spoken so confidently to Althea, I was very far from feeling so; and as I hurried through the deserted streets I wished the Baron had been at Jerusalem and all his mad-brained schemes and cause and associates with him before he had come to plunge us all into this unsavoury mess.

There was, of course, only one place in the whole city where I could go in search of him—the wharf of W. Mischen; and it was no more than a bare possibility that he or any one else would be there at that time of night.

Moreover, if I did succeed in finding him there it was anything but clear how I could get him away. Already he entertained the gravest suspicions of me; and the moment he spoke to any of his infernal associates, all the fairy tales I had told him would be exposed.

He would show the bomb which I had given to him; and it needed no gift of prophecy to understand the feeling which would be aroused against me. Every man in the crowd would be itching to slit my throat or put a bullet into me.

There was just one chance in a million in my favour—that he had set out to blow up the "warship" by himself. But even that would not help me; as I should most certainly be unable to trace his movements.

If it had not been for the sham bomb which I had given him with its compromising history connecting me closely and certainly with it, I should have given up the quest altogether and left him to find his way back to the house. But I dared not leave that broad trail without at least a desperate effort to efface it. If it were discovered and my purchase of it proved, it would taint the whole story I had to tell of my possession of the paper I had secured from von Felsen. It would all be set down to my connexion with these infernal Poles.

In a word I was just at the end of my wits; and when I turned into the lane leading down to the wharf, I did not know whether to hope that I should find it empty or not.

I went very warily as I neared the place, pausing many a time to look about me. If any one was in the building, it was almost a certainty that spies would be somewhere in hiding to give warning to those within of the approach of any unwelcome strangers.

I scanned every possible hiding spot, therefore; and satisfied myself that no one was about; and so far as I could judge, the building itself was empty. It was shut up and in total darkness.

155

I pressed my ear against the door, and listened intently for any sound within. It was as still as the grave. I think I was relieved to find it so.

I was turning away to think what I could do next, when I heard a faint sound of cautious footsteps in the lane above.

Whoever might be coming, I had no mind to be caught in that equivocal position, so I crept away stealthily, keeping close in the shadows, and hid myself behind a heap of rubbish which stood against the adjoining warehouse, as two men came cautiously down the narrow street.

I was soon satisfied that the newcomers were not the regular police patrol; but they might be detectives. I should be in a pretty mess if they were; and I held my breath as they came near, watching them the while with straining eyes and quickened pulse. And then I saw that they themselves were being shadowed.

CHAPTER XXIII

IN THE GRIP OF AN ENEMY

The appearance of the third man was as disconcerting as it was mystifying. That he was sleuthing the other two was clear from the stealthy manner of his approach and the care he displayed in taking advantage of every scrap of shelter. He was an adept at the work. More than once the men looked round to make sure they were not followed; and each time, as if by instinct, the other had gone to cover.

As they reached the warehouse the couple became even more cautious, and the spy did not venture to show so much as the tip of his nose. With a last look round, they opened the door quickly and disappeared into the building.

I dared not show myself, of course, until I knew what the spy would do; and I felt extremely uncomfortable as I waited.

It was some minutes before he ventured any nearer; and then he came down the lane with cat-like stealth and absolutely noiseless tread, and at first did what I had done, listened intently for any sounds within the warehouse.

Presently he stepped back a pace and scrutinized the front, and

156

then turned his attention to the adjoining building. While doing this, he came right up to the rubbish heap behind which I lay; and a few seconds later began to glance about him as if for a place in which to hide.

The heap appeared to suggest itself to him in the same light as it had to me; and I saw that discovery was inevitable.

I scrambled to my feet, therefore, not willing to be taken at a disadvantage; and without a sound he turned on the instant and bolted up the lane.

I was completely mystified by this sudden flight. He was a spy, of course; but whether he had been set on by the police, or was shadowing some suspected members of the band, I had no means of even guessing.

Nor had I the time. If he was from the police he would soon be back with help; while if he was one of the men, he would carry the news to his friends that some one else was dangerously interested in the proceedings.

It was clear that something was going on inside the place, and I had to find the means of ascertaining whether Althea's father was there.

My previous visit had shown me that access to "W. Mischen's" premises could be obtained without much trouble from the water front; and although I was by no means a professional housebreaker, I had no difficulty in finding a way into the unoccupied warehouse.

One of the windows was unfastened, and raising this cautiously I squeezed through. It was a large empty room, and as dark as a chimney; but I felt all round the walls until I came to a door and shutting that behind me I struck a match and found the way out on to the wharf.

Then I had a stroke of luck. Tied to the wharf on the opposite side from "W. Mischen's" was a small boat with the oars in it; and, perceiving the possible value of having a means of retreat by the river in case of trouble, I decided to borrow this and fasten it in readiness for use in emergency. I hauled it along to "W. Mischen's" landing stage and made it fast.

The night was very still. The silence on the river was unbroken except for the lapping of the water as it eddied past, and the occasional creak of the small boat as it gritted against the wharf.

On my former visit I had noted the position of the two doors opening from the building to the wharf. One was from the warehouse portion; the other from the offices; and the latter was unfastened. I would have given a good deal to have known whether this was due to the carelessness of the obliging young clerk, or whether it had been used that night by those who were in the building. If they were expecting any fresh arrivals by water the discovery of my boat might be very awkward.

Still I could not stay to count the risks, so I pushed the door open and entered. I remembered that there was a flight of stone steps leading to the upper part; but before going up, I crept into the offices and made sure that the men I sought were not there.

I found them empty, and retraced my steps and crept up the stairs, carefully feeling each step with my hands as I went. At the top the way was blocked by a door.

No light showed from the other side of it, however; and after listening intently, I turned the handle very slowly, pausing at each creak it gave, until it yielded. It was another big barn of a room with windows looking out over the river.

My eyes were now getting accustomed to the darkness, and, by the aid of the very faint light from the windows, I made out a heap of empty sacks in one corner. I was crossing towards these on tiptoe, when I heard the murmur of voices.

Glancing in what I judged to be the direction of the sound I saw a light through the crack of a door; and after a pause I stole over the sacks and concealed myself among them.

It proved a lucky step. I had just lain down under them when the door opened and a man came out.

I recognized him as the more reckless of the couple who had been at Ziegler's with the Baron on the night of the murder.

The light from the door enabled me to see more of the place. The room from which he came was at the end farthest from the stairs by which I had come up; and between that and the stairs there was another door. I judged that there were two offices each communicating with the big warehouse and probably with one another.

This discovery was to prove of much value a little later on.

"Hush!" called some one from the room at the noise he made.

"To the devil with your hushing," he muttered with an oath. "Who's to hear?" and he opened the door leading to the stairway and went down.

I had had ample proof of his recklessness before; and I knew that if there were any others like him in the company, my life would not be worth a pinch of snuff should they discover me. I lay as still as the sacks which covered me, therefore.

Those in the room were of a much more cautious nature, however, than the fellow who had just left them; and, although they spoke together, their tones were so low that I could not make out what they said. Occasionally a single word would reach me; but I listened in vain for any indication that the Baron was among them.

In my eagerness to ascertain what was being said I was about to risk crawling to the door when I heard the man returning, and soon learnt then why the door leading to the wharf had been left open.

"Not a sign of them," he said, as he entered, to the others. "I expect the plan has missed fire. If I thought he was still fooling us, I'd shoot the old fool off hand." He left the door wide open, and I could hear distinctly.

"Not so loud, Gassen," said some one hurriedly. "Your voice carries so."

"I wish it would carry to that cursed Englishman and bring him here to the old lunatic's rescue."

"We have no proof. It's only your guess work."

"I want no more proof than we have. Who else was likely to betray us? Tell me that. Who else would have been able to get that cursed news into the papers and have the plans about the ship changed? Wasn't he a newspaper man of some sort? Tell me that. And how else could he get the news except from that blabbering old fool in the corner there when he was at his house."

"The news came from Paris."

"Paris be hanged," he cried fiercely with an oath. "How could they know in Paris if some one here hadn't told them from Berlin. Tell me that."

There was a long pause during which one of the men struck a match and began to smoke.

So Althea's father was there all the time, and this meeting had apparently been held for my punishment rather than in connexion with the meditated outrage. He was suspected of having betrayed everything to me; and my trick of getting the news published had been guessed.

"We shall have to give it up for to-night, Gassen," said the man who had spoken before. "They have failed to get him to come."

"Why don't they come back and say so then?"

"They may have been stopped in some way. Or perhaps they came while we were away."

"Schmidt has been here all the time taking care of the old fool there. Or are you another of the white-livered ones?"

"I've been here all through, of course. You needn't talk like that to me," said a man who had not spoken before.

Gassen laughed. "I shall say what I please and you can do what you like."

I wished with all my heart that the man would have started a quarrel; but he appeared to be afraid, and held his tongue.

"I don't mean to stay here all night," said the former speaker, whom I judged by his voice to be an older man than the others. "It isn't safe."

"What will you do with our precious 'leader' then?" was the reply with a very scornful reference to the unfortunate Baron.

"He can be kept here. There's plenty of room in the cellars."

"If you do go, we shan't want more than enough room to bury him. You can take my word for that," was the retort with a brutal laugh.

"I won't have any violence here, Gassen."

"Then you'd better stop and prevent it. I shall keep my word. But you know that pretty well by this time, I fancy."

The man addressed shifted uneasily and his chair scraped on the floor.

"You'll do what I say, Gassen," he replied with an effort to put authority into his voice.

"Then you'll have to say what I say. That's all. I haven't come here to-night for fun. Do you suppose there will be no violence, as you call it, if they succeed in persuading the Englishman to come to the rescue of the old dotard? Tell me that."

"Nothing must be done here any way."

Gassen swore contemptuously. "Well, it doesn't matter. You haven't seen him and I have; and you can take it from me that he isn't the man to take what's in store for him here without putting up a fight for his life."

This unexpected tribute to my fighting instincts was flattering perhaps; but I knew what lay behind it; and it came out the next instant.

"I may as well tell you what I mean to do. If they do get him here, I shall shoot him straight away without wasting any time in talk."

"You're too reckless. You'll get us all into trouble."

"Reckless?" he repeated with a curt laugh. "I'm not reckless enough to give him a chance at me."

It was a novel experience to listen to the plans for one's own murder; and I found it sufficiently depressing. I knew that the fellow was quite capable of making his words good; and that when we two did meet, it would be a question of which of us was the handier with his weapon.

That the others were against the violence he threatened with such sinister bluntness, would not help me in the least. He would not let their reluctance stand in the way of his purpose. He had persuaded himself that I was the traitor who had baulked their plans; and was fully set upon taking my life in revenge.

160

My plight was indeed about as desperate as it could be; and what to do constituted the toughest problem I had ever had to face.

There were three courses. One was to sneak out of the place and fetch the police, taking the risk of what might happen to Althea's father when they came or in the interval before I could get them there. Another was to wait where I was, trusting to my luck to prevent my being discovered. In this event I should have to run the risk of allowing the other men who had gone for me to return and to the hope that the milder counsels of the elder man would prevail in regard to the Baron. The third was the bolder course of facing the three men there and then before the party was enlarged.

I decided at once against the first. The delay might prove fatal to Althea's father; for the man, Gassen, was quite capable of knocking him on the head or shooting him when he found that he was to be baulked of his revenge on me.

The same objection applied to the second alternative. And even more strongly. He might insist upon being left in charge of the old man; and in that event I could not entertain a doubt that Althea would never see her father again alive.

The third course appeared at first sight the most dangerous; but was not so in reality. There were only three men in the room beyond; and two of these were opposed to Gassen's policy of violence. And with him I need have no scruples; and should have the advantage of surprise.

I was very unwilling to take life; and the reluctance was so strong that, although I felt perfectly justified in creeping up to the room and shooting him before he saw me, I could not persuade myself to do it. But I would shoot him with no more compunction than I would have shot a dog, the instant he made any sign of an attempt to harm me.

I decided therefore that the bolder course was also the safer; and I began to edge myself free from the sacks under which I lay concealed. In doing this I made enough noise to attract the attention of the men.

"What's that?" It was Gassen's voice and he sprang to his feet.

"I heard nothing," said the other man.

Gassen came out and stood listening. I could have shot him then and ended the affair; but my reluctance to kill a man in cold blood stayed my hand.

"It must be the boat," he murmured, turning back for a moment into the room. "I'll go down and see. They may want my help; and we may be able to use your river scheme after all."

"Don't do anything rash, Gassen. A shot out there in the night would rouse the whole city. For God's sake, man, be cautious."

"Oh, to hell with your caution," he muttered as he came out again and went to the stairs. "If I don't come back, you'll know I've taken him down the river."

In a second I had another scheme and one that pleased me better. The only really dangerous man there was Gassen; and I resolved to follow him and tackle him alone.

He all but closed the door of the room after him, and I slipped from my shelter and crept as noiselessly as I could after him.

One of the others heard me, however, and just as I reached the head of the stairs he came out to listen.

"I'm sure I heard something. They must have come. Should we go down? I am afraid of Gassen's rashness."

"Oh, leave him to himself." This was from the man whom Gassen had called Schmidt and who had spoken so little; and at that his companion returned to the room.

I crept on down the stairs, pausing now and then in the half hope that Gassen would return, when I should have a double advantage in my attack—surprise and a greater height from which to strike.

But I reached the door leading to the water front before I saw him.

He was standing on the edge of the wharf, his figure silhouetted sharply against the sheen of the gliding river, shading his eyes as he looked anxiously up stream for some sign of those he was awaiting so impatiently.

I was on the point of making my rush for him, when he turned and looked straight in my direction. I thought he saw me and held my breath in expectation of his attack. But I had presence of mind enough to remain as still as a stone figure.

Then he turned away; and I concluded that I had been too deep in the shadow of the doorway for his eyes to pierce the darkness.

He moved off toward the end of the wharf, and then I saw him start and stare down intently at the river below.

He had discovered the boat which I had fastened there, and he stooped down to examine it closely. Intent upon this he did not hear my steps as I crossed toward him, and when he rose I was close to him and had him covered with my revolver.

His surprise was so complete that he all but staggered backwards into the river. "The Englishman!" he exclaimed with a foul oath, as his hand went to his pocket.

"You won't move," I said in a low tense tone.

He recovered his coolness on the instant. "You daren't fire here," said he.

"You'll see that, if you move."

"How did you get here?"

"Turn round with your back to me."

"What for? What do you want to do?"

"Do as I tell you. Quick."

For a moment he hesitated whether to try the risk of a fight for it; but with a shrug of the shoulders he obeyed.

"Now get down into that boat."

He paused again; and again obeyed.

"Throw those oars out here," I rapped out sternly.

I knew he had a revolver on him and watched him like a lynx. "Well, it's a fine night for the river," he said carelessly as he picked up one of the oars and tossed it on the wharf. I went a little nearer to the edge to watch him more closely as he picked up the other; not for a second suspecting his intention.

"Same place as the other?" he asked in the same indifferent tone.

"Don't fool with me," I cried.

But he did. Just as he seemed about to toss the oar to the side of the other, he swung it round and thrust it violently into the pit of my stomach.

A fool in my unpreparedness I staggered, my pistol dropped from my hand, and the next instant he was back on the wharf with his hand at my throat.

CHAPTER XXIV

FROM PERIL TO PERIL

Gassen was a very heavily built man as well as much more muscular than I; and I should not have had one chance in ten against him in a struggle, even had the conditions been equal.

But they were anything but equal. I had allowed myself to be caught at such a disadvantage that the fight was as good as finished even before it had begun. At the mere force of his rush upon me I went down like a throttled puppy, choking vainly for breath as his fingers played a lively tune on my windpipe.

I knew that he meant to have my life; and I have never been so near death as when I lay staring helplessly up into his eyes, ablaze with the joy of victory and drunk with the lust for vengeance.

My first effort was a desperate attempt to drag his hands from my throat; but although I put out all my strength and squirmed and wriggled and twisted to elude his grip, I could do nothing. His arms were twice as thick as mine and quite as hard; and to stop the twistings of my body he knelt on me, pressing his knees into my ribs and stomach until I thought the bones would crack.

I made frantic struggles for breath under the grim iron ruthless grip of his steely hands; and as I felt the blood congesting in my brain and the deadening sense of suffocation growing, I abandoned all hope and had no longer power to offer resistance.

But even at that instant the luck turned. I was throwing out my hands wildly in vague convulsive movements when my left hand struck against my revolver.

On the instant hope and the love of life revived.

To distract his attention I recommenced to struggle, using my right hand only; and just as he was lifting me up to dash my head against the ground and finish the thing, I fired and shot him in the head.

Death was instantaneous, I think. His grip relaxed and he was falling forward on top of me when I had just sufficient strength left to push him to one side.

I lay still for some moments, incapable of movement, while the effects of the struggle and my terrible fight for breath continued. And at length I sat up, dazed, dizzy and bewildered, until the instinct of self-preservation roused me to effort.

I scrambled to my feet and stood, staggering and shaking like a drunken man, as I looked down at the still body and wondered in a vague dreamy way what I had better do with it. I was in very truth drunk with the peril through which I had passed and with the relief of my unexpected escape from death.

Then I remembered the men in the room above and wondered if they had heard the shot fired, and what they would do in consequence. I had still the work to do which had brought me to the place. For Althea's sake I must go through with it; and the thought of her put fresh strength into me.

My antagonist was lying close to the edge of the water; and this started an idea. I staggered along to the end of the landing stage, unfastened the boat, and dragged it close to where he lay. Then, having taken the precaution to exchange revolvers, that he might appear to have killed himself, I bundled him into the boat, and thrust it out for the stream to carry him where it would.

All the time I had been wondering dimly why the men above

had not come out to learn the reason of the shot; and now I began to wish they would come. I was recovering mastery of both wits and muscles; and perceived that if they would but help me by coming down, I could easily drive them into the river at the point of the revolver, to swim for their lives.

In this hope I waited for what seemed a long time. But either they had not heard the shot or were afraid to venture down.

When they did not come, there was nothing for it but for me to go up again to them. Now that the one desperate man, Gassen, was dead, I feared them no longer. The one man's persistent urging of caution and the other's fear of Gassen led me to believe that they were of the order of men who can plan trouble for others to do but don't care to take a hand in carrying it out.

As they would probably conclude that any noise I made was caused by Gassen returning there was no need for any particular caution; so I ran up the stairs and crossed to the room with a firm tread.

"Was that a shot just now, Gassen?" asked the elder man. "You weren't fool enough to fire at this time of night outside?"

He had barely finished the question when I entered the room, bringing them both to their feet with a cry of surprise.

"Who's Gassen?" I asked. "And where's the Baron von Ringheim?"

"It's the Englishman!" This was from the man of few words; and he clapped his hand to his pocket, so I covered him.

"You can take it out and lay it on the table there," I said sternly.

He fumbled at his pocket in hesitation; but a slight movement of my weapon decided him, and he laid a revolver on the table, which I pocketed.

"Put your hands up, you," I said to the other. He was a man of some fifty years of age and stood staring aghast at me. But he put his hands up and I ran through his pockets to make sure he was not also armed. He was not.

"Now we can talk with less strain. You sent for me to come here to help the Baron. I'm here to do it."

Both were still all but speechless with amazement. "What do you mean?" faltered at length the elder man.

"Wasn't it you who sent for me?"

He fell back into his chair and stared at me in silence, passing his hand across his brow distractedly.

"You'd better begin to think a bit. If you didn't send for me I shall come to the conclusion that you meant to harm him; and in that case we shall quarrel."

"Yes—yes. I did send for you," he answered hesitatingly. "We

165

have managed to save him from the anger of some of those who meant to harm him."

"Then hand him over to me and I'll relieve you of your guard. Where is he?"

He half-turned toward the corner, in where I saw the poor old man lying bound.

"He was very violent and—and we had to—to restrain him, or he would have run into danger."

"You make a poor show as a liar. But never mind; release him."

"We can do it safely now," he said to his companion, adding to me, very nervously: "I am not—not lying. We have saved his life."

"Quick," I said sternly. "As for your not lying, I have been concealed in the warehouse there long enough to hear what has passed."

"Then you know what has become of our friend?" he asked as the other began to set the Baron free.

"He has gone off in a boat."

"But that noise—that pistol shot—was it a shot? It may bring the police here to us."

"I should think it's very likely. You'll be able to tell them how you saved this old man's life," I replied drily. "Not that there seems to be much life left in him," I added as the Baron was brought up to the table and the light of the lamp fell on his bloodless features. It was like the face of the dead.

He was unconscious and I laid him full length on the table and set to work rubbing his hands and chafing his limbs to restore the circulation. While doing this I found the bomb in his pocket and transferred it to mine.

"If he is dead you will answer for it," I said, hot with rage against them. I could detect no pulse and my efforts to restore him appeared to have no effect.

"We have not harmed him, I swear that," declared the elder man.

"Well then, you'd better do your best to restore him."

"He is in your hands now. I cannot remain here any longer."

"Can't you?" The look with which I accompanied the words was enough, and the two of them fell to work with me on the instant.

We succeeded in bringing him round at length; but he was as helpless as a newborn babe; and to get him away from the place by any means short of carrying him was impracticable.

What to do perplexed me infinitely. The time was running away fast; and this threatened a double trouble. The men who had gone in search of me might return; or the police might arrive, either roused

166

by the shot which had killed Gassen or brought by that spy whom I had seen on my arrival.

Either event would be fatal to me.

To add to my exasperation I saw how, fool-like, I had myself destroyed what would have been a feasible means of escape. If I had not sent that boat off with its ghastly burden, I could have used it now; and I cursed myself for my stupidity.

To get another was impossible. I could not leave the place to go and hunt for one, neither could I send the others. I might whistle for a sight of either of them again if once he got his nose outside.

And so far as I could tell, the old man would not be fit to walk for hours. That we should remain there all that time was out of the question of course. But I had to do something; and at length decided to carry him down to the waterside, let the two men go where they would, and hunt up some means of getting the Baron away by water.

"You must carry him down to the air," I said. I was compelled to make them do it lest they should attempt some treachery.

Both were only too glad of the chance of escape thus offered them; and they were in the act of picking him up, when sounds from below reached us.

They dropped him again and stood looking at one another and shaking with fear.

It flashed on me instantly that the police had come; and in order that I might have a plausible tale to tell and appear to have been threatened by my two companions, I ordered them back into a corner of the room and drew out my revolver again.

"Don't you move so much as a finger," I cried. My intention was, of course, to act as if I had rescued the Baron.

But I blundered. It was not the police. Three men came hurrying up the stairs and into the room, and in one of them I recognized the fellow who had been with Gassen at Ziegler's house on the night of the murder.

He recognized me at the same instant. One of the three, not understanding the position and addressing the elder of the two, exclaimed as he entered:

"We haven't got him, general."

"But we have. There he is," cried his companion.

The pause of surprise was broken by a laugh from one of the newcomers. "What the devil does all this mean?" he asked.

At this point the cowardice of the man they had called the "general," promised to stand me in good stead. Watching me carefully, lest I should carry out my threat to shoot him, he stepped forward a pace and said: "There has been a great mistake. Gassen was wrong, and there has not been any treachery. We were just about to leave here."

But the statement was received with a jeering scoff.

"Where are your wits, general?" cried the man who had spoken first, and who appeared to exercise some amount of authority. "We all know that some one betrayed us; and Fritz Gassen was right—it could only be this man." He jerked his hand in my direction. "And we know where he got it from"; and he emphasized this with a nod toward the old Baron lying so still and white on the table. "Didn't he tell us so himself?"

"He does not know what he says; he's out of his mind," was the reply; and for a while they wrangled.

"Well, where's Gassen? He can settle this between us," said the newcomer after a while.

"He has gone"; and the speaker added the story about the supposed shot and subsequent disappearance of Gassen.

The men listened very intently, and kept shooting black angry glances of suspicion at me. They guessed what had occurred.

"Where is he?" they demanded, turning to me, when the "general" finished.

I was on the horns of a dilemma. If I made any show of force I should be giving the lie to the "general's" statement.

"He went off down the river to look for you," I answered.

"'Down' the river?" cried another quickly. "You hear that?"

"Well, up the river then," I said sullenly.

"You shot him. That's the truth," came the retort, sharp as a pistol report.

This appeared to give me the opportunity I sought of being able to take out my revolver without any apparent hostile intention. "Here's my revolver. You can see for yourself it hasn't been fired."

But it was as bad a blunder as I could have made. One of them craned his neck forward as if to satisfy himself of the truth of what I had said; and then gave a cry of rage. "It's Gassen's pistol. There's his mark on it. I know it."

The rest followed his pointing finger.

"Well, anyway it's loaded in all six chambers; and it's the only one that's going to be drawn now." I spoke very coolly and watched the three newcomers closely.

"What about no treachery now?" cried one, turning to the elder man.

"You've brought this on yourselves by suspecting me. You'd better go before there's any trouble," I said to the three. If I could get rid of them, the others would give little trouble enough.

"You'd better go," said the "general" nervously.

They were perplexed what to do, and stood hesitating near the door. The sight of my weapon had a very wholesome restraining effect. One of them began to back out, and it looked as if I was going to get my way and frighten them off.

But just as this appeared most probable and I was beginning to breathe more freely again, trouble came from the man, Schmidt, whom I had treated with contemptuous indifference as of no account.

He had been standing in the corner to which I had thrust him on the arrival of the others, and had not spoken a word. I had almost forgotten him, indeed; but I was to pay for that forgetfulness now.

As I stood facing the others he was on my left hand, and he hurled something at me with great force. It struck my revolver hand and the weapon dropped. When I recovered my surprise I was looking down the barrels of three pistols pointed straight at my head.

"No shooting here, Marx," cried the elder man earnestly. "It isn't safe."

"Why didn't you say that when he was covering us?" was the angrily spoken reply. "He shall pay for Gassen's death."

But terror of the consequences made the man earnest, and for a second he stood right in the way of the pointed weapons. They pushed him hurriedly aside; but I had been able to use the moment. I clapped my hand to my pocket feeling for the weapon I had annexed, but instead I felt the bomb I had taken from the old Baron, and raised it high so that all should see it just as the man was thrust to one side.

"I'll send him to hell for that," declared the more daring man.

"Then we'll all go there together," I cried in a ringing voice. "I can do it with this."

One of them fired at once, and that I was not killed was due only to the "general's" terror. He threw up the fellow's arm as he fired.

"For God's sake," he exclaimed. "Are you all mad?"

"You fool," was the reply. "The thing's only a sham."

Again he was being pushed aside when another man came rushing in.

"The police!" he cried. And at the same instant we heard a loud peremptory knocking at one of the street doors below.

In a moment panic held every man in the room in its thrall. Dead silence fell on us.

But I doubt if any one of them was more utterly confounded than I or more desperately embarrassed. To fall into the hands of the police was better than to be shot down like a dog; but it meant a hundred hazards for me to be caught under such circumstances.

We all stood staring at one another like a set of wax figures, the common peril knitting us together in a bond of panic.

Then the knocking was repeated with even louder clamour than before.

CHAPTER XXV

AN AWKWARD PLIGHT INDEED

The second clamour of the police at the doors below brought me to my senses; and luckily I was the first man to throw off the apathy of alarm which their coming had caused.

If any of us were to escape, it could only be by the river; and I set about making a desperate attempt to get away by that means and to take the Baron with me.

As I had had to carry my life in my hands when coming into the building, and had been fully alive to the fact that my safety might depend upon my knowing how to get out of it again without even a second's hesitation, I had observed with scrupulous care the means of exit.

The room in which we all were was the larger of the pair of offices, the two doors of which I had seen when hiding in the outer warehouse. The partitions were of rough matchboarding, and I noticed now that the door fastened with a spring lock.

The only light we had was from a lantern standing on the table, and my first step was to knock this off the table. I used the instant of consternation which followed to spring at the fellow who had entered last and was holding the door, thrust him away, and slam the door.

The hubbub and confusion which followed were indescribable, and the air reeked with the curses and execrations of the men, who appeared to have only a very slight acquaintance with the plan of the place.

They were all jammed together in a body, close to the door, and struggling, swearing, and fighting one another in their frantic efforts to get out.

170

Not one of them had a thought to spare for the helpless old man on the table, and I picked him up and ran through to the smaller room beyond. One of the five had known of this other exit, and he was at the door as I reached it. He got out before me and turned to call to the rest.

Which of them it was I don't know, but I struck at him and hit him hard enough to send him sprawling along the floor of the warehouse; and before he could regain his feet I was well on my way down the stairs to the wharf.

The police meantime were thundering at the doors which let out upon the lane and beginning to break them in, and as I reached the bottom I heard the men above rushing after me down the stairs. It was a question of seconds now.

I slammed behind me the door which let out on to the wharf, and a glance showed me where the boat lay in which the men had arrived. I darted to it, slid the Baron into the bows, and with my heart in my mouth cast the painter loose and jumped in, just as the rest of the men came streaming out on to the wharf.

They gave a yell of rage as they caught sight of me, and one of them—the brute who had been so in tent on taking my life—ran along the stage and jumped after me.

I had not been able to push the boat off any distance but had seized hold of one of the oars. He landed in the boat, nearly capsizing her; but before he could recover his balance, I thrust the end of the oar into his stomach and sent him overboard.

The next instant I was pulling down stream for my life. The wharf and all upon it were soon lost in the gloom, and the sounds of a struggle, presumably between my late companions and the police, grew gradually fainter and fainter as I increased the distance between us.

I had succeeded in escaping for the moment, but my troubles were by no means over. The men whom my flight had so enraged would tell the police all about me and the direction in which I had gone, and in a short time the river would be alive with parties searching for me.

To remain in the boat for long was therefore out of the question, and yet I could not leave it safely. The trouble was of course what to do with my companion.

But for him, I would have landed at once and have made my way home. But he could not walk a step, and indeed, when I stopped rowing for a moment to examine him, I found that he was once more unconscious.

I considered very carefully whether the really best course in both our interests would not be to abandon him and get my story of all that had occurred to Feldermann or even to Herr Borsen. It was all important that I should get my version of the affair to the authorities first; and I was confident that the knowledge I possessed in regard to von Felsen would enable me to secure the Baron's pardon as well as clear myself.

But I could not face Althea and tell her that I had found her father, that he was desperately ill, but that I had left him drifting in an open boat on the river while I made sure of my own skin.

I must find some other plan than that. By hook or crook I must manage to get him to some sort of shelter. Where to look for one, or even how to set about the search, puzzled me consumedly.

My vague idea was that I might be able to discover some cottage where a few marks would secure what was wanted; and as it was certain that nothing of the sort would be found down the stream and in the middle of the city, I pulled across the river and, hugging the banks as closely as practicable, I doubled on my tracks, and rowed as hard as I could upstream.

I did not get through without a couple of disquieting scares. I had been rowing for a long time and was resting to take breath when I heard the sound of oars in the distance. I could not be certain whether the sound was coming up or down the stream, so I paddled quietly into the side, shoved the nose of the boat into some reeds on the bank, and lay down.

It proved to be a false alarm, however. The boat was coming down stream, and I judged it to be either some early fishermen or some peasants taking produce down to the market.

But this decided me to abandon the river at once. It was now close to the dawn; and if we were seen, the news would be told to any one in pursuit; and my thought was to destroy all traces of our course by sinking the boat.

I rowed across the river again, therefore, and picked up my companion and carried him ashore. This roused him, and as I laid him down he began to babble and chatter with all the inconsequence of an imbecile.

I then undressed and pushed off into the river again, drew out the bung, and wedged the oars under the thwarts. When the boat was nearly full I plunged into the water, hung on to the stern until she sank, and then swam ashore.

While dressing I felt the bomb in my pocket and the revolver which I had taken from the men in the warehouse. The Baron had been watching me with the intent stare of lunacy; but the moment his eyes fell on the bomb, some chain of thought appeared to be linked up in his bewildered wits, and he came at me and tried to get possession of it.

But I flung it far out into the river and sent the revolver after it. This appeared to enrage him; for he began to fight with me with more strength than I could have believed possible after his experiences of the long night of hardship, and kept up an incessant stream of angry invective.

In the midst of it, I heard the throbbing of an approaching launch, and knew at once that this time it must be the police. There was sufficient light now for any one on the river to be able to see us where we were, especially if any sound of his voice attracted their attention.

It was an awkward predicament and a dangerous one too. I had no alternative but to use force. Some bushes were close by, so I caught him up in my arms, thrust one hand over his mouth, and dragged him to shelter, where I had to lie at full length upon him to keep him quiet until the launch had passed.

I told him that the police were close upon us, but he would not or could not understand; and he writhed and wriggled to free himself the whole of the time the launch was passing, and indeed until the snort of its engines was no longer to be heard.

When I released him, he got up and tried to rush away; and again I had to drag him back and use force to hold him. But his efforts had weakened him considerably, or perhaps the paroxysm of rage had passed; for he lay comparatively quiet, while I tried to think what to do next.

I was some miles from the city, in a district of which I knew nothing; the light was strengthening every minute; I had a madman to take charge of; and must either get him back safely and secretly to my house, or at least find some sort of shelter where he could remain under supervision.

The first step was of course to get far enough away from the river bank not to be seen by any one on the look out for us.

But nothing would induce him to leave the waterside. He retained in his poor crazed brain some remnants of recollection of the scheme to destroy the cruiser and the fact that it had to be done on the river, and for this purpose the impulse to stay near the water was irresistible.

I tried to reason with him and to make him understand the danger of his being arrested; every argument and persuasion I could think of: but it was absolutely useless; and when at length I essayed to force him to come away, he set up struggling and yelling.

I had to employ force again. I fastened my handkerchief over his mouth as a gag; for his cries were loud enough to be heard at some distance; and then carried him away across some fields for some few hundred yards.

I began to consider again very carefully whether in both our interests it would not be best for me to abandon him and hurry back to the city alone; but I could not bring myself to desert the helpless old man. I must find some other plan than that. I must get him to some sort of shelter, and that one consideration must determine everything else.

Another spell of weakness followed my last exercise of force; and when I took off the gag and released my hold of him, he remained quiet. I sat and watched him, hoping that he would sleep, and that the sleep would to some extent soothe his excitement and reduce his delirium.

He did fall asleep, and for an hour or so I watched him. He started every now and then and talked a little, murmuring some fragments of sentences. I heard Althea's name, and mine, and stray references to his country; but I paid little attention. The truth was I myself was so overcome with fatigue, that it was with the utmost difficulty I could keep my eyes open.

When he woke, he was much calmer and spoke almost rationally. I explained the position and he seemed to understand it; and when I said our safety depended upon our getting to some place of shelter, he agreed. But I noticed that he would not look me in the face, and kept eyeing me furtively with quick, stealthy glances, lowering his head each time I looked at him.

This was a small matter, however; and as he rose readily to go with me, I was more hopeful than I had been at any time before.

But I found that I was used up. I could scarcely drag one leg after the other; and when after some time I saw a cattle shed with the door invitingly ajar, the desire for rest, the imperative need for it, indeed, took too strong a hold of me to be resisted.

I found some fodder lying in one corner of the place and on this he lay down immediately, declaring that he was worn out, In the hope that the rest, even without sleep, would serve to refresh me, I sat up and watched while he slept as quietly and peacefully as a child.

But nature would not be denied; and when I caught myself nodding drowsily, I fastened his wrist to mine with my handkerchief, and lay back with an intense sigh of relief. I was a light sleeper at all times, and was confident that the least movement of my companion would rouse me.

My confidence was misplaced, however. I must have slept very soundly, for when I woke the sun was high in the heavens streaming in through the wide open door, and a man, presumably the owner of the barn, was standing over me with a pitchfork in his hand, demanding very angrily what I meant by sleeping there.

174

And the Baron was gone!

One end of the handkerchief was still fastened to my wrist, but the other was dangling loose.

"You'll come to the police, you rascal," cried the farmer. "Who are you and what the devil do you mean by being here? Where do you come from?"

He flung the questions at me as I sat up rubbing my eyes and blinking stupidly at him.

I made an effort to rise, but he threatened me with the fork. "Lie still, or you'll have something else than bread in your belly for breakfast," he threatened.

I saw the force of the argument and obeyed. "I am sorry you take it so ill. I have done no harm and——"

I began, but he cut me short.

"No harm, you dirty rascal. It's scoundrels like you that are the pest of the country—lazy, loafing tramps sneaking about and stealing whatever you can lay your hands on"; and he let himself go on what was evidently a sore subject with him. His fury was out of all proportion to the cause of it, even supposing I had been the tramp he deemed me.

To argue with any one in such a rage as possessed him at that moment was obviously useless, however, so I let him storm and abuse me as he pleased. While he held that fork, I knew that any retort from me might make him use it.

He mistook my calmness for fear, and as he warmed to the congenial work of abusing me, he grew more threatening with his weapon, and flourished it about in such a way that I expected any moment to find it plunged into my body. I simulated dire alarm, and cringed and winced at his gestures in a way that gave him huge delight.

But it also led him to give me the chance for which I was waiting; and when at last an opportunity came, I dragged the fork out of his grasp, jumped to my feet, and placed myself between him and the door.

For once at any rate I traded on somebody else's evil reputation. The farmer ran rapidly down the scale through surprise to almost abject fright. He stood shaking in every limb with his eyes darting from the fork to my face, as if he expected me to treat him to the same sort of breakfast as that with which he had so glibly threatened me.

"I didn't mean it," he stammered. "I know you have done no harm. It'll be all right, my man. You can go."

"I'm glad you've changed your tone, but you've made a mistake about me. I hope you can see that."

"I do. I do," he cried readily, his eyes still fixed warily on the pitchfork. I turned and tossed it away behind me, and he heaved a sigh of relief.

"If I have done any harm I'll pay you," I said, taking out some money. "How much? Five marks, ten marks? By the way, what time is it? My watch has stopped," and I pulled it out with a view to impress him still further.

It had the due effect, and his manner changed again; but he was not quite free from suspicion. "I do not charge for such a trifle," he said, with an air of nervous apology mingled with doubt.

"I am quite willing to pay you and quite able to. And if you can give me some breakfast, not of that sort"—I laughed as I pointed round to the fork—"I shall be happy to pay for that also. I lost my way in the night, and overcome with fatigue I lay down to sleep. I had a friend with me, but he must have got up and gone out while I slept. Here, you'll want this, I suppose;" and I picked up the fork and handed it to him. "Shall we walk up to your house? If I had seen it in the night we should have knocked you up."

As I handed him the fork, he looked at me and then a smile spread slowly over his broad face, as my easy manner drove home the conviction that I really was not the desperate character for whom he had mistaken me.

"You can have some breakfast, and welcome; but it's nearer dinner-time. It's close to midday."

I wound up my watch and set it to the correct time, which he gave me. "I suppose you haven't seen anything of my friend?" I asked carelessly.

"No—at least no one who has said anything about having a friend anywhere about here; but we had a stranger at the house this morning asking for some food. But he's a very old man and ill."

It was the Baron, right enough, and the good news excited me greatly.

"That's the man," I cried eagerly. "He is ill. Let's push on to the house at once"; and I hurried on at a rapid pace.

CHAPTER XXVI

A CHARGE OF MURDER

The farmer lumbered along at my side for a while, puffing and blowing hard, and as we climbed a hilly field we had to call a halt.

"I'm not so young as you," he said, gasping and wiping his forehead.

"I'm very anxious to get to my friend," I replied.

"He didn't seem very anxious to see you; at least he didn't say anything about any friend; but it was a hint from him which sent me down to that barn of mine to look for you."

"What did he say?" I asked, seeing that there was something behind his words.

"We've had a very rough character about these parts for some time past—a rascal that has been robbing right and left and has knocked one or two of the neighbours on the head—and I was speaking of him to my wife before the old stranger, and he turned and said he had seen a man of the sort in the barn there."

I laughed but held my tongue.

"You must excuse me, but is there anything funny about the old gentleman? He is a gentleman, of course; I could see that in a twinkle?"

The question gave a hint of the line to take. "Did you notice anything odd about him, then?"

"It's not for me to talk, of course; but my wife thought he was a bit strange in his head."

"Poor old fellow," I replied in a tone of commiseration.

"Ah, I thought as much," was the answer with a note of self-satisfaction. "My wife isn't often wrong. Are you in charge of him so to speak?"

"He is in my charge just at present; but I'm not his keeper, if that's what you mean? He's as harmless as a child; but he fancies himself a desperate conspirator. He's a noble."

"He told us that, but we didn't believe him."

"It's true; and of course his people are well able to pay handsomely for anything that is done for him."

The bait was taken readily. "I shall be glad to help of course if I can."

"If he's still at the house, you can. I want to get on to the city and send his friends out for him. If you could look after him meanwhile, you can name your own price, and I'll pay you something on account of it."

"I suppose he really is harmless. I mean he wouldn't be likely to give any trouble if we kept him in the house?"

"Oh, no chance of it. And certainly not, if you or I were in the room with him. Although of course I must get on to the city. I suppose two or three twenty mark pieces would pay you for a lost day?"

"I should think it would be worth five," he replied with Teutonic aptitude for driving a bargain.

"It's a lot of money; but we'll make it the five with an extra one for the wife, if she looks well after him. I always like the wife to have something."

We came in sight of the house soon after that, and with intense satisfaction I saw the Baron sitting by the door basking in the sunlight. Fearing that possibly he might take fright when he saw me and run away, or do something to scare the farmer from the bargain, I gave the latter a couple of gold pieces as an earnest, and sent him on ahead to get the Baron up into a room.

There was no difficulty. He went up to the Baron, who greeted him with a condescending smile. They spoke together, and I breathed a sigh of fervent thanksgiving when the two went indoors.

That load was lifted from my shoulders, and I followed to the house after an interval. Over a hearty meal I heard that the Baron had been put to bed, where he had fallen fast asleep. I did my utmost to ingratiate myself with both the farmer and his wife, and laughed as heartily as he himself did when he told her how he had treated me in the barn; and with a promise that they should be relieved of their charge as soon as possible, I set off in the farmer's cart for the nearest station on my way back to the city, to relieve Althea's anxiety and send her out to her father's assistance.

The stroke of good luck in finding a shelter for him had raised my spirits, and as I paced up and down the platform of the little by-station, where I had to wait over an hour for the train, I was able to view with comparative ease of mind the complications which still beset me.

My first step was obvious. As soon as I had seen Althea, I would get an interview with Herr Borsen and make a clean breast of everything, both in regard to myself and von Felsen. I was convinced in my own mind that the man who had fired that shot at me after leaving the station had been instigated by him. I had seen him at my house, had recognized him at the station, and again after he had fired at me.

In the face of that, it would be quixotic to wait for further proofs

178

before letting von Felsen feel the weight of my hand. That day should see the end of things so far as he was concerned; I would hand over to Herr Borsen, not only the confession of the theft of the papers, but also that of the murder.

As I recalled my interview with him I saw how he had fooled me, and that his prompt recovery from terror—which I had attributed to his relief at hearing that his life might still be saved—was in reality due to his belief that he could compass my death in time to save himself from all trouble through the revelation of what I had forced from him.

Such a snake as that deserved no mercy, and he should have none.

I anticipated very little trouble in getting out of my own troubles. I had committed no crime. My association with old Ziegler and the men who had been plotting against the Government was in reality innocent enough; and although it was probable that those whom I had outwitted on the previous night would tell of my presence at the wharf and would do all they could against me, the fact that I had gone in search of the Baron would put that right.

The one step which I did regret was that I had had to take the life of the man, Gassen. But it had been done in self-defence. I had not intended to do more than send him adrift in the boat, while his attack on me had meant murder and nothing short of it. But whether it would be prudent to open my lips about it was questionable, and I would await developments before deciding.

Altogether, I was in a very confident mood as I drove from the station to my house, and jubilant in my anticipation of Althea's delight at the good news I could give her about her father.

But instead of having to deliver good news I had to receive bad—the worst indeed. The servants were alone in the house and on the point of leaving it; and I found Ellen sitting disconsolately in the hall, her eyes red with weeping, dressed in her hat and jacket ready to go.

"What is the matter? Where is Fräulein von Ringheim?"

"She has gone, sir. There has been such trouble here. We had the police looking for you, and they searched the house from top to bottom," she wailed, her words interspersed with sobs. "Cook has packed, sir; and I can't stay, if you please."

"Very well, but before you go, try and tell me something more definite."

She fumbled in her pocket and brought out a telegram. "The Fräulein opened it, sir: I didn't; and she told me I must get it to you as it was very important."

179

It was from Bessie and announced her safe arrival in Brussels with "everything." This was one piece of good news at any rate.

"Now, Ellen," I said, turning to question her, "of course you must go away if you wish, and I shouldn't think of stopping you. But I assure you the whole businesss is a mistake somewhere, and you do not run the faintest risk in staying here. Martha has not gone yet?" This was the cook.

"No, sir; but she's just ready."

"Well, while I change and look round, go and tell her to see me before she leaves."

"But the police told us both to go, sir."

"I'm not at all sure that you've had the police here at all. Did the Fräulein go away with them, whoever they were?"

"No, sir. Herr von Felsen was here and was with her when the men were turning the place upside down. You never saw such a mess as they've made of things."

"Never mind the mess. Did he come with them?"

"Just before them, He was very excited and said they were coming."

"What time was that?"

"About midday, sir."

"And when did he leave? Did the Fräulein go with him?"

"Yes, sir. That was about an hour ago."

It was just four o'clock. If I had not had to wait for that train, I should have been in time to take a hand in the business.

"I am quite convinced from your answers that these men were not police, Ellen; but tell me were any of them the men who were watching the house yesterday?"

"Yes, sir. One of them spoke to me yesterday, and it was he who told us to-day that if we didn't go we should be in trouble. He behaved shameful, and wanted to put us out there and then without our boxes; but cook she up and told him she wasn't going without hers, and then he gave us an hour to clear out in."

"Well done, Martha," I exclaimed, as the cook came downstairs. I explained to her that the men had not been the police, and endeavoured to allay the fears of them both.

I succeeded after some difficulty, and they agreed to remain.

"That fellow said he'd come back in an hour to see that we had gone," said Martha, a woman with a great deal of spirit. "I hope he will come"; and she nodded her head with an emphasis which promised him a warm reception.

"I don't expect you'll see him here again. Now, a last question. Did they say anything to you about the supposed crime for which I was to be arrested?"

"They went on awful about you, sir," replied Martha. "You was a conspirator, and a murderer, and you'd either run away to get out of their hands or had killed yourself; and I don't know what else. But you were never coming back. That was certain."

"Well, here I am, you see; so you can tell how much to believe of the rest."

"They said they had warrants for you, sir," put in Ellen. "They showed me some papers; and the Fräulein told me afterwards they had, and that she was going away in order to prevent any harm coming to you."

"Well, we'll soon have things all right again," I replied, and went off to change my clothes and view the results of the men's work.

I thought I could understand it all, I guessed that the man who had fired at me on the previous night had mistaken my fall for the result of his shot, and had accordingly reported that the attempt had been successful. With me out of his way, von Felsen had only to recover possession of the stolen paper, the keys and the confessions he had written, to find his hand once more on the controlling lever of everything so far as Althea was concerned.

That was what the search meant, and that it had been complete, the evidence of my own eyes showed. But it had not been successful, any the more for that. The stolen paper was safe in Brussels, and I had been in such a cyclone hurry to get after the Baron on the previous night, that I had not stayed to look the other things up, but had thrust them into the first place which had caught my eye. This had been the large upright iron stove in the hall among the kindling wood and paper. And there I found them.

Almost every other conceivable nook and cranny in the house which would have served for a hiding-place had been ransacked, and every desk and drawer opened and searched. It was a stupendous piece of luck.

A moment's reflection decided me to leave them where they were. My first task must be to find Althea. Her safety was much more to me than my own, and she was not safe for a single second of the time she was with von Felsen.

It was an easy guess that his failure to find what he had sought so drastically would put him in a very ugly mood, and even his belief in my death would not suffice to ease his mind. So long as that evidence of his crimes remained in existence, it was liable to fall into the hands of some one who would be able to use it with disastrous results to him.

I would have given much to know the story he had told to Althea. He would not say a word about my supposed death, and the

181

servants' references to the warrants for my arrest suggested the line he had taken.

He would seek to prey upon her fears both for her father and myself, and pose as being still in a position to save us both. If he had done that I had no doubt that he would drive her to consent to marry him; and my fear was that, exasperated by not having found what he sought and needed so desperately, he would rush matters to a crisis at once.

I hurried at once to von Felsen's house, but only to find it shut up. I knocked and rang several times without result, and in the end had to turn away baffled and a prey to fresh fears and apprehension.

Where to look for him I had no idea, nor where to look for Althea of course. I had felt so certain of finding them both at the house that the sting of the disappointment was all the more disconcerting.

It flashed across my thoughts that possibly Althea might have gone back to her own house, or might have communicated with Chalice in some way during my absence; and acting on the impulse, I jumped back into the cab and told the man to drive me there.

On the way another thought occurred to me: Hagar Ziegler. She might know where to tell me to look for von Felsen; and I was putting my head out of the window to give the driver the fresh direction, when we pulled up at Chalice's house.

As I should lose no more than a few minutes in seeing her, I ran up to the door, and when the servant opened it I sprang up the stairs without wasting the time to be announced, dashed into her room, and, without an apology for my abruptness, asked if Althea had been there.

Chalice jumped to her feet on my entrance, stared at me as if I were a lunatic, and then backed and laid her hand on the bell-pull.

"Why do you come here? I can't help you, Herr Bastable. You must know that."

"You can answer my question at any rate. Fräulein Althea is missing from my house and I am searching for her. Has she been here?"

She fixed her eyes on me with an expression of bewilderment. "She can't help you to escape; and of all houses in Berlin this is the last you should have come to."

"For Heaven's sake do give me an answer. Can't you see I am on fire with impatience? Every minute may mean ruin to her."

She bent toward me and came a step or two forward. "Do you mean you don't know? You must not stay here. It will ruin me if you are found here. Do you mean that you don't know?

"Know what?" I cried angrily in my exasperation.

182

"Good heavens! Why, that you are accused of the murder of Hagar Ziegler's father!"

CHAPTER XXVII

ONCE AGAIN IN THE TOILS

When Chalice's appeal to me to leave the house at once elicited no response from me—I was indeed too staggered for the moment by her news, and sat groping blindly for some clue to its real significance—her eager insistence gave way to despair at the thought of the possible consequences to herself.

"You will ruin me!" she cried vehemently; and throwing herself on to a couch she burst into an hysterical flood of tears.

She could have used no stronger weapon, and I pulled myself together. I knew her grief was utterly self-centred; but the sight of her tears had that dismaying effect which most men will appreciate, so I rose at once. "Tell me quickly all you know and I'll go," I said. "And the sooner you tell me, the sooner I shall be away."

This had the desired effect. She choked down her ready sobs. "Fräulein Ziegler telephoned to the Steiners, the people of the house here, about half an hour ago to ask if you had been here; and the daughter came up to ask me where you were, adding that you were wanted by the police for—for that awful thing. For Heaven's sake don't let them find you here. They will connect me in——"

"Never mind that," I cut in abruptly. "They won't do anything of the sort. I had no hand in it at all. Fräulein Ziegler herself knows that perfectly well. But there is something you must do at once. Fräulein Althea has disappeared from my house and I am searching for her."

"She is not here and has not been here," she interrupted. "And if they find you——"

Not a thought for Althea. Everything for herself. "Listen, please, and then do what I tell you. I want to tell her that her father is lying ill in a farm-house, and that she must go at once to see to him and bring him back to the city. As she has been taken away, you must go and care for him;" and I told her where and how to find the Baron.

But she burst into vehement protests. "Why should I go? It is

Althea's matter. He is not my father. He has never done anything for me. Why then should I run this risk? Where could I take him?"

In disgust at this incessant note of self, I resumed my seat and said curtly: "I will wait here while you settle that."

"You wish to ruin me!" she cried again.

"No. I am only warning you. If some one does not go to him and take care that he is placed in safety, he will do some mad thing and then you will be ruined."

"But what can I do? He would not come with me. Oh, you are cruel. You know how helpless I am. No one thinks of me. Althea should be here."

"You can go out and stay with him, paying the people there to look after him until I can arrange something else."

"Stay with him! Are you mad? My concert! My practising! Herr Grumpel!"

"There will be no concert for you if he breaks loose. There will be a prison instead for you as well as for the rest of us."

"But you? Why do you not go?"

"I have to find Fräulein Althea."

"She would not have you sacrifice my future in this way. Oh, how selfish you all are! All in league against me!"

"I have warned you, and can do no more now. If you do not go out and arrange for him to be kept safely where he is, you may as well leave Germany by the next train for all the hope you will ever have of succeeding here. That is my last word; if you wish to sing at that concert, you will go instantly and do what I have said."

I turned to leave her then, and as I reached the door it was opened quickly from without and a woman of about thirty entered. She started at seeing me, and stood holding the handle of the door and staring at me.

"Fräulein Steiner!" exclaimed Chalice, in some dismay.

"Lotta told me Herr Bastable was here. I came to see."

"Yes, I am Herr Bastable."

"I beg your pardon," she said, nervously stepping back and making as if to close the door again.

"I will come with you," I said, following her out. "Probably you wish to telephone to Fräulein Ziegler that I am here. With your permission I will speak to her myself."

She was trembling a little. "She asked me to let her know," she faltered. "She is holding the 'phone now."

"She will recognize my voice over the wire. I will save you the trouble. A very serious mistake has been made"; and when we reached the hall, I went to the instrument at once. "Are you there?"

"Who is that?" came the reply in Hagar's voice.

"Mr. Bastable. I am just leaving the house here—Frau Steiner's. I must see you at once. I have just learnt that you have been deceived in regard to me, and I can tell you the whole truth about your father's death, and can put the proofs of what I have to say into your hands. I do not blame you for what you have done; but before you do any more, please see me."

"What have you to say? It is too late now."

"It will be too late if you do not see me at once. It is about Herr von Felsen. You will repent it all your life if you do not see me."

"Wait a moment." I heard the faint echo of a conversation; and then she asked: "Will you come here?"

"Who is with you?"

There was another pause. "Herr von Felsen," she replied then to my infinite surprise and relief.

"Yes. I will come at once."

"Wait a minute, he wishes to speak to you himself."

"Of course I will," I replied eagerly. I waited; but no sound came over the wire; and when I spoke there was no reply.

In a flash I saw the plan. I dropped the receiver and hurried out of the house on the instant. The intention was to keep me at the instrument until the police would have time to come and arrest me.

I jumped into the first cab I met and drove by a circuitous route to my own house. As they believed they could put their hand on me at once, I calculated that I should have time to get home, change into some sort of disguise, get the papers from their hiding-place and set out in search of Althea.

Von Felsen's presence at Hagar's house had at first baffled me as completely as this last move—the preposterous charge of murder; but I began to see the meaning of all. He had probably found difficulty in dealing with Althea and had also heard that the previous night's attempt on my life had failed. This had cornered him.

He knew that his breach of faith would cause me to denounce him, and in his desperation he had resolved to charge me with the murder and thus get me held by the police. This would give him the time he needed to carry out his plan with regard to Althea.

It meant more than even that to him, indeed. It would both prejudice any statement I might make impugning him, and at the same time very probably enable his father's agents to regain possession of the confessions he had made.

It was a very ominous outlook; but it had a redeeming feature. If my reading of the case were right, it was clear that so far Althea was safe. And the reasons which had forced him to leave her while he returned to Hagar, to use the latter in this way, were likely to be strong enough to prevent his purpose with her until he could satisfy her of my actual danger. In other words until he had secured my arrest and could carry to her the proofs from the police themselves.

But it was only a question of a few hours at most. If I remained in the city I should soon be caught; and remain I must of course.

My first thought was to get the papers which were of such vital import, and take them straight to Herr Borsen or to Feldermann; but there was a risk to Althea in that which alarmed me.

If von Felsen heard of it—and he was almost sure to learn it immediately—he would be driven to bay; and in that mood ready to do her any violence.

I guessed that in regard to her he was calculating that, if he could once force her to become his wife, I should hold my hand rather than bring all the shame and trouble upon her, consequent upon his having to answer for the murder of the old Jew. And the problem I had to face was how to use the hour or two of freedom so as to find the means of checkmating his designs upon Althea.

I could see only one way—through Hagar herself.

If she had not been hopelessly poisoned against me by von Felsen's story, I was confident that I could work upon her jealousy and set her to hound him down; and thus prevent mischief.

By the time I reached my house I had a crude sort of plan. Among the relics of my private theatrical days I had a suit of workman's overalls; and, dressed in these and carrying a small bag of tools, I could manage to escape the notice of any of the police to whom my face was not too familiar.

I told the two servants that, as I was now in some trouble they had better leave the house at once. Then I hunted up the disguise, slipped the overalls over my own clothes, secured the papers and set off to find Hagar.

As I hurried along in the direction of her house I had to pass my old office and the thought occurred to me to put the papers I carried into safe hands. Bassett was the very man for such a purpose. So I went up to him, and explained that I was likely to be arrested on a false charge. I wished him to hold them for me until I could communicate with him again. This precaution would, at any rate, frustrate the efforts of von Felsen to get hold of them.

To obtain an interview with Hagar was a very different matter, however. I hung about the house for some time at my wits' end for an excuse to get inside; and when at length I began to fear that my movements would be regarded as suspicious, I put as bold a face on matters as I could, and rang the bell intending to ask for her openly.

Just as the servant opened the door I changed my tactics. "I'm sorry to have been so long in coming, but the boss kept me. I'll soon put it all right, however," I said coolly and stepped inside.

The girl stared at me as if I were a lunatic. "What is it?" she asked.

"This is Fräulein Ziegler's, isn't it?"

"Yes, of course. But what do you want?"

"She has just telephoned to the exchange that something is wrong with one of the instruments. Is it the office one?"

"What is that, Rebecca?" It was Hagar's voice.

"There is a man here who says he has come to see to the telephone," was the reply as the servant went toward her mistress.

"I'll soon have it right," I declared, and took advantage of the moment to step into the office. I knew the way well enough, of course.

"There is a mistake somewhere," said Hagar; and, as I had calculated, she followed me into the office.

I began to fool about with the instrument, keeping my back to her for the moment. "We had a message," I growled, altering my voice, and speaking in a tone of a man with a grievance.

"There is nothing the matter with that," she said quickly, crossing to me.

"I'll see to it all right," I mumbled, bending over the instrument.

"I tell you it's a mistake," she rapped back sharply, and tapped me on the shoulder. "Don't meddle with it."

I affected to take umbrage at this. "Oh, all right," I muttered and crossed to the door as if in a huff. A glance showed me that the servant had gone; so I shut the door and turned round.

She recognized me instantly. Her lips moved as if uttering my name, but no sound came. She flashed one rapid glance over my workman's garb, and her eyes lighted angrily as they met mine in a long steady stare, while she was thinking what to do.

"I have come prepared to answer the charge Herr von Felsen has induced you to bring against me; but we must have a square talk first. Then you can send for the police if they are not already in the house."

She did not take her eyes from mine while I spoke, and made no reply. Her eyes were as hard as flints; and my task began to look hopeless.

"I see you have made up your mind; yet you might remember that I saved your life that night."

Her lip curled. The only comment; but more eloquent than many words.

"I know the whole truth about that night's black work, and what brought those men to your house."

Her agitation and rage were mounting fast and after a pause she burst out bitterly: "Of course you do. The chief of them slept that night in your house and has been concealed there ever since. Do you dare to deny it?"

"Whom do you mean?" Her lip curled again and she shrugged her shoulders. "You mean Baron von Ringheim? Von Felsen has told you that?"

She gave an impatient gesture. "It is the truth that matters, not how I know it," she retorted.

"On the contrary his motive is everything. But he kept that to himself, of course. Did he tell you that he came here with these lies in order to get you to accuse me so that he should have time to force Baron von Ringheim's daughter to marry him?"

"You lie," she cried fiercely. "You were seen to enter and leave this house shortly before I met you that night. The ring I saw on your finger was his and he had left it with my father that afternoon. And if that is not enough proof, one of your associates has shot himself, leaving behind him a confession that he and you together murdered my father in revenge for his supposed betrayal of you. Do you think I have forgotten your agitation when I recognized the ring?"

Von Felsen had told his story cunningly, and what she had termed my agitation at her recognition of the ring on the night of the murder lent colour to it. My conduct was quite open to such a misconstruction as she had placed upon it; but there was no time to attempt to shake her conviction by argument.

I paused a second in doubt as to the line to adopt, and she read this hesitation for guilt. "You cannot answer me; but you shall pay the price."

"If you persist in this folly, it is you who will pay the price. Von Felsen went to my house to-day in my absence and compelled Fräulein von Ringheim to go with him and consent to become his wife upon certain conditions. In order to be able to appear to be in a position to fulfil these conditions, he came here to you to get me arrested on this ridiculous charge. No one in the whole empire knows better than he that there is not a glint of truth in the story. But you have fallen into the trap, and within an hour of my arrest, Fräulein von Ringheim will be his wife."

"It is false," she exclaimed vehemently. "To-night we are to be married."

I smiled. "Where is he? Set him face to face with me and force him to let her be present; and you will see."

This fired her jealousy. "It is false," she cried again; but her tone was less vehement and her eyes signalled doubt. "You say this to turn my anger against him, that you may escape. You shall not."

"Can you find him? He is not in his house in the Coursenstrasse. He knew I should seek him there. Can you take me to him?"

She paused and then with a hard contemptuous smile replied: "So that you may find a chance to escape on the way? I can trust you no longer."

"Did I not come here knowing full well the charge you have made against me? Should I have come if I were guilty? Be reasonable."

"I do not trust you," she repeated.

"It is sheer madness," I cried in desperation. "You are wasting hours that may mean everything to both of us for all our lives. Name what conditions you please, and I will accept them. I will go to him with you under arrest, if you like. Will that prove to you I am in earnest?"

She paused and then nodded eagerly. "Yes, yes. If you dare to do that."

I crossed to the telephone to call up Feldermann.

She watched me closely and as I passed her, shrank out of my way lest I should touch her. I affected not to notice the gesture and stood at the instrument with my back to her.

But the next instant I heard her open the door and turned to meet her eyes fixed on me with a glance of vindictive triumph. "You shall be arrested, as you say," she cried, and rushed away slamming the door behind her.

Just then the answer came through. "Is that Herr Feldermann?"

"Yes. What is it? Who are you?"

"Mr. Bastable. I am at Ziegler's house and have heard I am charged with having murdered him. Can you come at once? I have a——"

"Charged with what?" The tone was one of intense astonishment.

"Murder. I want you here at once."

"Are you out of your mind? There's no such charge——"

I heard no more, for the door was flung open, and two men in police uniform rushed in and dragged me violently away from the telephone, as Hagar followed.

"That is the man. I charge him with the murder of my father," she cried.

Too late I saw the trap into which I had walked. "These are not

189

the police," I protested to her. "I have telephoned to Herr Feldermann. This is a trap. They are von Felsen's——"

"We'll show you if we're not the police," cried one of them as he slipped a pair of handcuffs on my wrists. "No more talking here"; and he whipped out a revolver and ordered me to hold my tongue and go with them. "Bring her on to the station to make the charge there," he added to a third man who had entered.

I shouted a last protest to Hagar, but a hand was clapped over my mouth and I was hurried out of the house toward a carriage which was waiting at a few yards' distance.

At that moment a motor car came slowly along the street and passed me as I walked between the two men in uniform.

I called out and this drew the eyes of the occupants upon me.

One was von Felsen, who leered at me in triumph; and by his side sat Althea, pale and distressed at seeing me thus handcuffed in the hands of the police.

As she fell back, burying her face in her hands, the chauffeur quickened the speed of the car and it whisked round a corner just as I was bundled into the carriage.

CHAPTER XXVIII

DRAGEN AGAIN

I had made a pretty mess of things, and now that it was too late I began to appreciate what a fool I had been.

Von Felsen had outplayed me at every point, and chance and my own folly had helped him to score a complete victory.

The charge of murder was the merest bluff, and he had imposed upon Hagar for the purpose very cleverly. He had probably found Althea unexpectedly resolute not to yield to his wishes without some actual proof of my arrest, and had then vamped the charge, through Hagar, and planned that Althea should see me in the hands of men in police uniform.

He had calculated that, relying upon my ability to clear myself of the charge in Hagar's eyes, I should go at once to her to get her assistance in tracking Althea; and I had walked straight into the trap.

I had of course been closely shadowed, and as soon as I had reached Hagar's house, he had been informed, and had brought Althea in the car to be a witness of the arrest.

With one cunning stroke he had thus got rid of me, had convinced Althea of my arrest, and probably freed himself from the embarrassment of Hagar at the same time. I did not doubt that the men he had taken to her house would see that she gave no sort of trouble.

These thoughts flashed through my mind in the few seconds after I was in the carriage, together with some exceedingly disquieting speculations on my own plight. It was about as bad as it could be, but I was not going to give up all hope without an effort.

The men thrust me into a corner of the back seat, and one of them held a revolver close to my head, threatening to fire if I made any trouble.

But this did not scare me as badly as they thought. I knew they would not dare to shoot me in the street. Their own safety would be endangered, and the risk was too great for them to run it except in the last resort.

I affected to be very frightened, however, and waited for a chance to try and attract attention and bring help. The opportunity came as the carriage had to stop when crossing one of the main streets.

With a sudden kick I broke the glass of the window near me and gave a yell for help. The fellow opposite seized my legs while his companion thrust his hand over my mouth. But I wrestled violently, and in the midst of the struggle a policeman's head appeared at the window of the carriage.

"What's the matter there?" he asked.

"I think you'd better get in and give us a hand," answered one of my guards very coolly. "He's a lunatic; just cut his wife's throat."

The man's coolness and his uniform had the effect of quieting all suspicion. "All right. Strap his legs and gag him, why don't you? Don't let him make that racket."

I got my head free then. "I am an Englishman, these are not——" I began when I was silenced again.

"He's been yelling that all the time," was the reply, with an oath and a laugh. "I wish you'd lend a hand. We don't want to hurt him."

"I can't come. Drive on there," he told the coachman; and on we went.

As soon as the policeman's face disappeared from the window, the fellow at my side flung me heavily back into the corner of the carriage, and together they fastened a large handkerchief over my mouth, one of them twisting his fingers into it so tightly behind my head that I was powerless to open my lips. And he held me in this fashion for nearly all the rest of the drive.

Further resistance was now out of the question. I had made my effort and it had failed, and all I could do was to keep still and wait with such resignation as I could summon for what was to come to me.

If I escaped with my life, I should have reason to be thankful. I had already had ample proof that the men whom von Felsen employed were quite capable of going to any extreme. My life had been attempted more than once; and at the time of the previous abduction, when I had not been nearly so dangerous to him as now, I had only escaped death by the narrowest of margins.

Yet it was not for myself that I was mainly afraid now. Von Felsen had so planned things that Althea had been persuaded of my arrest; and I could not doubt for an instant that she would at once agree to do anything he demanded. That night she would certainly consent to the marriage; and the thought was like the sear of a hot iron on a nerve.

Compared with the agony of that dread, nothing else seemed to matter. I would cheerfully have given my life to have saved her from such a fate; but even if I lost my life now, I should be powerless to help her.

Maddened by this reflection, I made another and desperate struggle with my captors. Wrenching myself free from the gag which held me like a vice, I fought and kicked and writhed, yelling for help at the top of my lungs all the while in a furious effort to escape.

But it was useless. Both were strong men, and they overpowered me and forced me down, this time on to the floor of the carriage, and held me there until we stopped. One point only did I gain by the effort. One of the handcuffs came unfastened and could not be relocked on my wrist.

But this did not help me much. One of the brutes seized my arms and held them behind my back, and twisted them till I thought the very sinews would break.

I did not give in until my strength was utterly exhausted and my head reeled dizzily; and in this condition, with no power left for resistance, I was hauled out and carried rapidly into a house.

There I was gagged again, my arms and legs were tied, and I was flung down on the floor of an empty room, the door of which was locked upon me.

Bruised and sore from head to foot although I was, and aching in every muscle of my body, I thought nothing of my hurts. I was on fire with impotent rage and belated repentance for my stupidity. Only an hour or two before I had had the upper hand. There was apparently nothing to prevent my gaining a complete victory. If I had only gone straight to Feldermann or Herr Borsen, von Felsen would now have been grovelling at my feet begging for mercy.

What a credulous fool I had been to believe for an instant that that ridiculous charge of murder had really been made! What would I not have given to have been able to set the clock back for those few hours!

Gnashing my teeth at my idiotic blundering, I passed hours of torture. I was left alone, except that now and again the door was opened and some one came in with a lantern to see that I was still securely fastened.

I abandoned all hope, and each time I heard the key turned in the lock, I made up my mind that some one was coming to take my life. I grew utterly reckless also, and slowly a fresh thought began to take shape in my mind.

Save my life I could not, but if a chance came I would at least send one of the scoundrels who had taken a hand in the business to his last account. It was just a wild impulse to have revenge; but I hugged it close to my heart until it became my one cherished object, the one thing I could do before they took my life.

That thirst for revenge, that lust for blood, if you like, put strength into me, gave tone to my nerves and purpose to my thoughts when all else in that hour of black despair had failed.

I began to test the strength of the bonds which held me, and gradually to loosen them slightly, as I tugged at the cords which bound my arms and strove with frantic struggles to ease the pressure of those on my legs.

The exertion brought the sweat of effort and pain to my brow; but I was nearly what they had termed me, a madman, in my furious desire for revenge; and although every movement racked and tortured me, I did not cease until I had so far succeeded that the blood began to flow freely once more in my veins.

Faint and exhausted at last with the struggle, I was lying quiet, to regain strength for a further effort, when the key was turned in the lock once more. This time two men entered; the gag was taken from my mouth, and I was ordered roughly to sit up.

I took no notice of this. It was my cue to affect to be helpless. One of them dragged me to the wall and propped me up in a sitting posture, while the other held the lantern close to my face.

A movement of the light enabled me to see his face, and I recognized him. He was Dragen, the man who had carried me off before.

"Ah, you know me, I see," he said with a chuckle. "That will save

193

trouble perhaps, as you'll know I'm not likely to let you fool me a second time."

The wild desire to take life which had so possessed me before now focussed into a set purpose that his should be the life; and I lowered my eyes quickly lest he should read something of the thought in my mind.

"You know what we want, Mr. Englishman, and what we mean to have. Those papers. Where are they?"

I made no reply, and he thrust his hands into all my pockets to search for them. A bitter oath showed his disappointment. I smiled in triumph; and this so exasperated him that he struck me in the face.

Then I understood why I was still alive. Until those papers were regained, von Felsen knew that he would be in danger of losing everything despite his present victory over me.

"You are a brave fellow, Dragen, to strike a helpless man."

He raised his hand to repeat the blow, but his companion stopped him. "What's the good of that?" he said gruffly. "You know what we were told."

"Hold your tongue, curse you," cried Dragen. "I mean to get them, and shall go my own way to do it. Where are they?" he demanded of me.

"What papers do you mean?"

"To hell with your questioning me. You know what I mean. Where are they?"

"You think you can make me tell you?"

"I'm sure I can," he retorted with an oath.

"Try then;" and I looked up and met his angry eyes firmly.

"Give them up and no harm shall come to you."

"This looks like it, doesn't it?"

"Don't you anger me, or it'll be the worse for you."

"You can only take my life, but even then you can't save your employer's; nor your own, for the police know all about that other affair."

"You'll be short of breath long before you get a chance of saying any more about that or this."

"That's only what I know already. If I were to tell you where the papers are, I might whistle for a chance of getting out of this. But I'll tell you one thing. They are in the hands of those who will know how to use them, whether I am alive or dead, by this time to-morrow morning. Do what you will."

This infuriated him, and he seized and shook me violently in an uncontrollable frenzy of rage, and then flung me down violently on the floor. He caused me severe pain; but except for this, the rough handling benefited me rather than him. He had seized me by the arms, and the cords on my wrists were perceptibly slacker for the severe shaking.

My head struck the floor heavily when he threw me down, and I lay still as a corpse, letting all my muscles relax and breathing as slightly as possible, that he should think I was on the verge of unconsciousness.

He questioned me again about the papers, but I gave no sign that I even heard him; and when he kicked me and then tugged at my arms and lifted my head in the effort to rouse me, I made no sign of life.

The second man was scared at this. "You've done for him now," he muttered.

"Serve him right," growled Dragen, with a savage oath. "He tricked me before."

"But what about serving me? What's the good of this to me? How are we going to earn the money, with him in this state?"

Dragen swore again and was aiming a vicious kick at my head when his companion stopped him so suddenly that he overbalanced and fell to the ground close to me. In the fall something dropped from his pocket and rolled near me. It was a small sheath knife, and to my infinite delight neither man saw it.

Dragen rose in a rage and a fierce quarrel broke out between the two. This enabled me to shift my position unobserved, so that I first lay on the knife and then rolled forward until my hands could reach it, when I tucked it up underneath the back of my waistcoat.

The quarrel ended without blows; and presently they drew aside and talked together in low muttered tones, the purport of which I could not hear. After a time they crossed and looked at me, and the fellow who had been protecting me from Dragen's violence knelt down and tried to feel my pulse. He was clumsy at the business, however, and could not find it. "I believe you've finished him," he muttered and laid me down gently at full length and loosened the cords on both wrists and legs, and began to chafe my limbs to restore circulation.

"That's better," he said at length, feeling again for my pulse and finding it this time. "Get him some brandy or something. But you'd better do what I said, Dragen," he added, rising. "If those papers are in safe hands, as he said, we'd better know what to do next."

The man's evident alarm infected Dragen. "Curse the whole business," he growled uneasily.

"That won't help us far. If you hadn't been in such a devil of a rage, this wouldn't have happened." Then he knelt down by me again. "Can you hear me?" he asked anxiously. "No harm will come to you. Can you hear me?"

My reply was the faintest of faint moans.

"He's coming round all right. Get him some brandy and don't let him see you, and we'll have him round all right," he said in a tone of great relief, as he rose once more. "I'm for fetching him; let's see what the others say," he declared as he picked up the lantern. "We must know what to do next."

There was another conference, and then they went away together, leaving the door unfastened.

In another moment I had slipped my hands out of the cords which had been so considerately loosened and with the knife I cut those which bound my legs. Then I kicked off my boots and stole out of the room in my stockinged feet, resolved to make a fight for my freedom.

The passage outside the room was in darkness; but I knew in which direction I had been carried into the room, and crept noiselessly toward the front door of the house.

But there was a room between, the door of which stood open. I heard the voices of the men there, and one of them was standing close to the door. To pass this meant a great risk of being either seen or heard, and as I hesitated whether to take the chance I caught fragments of the talk.

They were discussing the advisability of fetching some one or of going to some one for further instructions in view of my statement about the papers being in the hands of those who would use them.

Presently the man by the door, interested in the discussion, went a little way into the room, and I seized that moment to creep past.

The house had double doors, and the inner one was pressed back against the wall. I ran my fingers lightly up and down the outer one searching for the fastenings, when a general scuffling of feet in the room announced that the men were moving, having apparently come to a decision.

I slipped back and hid behind the inner door and held my breath as they came out into the passage, talking excitedly.

The suspense of those few moments was more trying than words can describe.

I had failed to find the means of opening the front door; and if they went back into the room where I had been lying, I should be caught like a rabbit in a snare. The instant I was discovered my life would not be worth a spent match.

They stood wrangling in the passage for a time that seemed an age to me in my excited suspense; and every second I expected one or other of them to go back to the room and then announce my flight.

"Well, let's have a look at the beggar first and see if we can't drag it out of him," said one, whose voice I recognized as that of the man who had been standing by the door.

They moved in a body toward the room.

My heart sank and I gave myself up for lost. My only chance, and that the faintest and feeblest, was that I might seize the moment of respite to get the door of the house open.

CHAPTER XXIX

JUST IN TIME

But just when matters appeared to be at their worst, the luck turned. The man who had prevented Dragen before intervened now.

"You can get him some brandy and he'll be all right."

"Where is it?" came the reply; and there was a pause.

"I shan't wait," said the former speaker again. "I shall take the risk of going. Fritz is just below with the horses. If there's any violence before we get back, you'll have to answer for it."

"Answer to hell," growled Dragen fiercely.

"I shall split on the whole thing if there is, mind that," retorted the other in quite as angry a tone; and he passed my hiding-place, opened the door, and went out.

He tried to close it sharply behind him; but I took a risk at that moment and thrust my foot in the way. Fortunately he was in too bad a temper to care whether he left it open or shut, and ran down the steps.

Some one laughed.

"Pigheaded fool," growled Dragen.

"Would he split?" asked another nervously.

"Perhaps the beggar's well enough to talk now. Let's see."

"Bring the lantern," said another, and the shuffling of feet followed.

I dared not wait any longer; and moreover I had another plan now than merely to escape. I guessed that the man I was following meant to go to von Felsen; and I meant him to take me with him.

I opened the door stealthily and slipped out. The carriage was some twenty yards away, and I darted toward it. My lack of boots rendered my footfalls absolutely silent, and I reached it, unseen and unheard, just as the man had got in and was turning to shut the door.

In the darkness he mistook me for one of his companions, "Coming, after all, are you?" he asked. I jumped in and he himself closed the door with a slam, and the carriage started.

Before he had time to see his mistake my hand was on his throat and my knife threatened him. "If you care for your life, keep silent," I cried between my clenched teeth.

For a few moments, precious as gold to me, surprise kept him quiet. I knew that my escape must already have been discovered, and I expected to hear the cries and shouts of the rest calling to us to stop.

Then he began to struggle.

"Keep still," I said fiercely. "I mean you no harm; but if you try to resist, I'll plunge this into your heart as surely as there is a living God."

At that moment came the cries behind us which I had feared; and the driver began to check the horses.

"Tell him to drive on, or you'll not live another second," I hissed, releasing my grip on his throat so that he could speak.

He hesitated and I raised the knife higher as if to strike.

"It's all right, Fritz. Get on as fast as you can," he called.

I drew a breath of intense relief. I had him now, and he was in deadly fear for his life. I ran my hand quickly over him and found his revolver and took it.

"Have you a knife?" His hand went to it. "Throw it on the front seat there."

He obeyed me and I tossed it out of the window. Then I sat down opposite to him and let him get back his scared wits.

He stared at me helplessly cowed by the suddenness of the attack and overawed by the weapon with which I kept him covered. I, in my turn, watched him quite as closely while I considered what line to take.

That he was going to von Felsen I had convinced myself; and I meant to go with him if I had to compel him to lead the way with my pistol at his head. But I had no wish to use force if any other means could be found.

I was not without hope of this. His fear about the money reward being lost if I came to harm, his squeamishness on the score of violence, his threat to tell what he knew, and his ready submission now, all tended to suggest that he was of a very different type of scoundrel from Dragen and the rest.

I gave him five minutes in which to pull himself together and then opened fire.

"You've made a pretty bad mess of all this," I said sharply.

He gave an uneasy start at the sound of my voice, but did not reply.

"You were in the thing to take my life, you know, and you can probably see your finish by now."

"I didn't threaten your life. Dragen would have done for you just now when you were insensible if I hadn't stopped him," he answered after a pause.

"I wasn't insensible. I know what passed."

"Then you know what I say is true," he said with a note of eagerness.

"Yes, I know it." I paused to see if he would volunteer anything more. He did not however. "If you like to answer my questions I may make things easier for you. Where are we going?"

He paused a long time before replying. "What are you going to do with me?"

"Shoot you if you try any pranks; hand you over to the police if you force me; give you your liberty and pay you well if you come over to my side in the affair and make a clean breast of the whole thing."

He chewed this in silence for a while and then asked: "How do I know that?"

"The first two you can judge for yourself; the last you'll have to take on trust. You can please yourself. How much were you to make by this job?"

"Five hundred marks; but it wasn't only the money. Dragen has the whiphand of me."

"He'll want all his hands for himself after this, and you'll stand by his side in the dock—unless you go in the witness box against him. Tell all you know, and you shall not have five hundred, but a thousand marks."

"They'd have my life."

"Not if you leave the country. I'll add the passage money to America. You're not tough enough for a real scoundrel, you know; and you'll get a fresh start there."

"I shouldn't be in it at all if it weren't for Dragen and the gambling."

"Well, you must make up your mind quickly."

"I'll do it," he said, after another long pause, drawing a deep

199

breath. "But you must keep me safe from the rest until it's over;" and then he began to tell me.

He said his name was Lander, and that he had been forced into the affair by Dragen. He had been one of the men who had made the search for the papers at my house, and afterwards had played the part of a plain clothes police officer at Hagar's, where he had found out that von Felsen was at the back of everything.

The latter's orders had been to recover possession of the papers at any cost; and when that had been done I was to be kept a close prisoner for a week. But von Felsen's terms had been, no papers no pay; and thus my declaration that they were in safe hands had caused a split and a quarrel; and Lander and one of the others had decided to go back to von Felsen for fresh instructions.

He had barely finished his story when the carriage stopped at von Felsen's house. Remembering that I had found it close shut when I was there before, I was surprised to see lights in several of the windows. I concluded that he had thought it safe to return there when he knew that I had fallen into Dragen's hands.

We got out and I told Lander to ask for von Felsen and say that we had a message from Dragen; and when the servant opened the door, I stood on one side and kept my face out of the light.

The fellow was inclined to be suspicious; and was going to shut the door in our faces on the pretence of going to call his master when I lurched against Lander, pushed him into the house and followed. Answering the servants' protests with a drunken oath, I staggered to a chair and flopped into it.

He stared at me for a moment, hesitating whether to try and put me out; and then knocked at the door of von Felsen's private room.

The sound of several voices reached us as he opened it; and after a pause von Felsen came out. I let my head loll forward so that he should not at first see my face; and he spoke to Lander. "Who are you, and what do you want?" he asked sharply.

Having no cue from me, the man was at a loss for a reply; so he motioned toward me and muttered something about the papers.

"Turn up the light in the library," he told the servant; and then to us: "Come in here;" and he led the way.

I rose and staggered after them, lurching first against the servant as he came out of the room, and then against von Felsen, who stood holding the door. In this way I shouldered him into the room and then shut the door.

"Who is this drunken beast?" cried von Felsen, as I was fumbling with the door fastening.

Then I turned and faced him and waited for the recognition.

I was not surprised that it did not follow at once. I had on the suit of workman's overalls; they were torn and dishevelled as the result of the scrimmage with Dragen; I was as dirty as a sweep; a soft, rather greasy cloth cap was drawn well down over my face; I was bootless, and had just been assuming drunkenness. I have no doubt I looked a very low grade sort of scoundrel.

"Why do you bring this fellow here?" he demanded of Lander angrily.

"Have another look at me, von Felsen," I said quietly, fixing my eyes on him, and crossing toward him.

He fell back from me as if I were the devil in the flesh and leant against the table behind him, staring at me wide-eyed, breathing hard, deathly white, speechless, and shaking like a jelly.

I was human enough to enjoy his discomfiture, and just stared at him while he tortured himself with the thoughts which my most unwelcome arrival had started. Lander glanced from one to the other of us in perplexity and for more than a minute the tense silence was unbroken.

Then von Felsen clasped his hands to his head with a faint groan of agony.

"Where is Fräulein von Ringheim?" I asked.

At the sound of my voice he glanced up at me and then cowered and shrank like a beaten cur.

The silent gesture chilled me with sudden dread. My confidence and the sense of victory fell away from me like a dropped cloak. I was too late after all. A frenzy of rage seized upon me; I rushed upon him and seizing him by the throat, shook him till his teeth chattered, and flung him away, and sent him asprawl to the ground.

"You shall pay with your life for this," I cried fiercely. "Go for the police, Lander," I said turning to my companion. "Here, take this card to Herr Feldermann;" and I scribbled a message to Feldermann to come.

"No, no, wait," said von Felsen in a weak voice as he struggled to his feet. "Wait till we have talked together."

"We've passed the time for talk," I answered with an oath. "Where is Fräulein Althea?"

"Send him away;" and he motioned toward Lander.

"Where is she?" I asked again. "I'm not safe to fool in this mood." I was beside myself with the lust for revenge, and could have found it in me to tear the life out of him there and then. "This is the end of things for you."

"I will tell you all. Send him away. She is safe and well."

"Wait in the hall there till I call you," I told Lander; and I unlocked the door, let him out, and relocked it.

"Now you treacherous devil, out with the truth," I thundered. "Have you forced her to marry you? If you have, I swear on my soul that you shall pay for it with your life."

He fell back before me, grey and sweat-dappled with terror.

"For God's sake!" he exclaimed. "I admit everything."

"Tell me," I stormed.

"She is in the room across there with the others."

"Come then;" and I twisted my fingers into his collar and hauled him toward the door. He hung back and squirmed like a reluctant puppy at the end of the leash.

As we reached it some one knocked sharply on the panels.

"Help! Help! I am being murdered," yelled von Felsen.

"Break in this door," cried a voice.

Keeping my grip on his collar I unlocked the door and threw it open.

Herr Borsen and a couple of strangers rushed in, and at the door of the room opposite stood two women with Althea behind them.

Borsen did not recognize me, and he and the other men were throwing themselves upon me to rescue von Felsen from my clutches when Althea broke past the women and called me by name.

"Bastable!" exclaimed Borsen with a great start of surprise as he held the others in check. "What on earth is the meaning of this?"

I took no notice of him and hurling von Felsen back into the room pushed through to Althea and took her hands.

"All is well with you?" I asked.

"Yes. You came just in time," she cried, pressing my hands and trembling. "But with you? I have been mad with fear."

"Nothing matters now," I replied, with a smile of intense relief.

"I insist on knowing the meaning of your forcing yourself into this house in this disguise, and of your attempt on Herr von Felsen's life, Mr. Bastable," said Borsen angrily, coming up to me.

For the moment I could not answer him. The reaction from the furious rage which had maddened me in my fear that I had arrived too late, and the sense of infinite relief at Althea's assurances, rendered me as weak as a a girl. I leaned against the lintel of the door and met his angry look with a fatuous smile.

Quick to see this, von Felsen made an attempt to get out of the room. "I'll send for the police," he said with an effort at bluster.

This roused me. I pushed him back. "Get me some brandy," I said to Borsen. "I am faint a bit. You shall have all the story you want; but that little beast must stop here."

"This is monstrous," cried Borsen indignantly.

"Lander, take my message to Herr Feldermann. If he wants the police, he shall have them," I added to Borsen.

"No, no," cried von Felsen hurriedly. "We'd better talk first."

Borsen looked at him keenly and then at me.

"You see?" I said. "You needn't go, Lander."

Borsen crossed and spoke eagerly to von Felsen, and I turned to Althea, who brought me a glass of wine.

I drank it eagerly, and as I handed her back the glass our hands touched and our eyes met. "I can scarcely believe it all yet. You are really not hurt?" she asked wistfully.

"I've lost my boots and worn out a pair of socks, but otherwise I'm all right;" and I smiled and held up one foot, the sock of which was dangling in tatters.

"How can you smile at it like that?"

"Because we've won. A narrow margin; but it's a win all right."

"But you were in the hands of the police. I saw you."

"No. That was only a make-believe. That little brute planned it to deceive you. But he won't do any more planning for a while. They were his men dressed up, and he worked it so that you should see it all for yourself."

"He told me in the afternoon that you had been arrested, and that he could get you out if I would marry him at once. I insisted on having some proof. And when I saw you to-night I—I gave in."

"These people were here for the marriage then?"

"I insisted on having witnesses and on hearing from Herr Borsen that what Herr von Felsen had promised would be done. That caused the delay. If you had been half an hour later——"

"Von Felsen would have gone to the scaffold," I finished, when she paused.

"Oh, Paul!"

"It's true. But here comes Borsen. You had better go home to Chalice's I think."

"I don't want to leave you again. You get into such troubles."

"I've only lost my boots," I laughed. And at that she smiled too.

"We had better come to an understanding, Mr. Bastable," said Borsen, coming up then. "You know of course that you have to explain many things in regard to your association with the Polish plot."

Althea started in alarm at this.

"You can take that threat back, Borsen, or I shall say what I have to say before the rest of the people here," I returned sharply.

"I didn't mean it as a threat," he replied.

"So much the better. Let some one see Fräulein von Ringheim home, and then we'll talk."

The minister who was to have performed the ceremony agreed to go with her; and then Borsen, von Felsen and I were left alone.

CHAPTER XXX

THE END

As soon as we three were left alone, I drew an easy chair close to the door, threw myself into it and begged a cigar from Borsen.

"Now, Herr Borsen, what has von Felsen told you?" I asked sharply. "I'm dead beat and want to get to bed. We'll have this thing over as soon as possible. I'm going to let him tell you why he wouldn't allow me to send for Feldermann just now, and I'll sit here and check what he says. He can tell you as much as he likes."

"You don't appear to understand that you have to explain your connexion with the Polish party," he retorted.

"My explanation is easy. I had two objects—one, to save the Baron von Ringheim; the other, to catch von Felsen tripping. I have succeeded in both. He knows that and more than that. And I can of course prove everything."

"What does this mean?" he asked von Felsen, who was staring at me in dire fear about what I meant to tell.

"I gave him twenty-four hours in which to get out of the country. Let him tell you under what circumstances. That'll clear the ground."

Von Felsen was too frightened to attempt a reply, however; and he sat eyeing us both uneasily, and pulling at his fingers with little nervous jerks.

"The matter's a thousand times more serious than you think, Borsen, and if I did the right thing, I should send straight for the police and hand him over to them. But if he makes a clean breast of it, and if the things are done which I require, I'm willing to hold my tongue."

"You think you are in a position to make terms," cried Borsen with some show of indignation.

"I don't think it. I know it. You have two things to get into your head. In the first place, that this fellow is a most infernal scoundrel, and that I have found him out; and in the second, that I am in possession of that paper which was stolen from the Count's office, and of the set of duplicate keys which enabled the thief to steal it."

"What do you mean?" He was intensely excited on the instant.

"Look there;" and I pointed at von Felsen, who was cowering down in his chair in a condition of abject terror.

"Do you mean that he——? My God, is it possible?" he cried horror-struck.

"Yes, that is just what I do mean. Let him tell you himself. If he won't then, I will; and I shall add the rest. The rest is blacker still."

It was some time before von Felsen could bring himself to speak, and then he gave a long rambling story of how he had been in Ziegler's power, and had been forced to disclose secret after secret, until the theft of the papers had been the climax. Questions from me brought out the rest—that he had brought Baron von Ringheim to Berlin; had let him know where Althea was in order to entrap me; and all the rest of it, including my abduction by Dragen, and the attempts on my life.

Borsen was almost unnerved. He sat with his head buried in his hands as he listened, and at the end his face was grey and drawn, and he looked across at me with a deep sigh of anguish. "We are in your hands, Mr. Bastable. It will ruin the Count."

"There is even worse yet, if it has to be told," I replied grimly.

"What are your terms?"

"A pardon for Baron von Ringheim and the restoration of his estates—you have already obtained the promise of that, you know— and the clearance of all complications affecting myself; a confession that he lied to Hagar Ziegler in accusing me of her father's murder; a letter from you now that you have heard von Felsen's confession; and a written undertaking that you will be responsible for his safe keeping until all is settled."

"You shall have them to-morrow," he said after a pause.

"Thank you, I prefer to have them now."

"But I cannot promise all this on my own account."

"Then we'll have the police here. I don't mean to lose sight of that scoundrel again until I know where I stand."

"I must see the Count first."

"Then see him to-night. You have my last word."

"You might take my word of honour, I think."

"I don't doubt you, but I'll take nothing but the actual evidence. You might not be able to prevail with the others."

"I'll go to him," he agreed.

He went at once, and I locked the door behind him and sat smoking in silence.

"Do you mean to accuse me of that murder?" asked von Felsen after a long pause.

"Yes, if I don't get my own way. And of everything else."

Not another word passed between us until Borsen returned after an hour or so and brought what I needed. The rest of the business was very soon completed.

I wrote a very short note to Althea, telling her that all was now well and that I would see her early on the following morning, and then turned to consider my last problem—where to sleep that night. It seemed a very trifling thing indeed, but it was to have consequences none the less.

Count von Felsen had insisted upon his son going to his house, and Borsen was to take him. I could not stay where I was; I was not inclined to run the risk of going to my own house lest Dragen or any of the men with him should come to make trouble; and in my bootless and generally dishevelled condition, I was doubtful of being received into any hotel.

I explained the position to Borsen, and he agreed to take me in the carriage with him and von Felsen and drop me at an hotel, where he would vouch for me. Lander accompanied me.

The matter was thus soon settled with the hotel people, and Borsen returned to the cab. I was just entering the lift, feeling as tired as a dog, when he came rushing back.

"He's gone," he exclaimed excitedly.

"Who's gone?"

"Von Felsen. He bolted while I was talking to the people here."

"Perhaps that's the best way out of it all. Anyway, I'm too dog-tired to look for him to-night. I'll see you in the morning;" and with that I left him staring blankly after me as the lift started.

It was close to noon before I rose, and I should not have woke then had it not been that some one was thumping vigorously at my door. I opened it and found Feldermann waiting impatiently to see me.

Dragen had been arrested, and the whole story of my treatment by him and his fellow-scoundrels had been told to the police by one of the gang, who had made a full confession. Feldermann had been to Borsen, as von Felsen's name had been mentioned, and he had come to me to learn what I should do.

"I can't tell you yet," I replied. I could not. I wished to see Althea first and ascertain her wishes as to our movements. For my part I was anxious to get away from Berlin as soon as possible. The last few days had been quite strenuous enough to satisfy me, and I realized the necessity of putting as great a distance as possible between myself and the Polish party.

"Has von Felsen turned up?" I asked him.

He shook his head and grinned. "I think we could trace him. I have a clue, but it may not be desirable to follow it up."

"Which means?"

"I expect you know more than they have told me; but I know enough to make me doubt whether his father is very anxious to see him again. Of course if you take steps against these men, it may have to come out, the whole of it."

"What's the clue?"

"That Jew girl, Hagar Ziegler, left the city this morning for Hamburg, with a companion. There's a boat sails to-day for Philadelphia."

"And the sex of the companion?"

He shrugged his shoulders and smiled significantly. A woman— apparently. "But only one berth has been booked for a woman, by wire of course; although, by a coincidence, a steerage passage has been reserved for a male passenger."

"And what does Herr Borsen propose to do?"

"Nothing. And you?"

"Nothing," I replied, adopting the same laconic tone.

He looked relieved. "And Dragen and the rest? Are you eager to push the charge hard against them?"

"What has Borsen said to you about that?"

"Nothing," he said again, looking at me very meaningly.

"You have something to say on your own account then?"

"No more than a personal opinion as a friend of yours. I have a sort of idea that if the whole matter were dropped, the other things you wish might be more easily arranged."

I understood and smiled. "Is that a bargain?"

He nodded. "Speaking as your friend I should think you may regard it as settled."

"The brutes meant to take my life. They ought to be punished."

"I think you may leave that to us."

"Very well, I will," I agreed.

"I'm glad you see it as I do," he said as he rose. "Oh, by the way, are you leaving Berlin?"

"Probably. Why?"

"Oh, there was a row and some fighting in a riverside warehouse the other evening, and a man was found with a bullet in his head in an open boat."

"Suicide?"

"I suppose so. No proof of anything else. The affair was political, we think. We caught one or two of those concerned, but some escaped. I don't suppose we shall catch them. They are either out of the country by this time or will be before we can lay hands on them."

"I expect you're right, Feldermann. I had an idea that there was something to be done against the Wundervoll, you know. She was to have been moored just off that warehouse, and I got Bassett—the man who followed me on my old paper, you know—to print a word of warning from Paris."

He gave a little start of surprise. "They wouldn't thank you if they knew; but I don't suppose you'll delay your going to wait for their thanks." And with that he left me.

I got up, then, borrowed a pair of boots, telephoned to Althea that I had been detained, had my breakfast and drove to my house and dressed myself in decent clothes, and packed a trunk and returned with it to the hotel, where I found Borsen awaiting me.

He had heard the result of my interview with Feldermann and had come to arrange for the papers to be handed over.

"They are in Brussels," I said; "but I am going through there myself, and the little interval will just allow time for your part of the matter to be concluded. By the way, that State concert is to-night, isn't it?"

"Yes, and if the new Prima pleases the Court, it's very likely the announcement of the Baron's pardon will be made by His Majesty. And the more likely, because the Prince von Graven will be present with his future bride, the Princess von Altenwelt. I suppose you know that the Imperial marriage is now definitely settled. Everything is going your way."

"I hope to-morrow that way will be the way toward England; in which case your messenger can meet me in Brussels."

"You might do worse than take the Baron with you. A temporary absence would be a good thing."

I hurried off to Althea, with this budget of good news; but only to meet with a disappointment. She was not at home, and Chalice had just returned from a final rehearsal with Herr Grumpel and was busy with the dressmakers trying on her costume for the evening.

She received me with very scant courtesy. She was in high spirits about the concert, but in a bad temper about her dress. "I can't see you now, Herr Bastable. I haven't a moment."

"Where is Althea?" I asked.

"Would you believe that she could have been so inconsiderate as to go rushing off at a time like this, when every minute is precious to get my costume perfect for this evening? I could cry with vexation. No one ever thinks about me, and I have to do everything for myself, and for them too. And there isn't the slightest need. At

208

the risk of sacrificing everything, I went out to that horrible farm yesterday and arranged for the Baron to remain there."

"She has gone to her father, then?"

"Yes. Imagine doing such a thing! And all these things here to be settled! And she really has good taste in such things. I do wish people would not be so selfish. I can't understand it. I shall never be ready, I know."

"How did you find the Baron?"

"Why, of course there was no need at all for me to go to him. I think it was horrid of you to make me waste the time in rushing out there at all."

"I will go out there now myself. By the way, did Althea say anything to you about your leaving Berlin for a time?"

"About my leaving?" she cried with positively indignant surprise. "Directly after my appearance when every one will be talking about me! Herr Bastable!"

"Her father will go and she will go with him. You can scarcely remain by yourself, can you?"

"Are you all mad or in league to ruin me? Why, to go away at such a moment would be——" The tragedy of such a prospect was obviously too terrible to be put in words.

"But the Court will prefer you to be away for a time," I said rising. "Our letter to the Emperor did all that we hoped, and the Imperial marriage is now definitely settled. The happy pair will be among the guests to-night to witness your triumph. I hope it will be great enough even to satisfy you."

She was a singular girl. She showed her lovely teeth in a smile, cast down her eyes, sighed, and then looked up and held out her hand. "I didn't understand you at first. Of course you mean that I should show that I really do feel the separation keenly. Oh, I wish I had always had some one so clever to advise me."

"I should not break my heart if I were you," I replied gravely.

She flashed a quick glance at me. "I shall get over it; but don't you think we might contrive to let it leak out that, if I really must go, it is because I am so—so upset."

"We can try," I laughed.

"You have a knack of putting things so nicely, Herr Bastable," she said as we shook hands. "Do that if you can for me. Oh, by the way, there's a letter for you from Althea. I quite forgot it."

It was only a line to say that she had gone out to her father and intended to bring him back with her; and she hinted that until we knew more of his feeling toward me it might be better for me not to see him. Would I wait for her return?

I set off to see Bassett and get the papers which I had given him over night, and then hurried on all the preparations for my leaving the city. I went two or three times to see if Althea had returned, but it was not until quite late in the evening that I saw her.

"I was sure you would understand my going off to my father," she said when we met.

"Of course. It is just what I would have had you do. How is he?"

"Surprisingly well. Just like himself; but I have persuaded him to go to bed. Besides, I thought you would rather tell me all there is to tell alone. I am dying to know it all. I never passed such a day of suspense in my life."

"It is all just what you would wish it to be, except perhaps in one respect. I'll tell you that presently;" and I went on with a long description of everything except the truth about Heir Ziegler's murder.

She put many questions, and insisted upon having all the details, her tell-tale face showing how intense was her interest.

"And now what is there I shall not like?" she asked at length.

I looked very grave. "It is about you and——"

I paused and appeared reluctant to speak of it. "I tried very hard to arrange so that—— You will give me credit for having done my best in your interests, I'm sure; but——"

"What is it?" she cried impatiently.

I sighed and then asked hesitatingly: "It was made a sort of condition you know, and although he was willing to leave everything else to you, I couldn't get any relief."

"But what is it?" she cried again.

"I scarcely like to—— It's so difficult that—— But I'm afraid you'll have to—to give in. You know how hard I tried to save you from that—well, from von Felsen; but—I don't like putting it on the ground that it would help me; but it would really mean that. Would that marriage——?" I paused as if in great embarrassment.

"Tell me. This is cruel," she said quickly.

"Could you make the sacrifice?"

"You said he had left the country."

"I wasn't speaking of——"

She did not let me finish. She laid her hand on my arm and looked up all smiles and blushes into my eyes. "It would serve him right if I refused, sir. To frighten me like this!"

"Does the condition frighten you then?"

She crept into my arms and laid her head on my shoulder with a little sigh.

There was no need for any other answer; and we were nearly

caught in this silent enjoyment of our victory by Chalice, who came rustling in to tell us of hers.

"It's been an absolute triumph," she announced boisterously. "The Kaiser was so delighted with my voice that he sent for me to say that he should pardon the Baron on my account. He is the loveliest man in the world."

And to this hour she believes that it was that and that only which had secured the Imperial clemency.

THE END